A DIFFERENT KIND OF LIFE

Pamela D. Holloway has written short stories and poetry but this is her first published novel. She is married with three children and lives in East Sussex.

By the same author

Claire's Story

PAMELA D. HOLLOWAY

A Different Kind of Life

First paperback edition 2017

A CIP catalogue record for this book is available from the British Lbrary.

ISBN 9 781 52072 2368

This book is dedicated with love
to my sister Babs

Chapter 1

Edinburgh 1982

On a bleak November day, three children watched as their father's coffin was lowered into the cold ground. Fiona felt a wetness on her cheeks and didn't know or care whether it was the wetness of the mist that swirled around the graveyard, or silent tears following the many others she had shed since Dada died.

She had known he was dying, though no-one thought to tell her. She watched as his big frame turned into a shadow of his former self. Her mind darted back to that last hug as bony arms pulled her to him. The smell of death hung around him, but Fiona neither noticed nor cared.

'Take care of the bairns my lovely,' he had whispered, so quietly she only just caught the words. She nodded.

'Of course Dada', she had said, slipping briefly into her baby name for him.

She came back to the present with a painful jolt. She could hear Stewart crying and holding her hand so tightly it hurt. Claire though, holding her other hand, seemed impassive, as if the whole event was something on television.

'It's alright Stewie.' Fiona bent and kissed the two year old. 'I'll take care of you.' It was at that moment Fiona realised her childhood was over.

As they left the graveyard she glanced at her mother. Mummy seemed so untouched – rather like Claire, she thought. A man was pushing the wheelchair, bending at intervals as he did so, to say something to Mummy. They walked in solemn procession; the wheelchair, then Fiona, then the bairns, as Dada always called them, and as Fiona would always think of them now.

Mr Lennard was his name. To Fiona he looked like the devil. Though she'd never met the devil personally, she was sure he looked exactly like Mr Lennard. He was tall, with jet black hair slicked and held in place by some greasy matter. His face looked as if he had forgotten to shave that morning and Dada's face was always so clean and fresh smelling – except when he died, Fiona added as an afterthought to herself.

Mr Lennard came in for tea. It was just the five of them. Dada had no relatives and Mummy's family lived in the south. She had moved north, as she always described it, when she married Dada and they had lived in Edinburgh ever since. She always alluded to it as 'the cold grey city'.

'What am I doing here,' she would say, 'so far from home?' Dada would hug her and sweep her up in his arms until she laughed again.

'That's what you are doing here my pretty one,' he would say, kissing her on the ear and swinging her around until she begged to be put down, saying she loved the place and loved Dada.

Fiona had memories of those days, but now they seemed a long way off. It almost seemed as if Mummy had been in a wheelchair forever – and that Dada had been dying for too long.

She still remembered her first day at school, spoilt because Mummy fell down in the playground and all the children teased her – all except Amanda that is - teased her that her Mummy was a drunk. It turned out to be multiple sclerosis and within a year of that first day at school, Mummy was in a wheelchair. Dada had widened doorways, moved their bed downstairs, made slopes of wood so that the wheelchair could be moved easily from house to garden, or house to car. But life had changed and it went on changing.

She could feel herself near to tears, but Mr Lennard, serving tea to her mother and looking as if he belonged there, made her fight back the tears and remembered what Dada had said about the bairns. So, she fussed over Stewie and her younger sister, trying to cut out the picture of that odious Mr Lennard bending over Mummy and whispering in her ear – making her laugh, and Dada not yet cold in his coffin.

Chapter 2

Life had changed for them all for ever, but most especially for Fiona. Every morning she was up before everyone; taking her mother tea and toast, laying breakfast for Claire and Stewie, tidying up from the previous evening, putting the school clothes out for Claire and Stewie and the back pack for her little brother to take to nursery. Then waking the bairns and chivvying them over and over until they struggled sleepy-eyed out of bed. Washing, dressing, hairbrushing, bedmaking; these became the start of every day for seven year old Fiona. She didn't think about it. She didn't care; she knew she had to do a good job or the Social People would say they couldn't stay together. She knew Mummy was alright. The nurse came to dress and bathe her several times a week and someone else helped her dress on the other days and did the shopping and cooked Mummy her dinner.

Stewie had his dinner at nursery and Claire and she had theirs at school. It often wasn't very nice, but it was something she hadn't had to do, so Fiona ate gladly. Claire picked at hers and then wanted crisps and chips and the things Dada never wanted her to have.

It was thoughts of Dada that kept Fiona going; what would Dada do, what would Dada think, would be the measure of her approach to everything. In the evening Mummy would put the wheelchair in the doorway of the kitchen and tell Fiona what to do. She was a quick learner and liked the cooking she did, but sometimes she felt tired and she knew she had homework (not a lot, but it had to be done, her teacher always said).

Several months went by and they were getting into a routine. After a cooked tea they would all go into the lounge, where Fiona would put her school books on the coffee table and sit crossed legged on the floor while the others watched television until bedtime. At the weekends they would play 'pairs' and children's scrabble, but Claire, still only five, was hopeless and Mummy got bored very easily. Still, they were happy – sort of.

It all changed so suddenly Fiona could hardly believe it. It was a Friday, a day Fiona usually looked forward to because Saturday was the next day and she could lie in bed until eight or even half past. It was such bliss. She would wake early as usual and then lie in bed wiggling her toes, revelling in the peace and warmth, snuggling her duvet round and then rolling over onto her tummy for another blissful hour in bed.

But THAT Friday – Fiona always remembered it in capital letters - THAT Friday when she got home from school, Mr Lennard was there. Mummy said he'd often dropped in while they were at school, but today he was going to stay for tea. Indeed, he was going to make tea for them all. What a treat! Fiona hated every mouthful – it tasted like sawdust to her. His speciality, he said, steak and kidney pudding. Stewie cried, because he didn't like kidney, but Claire smiled and simpered for Mr Lennard's benefit. Not that he took much notice; he seemed only to listen to Mummy and they seemed to be sharing something somehow. Fiona felt suddenly excluded. She felt angry. Why had Mummy let this man ruin her Friday?

It became a regular feature. Every Friday, Mr Lennard would be there, then Mondays as well. Then it seemed he was there all the time. One evening, after he'd told the children to play in the dining room – a room they hardly ever used, as the kitchen with its Aga and big table was warm and friendly – she'd overheard him tell

Mummy that 'They' (and Fiona presumed 'They' were herself, Claire and Stewie), 'They ask too much of you my dear. They're big enough now for you not to worry your pretty head about them.' She supposed Mummy's head was pretty. Dada had always said it was, but as she, Fiona, did most of the worrying, she couldn't really understand what he meant. She soon found out.

Mr Lennard moved in the very next Friday. Not only moved in, but slept in Dada's bed. Fiona thought she had cried before, but that night was the worst of her life. The future looked bleak.

It was only the beginning. It was gradual, but insidious. He undermined everything she did. Whatever time she got up, he was there first. 'I've given your mother her breakfast', he would say, in a voice that somehow implied she had failed. She would come home to be told that he was giving Mummy a special supper that evening (only he called it dinner). Soon, Fiona and the other two were eating supper on their own. The table seemed big and empty, no Dada and now no Mummy telling her what to do or how to do it.

After supper, Mr Lennard told them to play in the dining room and when Claire protested there was no television, a television appeared the next day. The dining room table was pushed into the corner of the room and a rather hard, small sofa and matching chair arrived. 'Mr Lennard is so kind,' murmured her mother when Fiona protested. 'He chose them himself, so you would have a room to play in and watch television and the dining room table will be better than the coffee table for your homework.' That was the only bit that was true.

The dining room soon became the 'kids' room'. Mr Lennard again: 'Go now kids,' he would say, 'to the kids' room. Your mother is tired.' Stewie particularly found it hard and sometimes Mr Lennard would relent and let Stewart spend a small part of the evening with Mummy, but it was never more than half an hour. Fiona would time it. It became so precise that she knew without doubt that Mr Lennard timed it too.

Fiona was now ten, Claire eight and Stewart five. He started at primary school and Fiona was doing well and due to go to the big school in a year or so. Amanda, her first and really only friend at school, was the person she was with most. The other children found her too quiet. In reality, she was quite tired a lot of the time and quite unhappy. She tried not to be; Dada would want her to be happy, but it was such hard work. One day she heard Mr Lennard (the other two called him Uncle Len now, but Fiona steadfastly stuck to Mr Lennard) say to Mummy 'Who does she think she is the little upstart'. She waited for her mother to protest but there was silence and this time she cried inside; a different sort of pain, this. Amanda knew a little bit about Fiona's life, very selected bits. She had invited Fiona around lots of times, including birthday parties, but the answer was always the same, 'I'm too busy,' Fiona would say.

By now, the three children lived a separate life to their mother and Mr Lennard. Fiona had stopped trying to do anything for Mummy and then been branded 'lazy'. The children ate together now on the dining room table in the kids' room because they were 'in the way' if they ate in the kitchen and they took 'too long'.

If she so much as left a fork out of place in the newly arranged drawers – where every fork now lay in a snug row with the next fork curled up beside it - would mean a reduction in her modest pocket money which was now fully controlled by Mr Lennard. Every pan had to be washed up before she could leave the kitchen to eat her meal, so frequently, Claire and Stewart had almost finished when she arrived to eat her now tepid food. Fiona kept thinking things could get no worse, but they did.

Chapter 3

It was Amanda's fourteenth birthday. Her parents planned to take her to Paris for the weekend – Disneyland, Paris – and she could invite one friend.

'Fiona,' she said immediately. Her mother looked doubtful.

'But Fiona doesn't ever go to anything does she dear?'

'This time she will – I'll make her.'

Her mother smiled. 'Well darling, if anyone can persuade her, I'm sure you can.'

The following morning Amanda grabbed hold of Fiona when she saw her.

'Fee,' she said, 'guess what? I'm going to Paris and you're coming too. See you at break.' And with that she was gone.

Paris, thought Fiona. How wonderful that sounds, and all through maths she let her mind wander.

'Fiona McInnes, are you on another planet today?' Her maths teacher looked both cross and concerned. They were all concerned about Fiona McInnes. She was diligent, produced good work consistently, but she always had about her a vague air of unhappiness. Her younger sister seemed alright, but Fiona caused one or two quite deep conversations in the staff room.

'Father's dead, you know,' said one.

'Mother's in a wheelchair I believe,' said another.

'There's a man living there – know anything about him?' Nobody did, but there was an unspoken question in the air, a sense

14

of unease.

This had happened before, of course, when a teacher at Fiona's primary school alerted Social Services about the family circumstances. Fiona had been told by Mr Lennard that the 'social people' were coming and they had better behave or they'd be taken away, and not together either. Fiona had dressed Stewie carefully; made sure she and Claire had clean dresses and they sat on the window seat, the three of them hardly daring to move in case they'd mess themselves up.

Fiona coached them. 'Tell them everything's fine,' she said to Claire. 'Smile when the people come,' she said to Stewart. He looked so appealing when he smiled.

The 'social people' had come. Fiona had no idea what to expect. In fact, it was quite a nice lady, about the same age as her mother. The children stayed in the kids' room.

'That's their playroom,' Fiona heard Mr Lennard say.

The social lady, as Fiona always thought of her, came to talk to them on their own. They remained sitting on the window seat. They looked healthy and clean. The little boy smiled adorably. The middle girl answered cheerfully, 'Yes, I'm happy.' She spoke enthusiastically. Fiona mentally patted her sometimes awkward sister on the back.

'And you, Fiona. How are you coping since your father died? Your mother's in a wheelchair, but you have this nice friend,' she phrased it carefully, 'living with you. It must be such a help.'

She waited, wondering what this thoughtful child would say. Fiona thought too. *If she knew we were banished to this room, if she knew we could hardly get to see Mummy, if she knew I cooked for us and we ate alone, they would take us away, they would split us up.* Thoughts of Dada entered her head. She blurted out, then bit her tongue.

'I, we – miss Daddy.'

The social worker nodded. 'Of course you do.' She sounded

sympathetic but Fiona knew she mustn't be lulled.

'But we're fine, Mummy and Mr Lennard.' She corrected herself hastily, 'Uncle Lennard.'

The social worker looked at her hard.

'Do you like him?' She looked from one face to the next. They all nodded vigourously and chorused together, 'Oh yes.'

The social worker breathed a sigh of relief; any lingering doubts that she might have had vanished.

'It's good to see such a happy household,' she said to the five of them as they sat in the lounge together, the first time in weeks they had even been allowed in the room. Mummy had smiled, so had Mr Lennard. Fiona's face ached with holding a controlled smile. Stewie had climbed on Mummy's lap and was enjoying an unexpected cuddle. Mr Lennard took Claire by the hand.

Wouldn't have dared do that to me, shouted a voice in Fiona's head.

'We're one happy family, aren't we?' he said, glancing around. His eyes met Fiona's and she saw the challenge. Again, they all chorused 'Oh yes.'

Amanda couldn't wait to tell Fiona all about the Paris trip. The girls sat on one of the benches. Amanda handed Fiona an apple. She often brought two pieces of fruit to school to share with her friend. Funny really, Fiona was her very best friend, yet, although they had known each other from the first day of primary school, she'd never once been to Fiona's home.

Fiona had told her that Daddy was ill. Then, two years later when he died, Amanda sensed that life for her friend had changed. Occasionally, very occasionally, something she said gave Amanda a clue.

'Fiona does all the cooking,' Amanda told her mother.

'Well, darling, her mother is in a wheelchair.'

'There's a man there too and I'm sure Fiona doesn't like him.'

Amanda's mother looked worried.

'Perhaps I should go round and see her mother,' she said to her husband that evening.

'I think you should keep well away, sounds a funny situation to me. Don't let Amanda go there.'

'She's never been invited,' Mrs Harrison replied, 'and that's what worries me.'

Her husband straightened his paper and harrumphed – a sure signal that he wanted the conversation to finish right there. Amanda's mother sighed. Men, she thought, men.

'I can't come with you, I really can't.'

'Yes, you can. I'm not going without you. You'll be responsible for ruining my birthday.' Amanda spoke using all her dramatic skills.

'How can I? I can't leave the bairns.'

'Tosh,' said Amanda, 'that's the trouble. You're still calling them bairns. For Heaven's sake, Claire is twelve and how old is Stewart?'

'He's only nine.'

'Nine!' Amanda exploded. 'Really, Fee, you pamper them. Just tell your mother and that Mr Thingamee that you've been invited to Paris for a weekend and they'll have to do the things you usually do.'

Fiona frowned. Amanda didn't know the half of it. She was tempted just for a moment to tell her all about precious Mr Lennard, but something stopped her; a fear that perhaps, even now, they might take Stewie away, or that Amanda's parents would come round, angry at what Amanda would undoubtedly tell them and finally, remembering Dada and his saying that 'it's only a family concern and no-one else's'.

Amanda looked so beseeching. For a moment, just a moment, Fiona dared let herself think about it.

'I can't, Amanda, I really can't.'

Claire was struggling with her maths. Fiona, who still hadn't finished the masses of homework she seemed to have these days, agreed to help her. The sisters were so different; Claire, still childish in many ways, seldom, if ever, helping Fiona. It was even a struggle to get her to make her bed, let alone put on a clean sheet and duvet cover. But they were fond of each other in an odd sort of way. Fiona was too bossy as far as Claire was concerned. It never bothered her that Fiona had looked after her more like a mother than a sister only two years older.

'Fee, stop doing that, I need help,' Claire wailed.

With a sigh, Fiona put down her pen. The history project was interesting but so time consuming. However, she also knew Claire's maths. For twenty minutes Fiona explained and re-explained and finally, Claire understood.

'Oh you're brilliant Fee. I'll do anything for you,' she sang, repeating the words of the song from 'Oliver!' which she had watched on television the night before.

'Would you really?' Fiona paused. 'Would you really do anything for me Claire?'

'Of course,' trilled Claire, happy that her maths was done and knowing if it was anything too horrible, like peeling potatoes, she would get out of it anyway.

'It's just that I've been invited to Paris for a weekend.'

'Oh Fee!' Even Claire was taken aback. 'But what's it to do with me?'

'You'll be in charge of you and Stewie.' Claire's face fell. She hadn't thought of that.

'Then you shouldn't go,' she said assertively. But Fiona had, surprising even herself, got the bit between her teeth. Why shouldn't she go? Why, for once, shouldn't Claire look after things?

'You said you'd do anything.' Fiona suddenly wanted to go to Paris more than anything she could ever remember, to get away from everyone, to be just plain, simple Fiona and not the big caring sister that Claire and Stewie relied on. For just one weekend! It took quite a bit more persuasion but Claire finally relented perhaps because she felt a twinge of guilt at seeing the look of excitement on her sister's face.

'Oh alright then.' She spoke with ill grace, but Fiona clutched her hands and danced around the room, singing 'Paris, Paris, Paris' as she danced.

The door opened. Mr Lennard stood framed in the doorway. The girls stopped their dancing, faces flushed and Fiona for once thought Mr Lennard looked quite attractive, more like her mother perhaps. But any softening in his attitude that there might have been at that moment was quickly quashed by Fiona's words 'I'm going to Paris.'

'You're what?' he exploded.

'Paris.'

Fiona spoke quietly this time. She had seen that cold look before. If ever she needed or wanted anything 'that look' would cross his face. Even now, she blushed when she remembered the first time; the time she had wanted to see Mummy, the morning she woke up and found blood on her sheet, the morning of her first period. She knew, of course, all about periods. She'd even bought a small packet of sanitary pads a year or so earlier when the school nurse told them all it was good to have them at home for when it happened. But she'd wanted to tell Mummy, tell her she was 'grown up', tell her that although she knew all about it, she was still a bit, just a teeny bit, frightened. But no, Mr Lennard wouldn't allow her saying Mummy was still asleep.

'But that's her breakfast tray,' she'd said.

'She's gone back to sleep. Anyway, what's so important?'

His expression had hardened and she'd felt herself flinch. He'd stepped towards her. She felt he knew; it showed somehow. She'd run back to her bedroom and lay sobbing on her bed. Then she'd heard Stewie calling, 'Fiona, help! I can't do my laces up.' Fiona had wiped her eyes and gone along the landing to Stewie's bedroom.

'What's this about Paris?'

Fiona was jerked back to the present. She knew she daren't let him know how much, how very much, this meant to her. With all the dignity she could muster, and trying to calm every last bit of excitement in her voice, she said 'My friend's parents have invited me to Paris for a weekend and I'm going.'

'Yes she is,' burst in Claire, enjoying the drama of the moment, but suddenly determined to help her big sister.

'And who's going to cook your meals, eh young lady?'

His tone was sneering. Before Fiona could speak, Claire cut across him.

'I am,' she said firmly, wondering at the same time how she would. Nevertheless, in her own somewhat selfish way, she loved Fiona and Uncle Len was a pain in the butt (an expression she applied regularly to anything or anyone she didn't like).

'On your own head be it.' The tone was ominous but it was a tacit agreement.

Half an hour later he was back again.

'Fiona, your mother wants to speak to you.'

Fiona's heart missed a beat. She hadn't seen her mother for several days and then only briefly. They never had conversations. Indeed, the children were no longer allowed to use the front door any more because their noise and clatter would disturb their mother, as she either slept in her bedroom or rested in the lounge on the other side of the front door. They were now permanently 'channelled' into the back of the house.

20

Her mother sat, or rather lay, on the sofa. She looked paler than ever, with deep circles under her eyes. Somehow she looked smaller too.

'What's this I hear about Paris? Aren't you being a bit selfish thinking of leaving your brother and sister?'

Fiona swallowed hard. *Selfish!* The rush of anger she felt gave her all the adrenalin she needed.

'Mother, I've never been away, not since Dada...' She corrected herself quickly, praying that Mr Lennard had not heard her special name for Daddy. 'Not since Daddy died. Claire will look after Stewart, she promised.'

'Oh very well,' said her mother in a weary tone, and as Fiona bent to kiss her 'thank you', she turned her face to the wall.

Mr Lennard was still glaring at her coldly.

'See how you've upset her. No wonder she never wants to see you.'

It was like a knife being turned in her stomach. Her mother didn't want her. She couldn't speak; yet more pain, unbearable hurting pain. When she didn't reply, Mr Lennard barred the door.

'Don't be insolent girl. I spoke to you.'

Mustering all the dignity she could, she finally managed to say 'And I DON'T want to speak to you.'

She ran upstairs and into the bathroom. She knew she was going to be sick and she didn't quite know why. But somehow, it did help her to forget the hurt.

Chapter 4

Fiona could hardly wait for Monday morning. She didn't want to telephone Amanda, she seldom used the telephone. Mr Lennard would be listening and she didn't want him to know how excited she was about Paris.

'You look like the cat who's swallowed ALL the cream,' said Amanda.

Fiona was waiting for her by the school gate.

'I feel like the cat!' was the reply. 'I'm coming to Paris Amanda!'

The girls hugged each other excitedly; Amanda, five foot nothing, dark haired and slightly rounded and her friend, several inches taller, straight fair hair just reaching below her shoulders and tied back for school.

'The weekend after next,' Amanda said, 'I just can't wait. We'll have such fun!'

Amanda had never known time go so slowly before. She made a casserole and froze it ready for Claire and Stewart's Sunday lunch. She re-told Claire about jacket potatoes and oven chips. She made sure there was plenty of fruit – they all liked fruit. The fridge was stocked with Stewart's favourite yoghurt and she had even bought some fruit and nut chocolate bars as a treat for Claire.

'Stop fussing,' said Claire, now rather looking forward to being in charge. 'You're only going to be away for two nights, not two weeks!'

Fiona laughed. She hadn't been so happy for as long as she

could remember.

On the Thursday evening before 'the weekend', she suddenly realised that she didn't have a small suitcase or overnight bag. She even contemplated Stewie's old nursery back pack, but even with the minimal amount she was taking, that was too small. Finally, and with great reluctance, she asked Mr Lennard if she could talk to her mother.

'No, she's resting.'

'But I need to talk to her.'

'That's right, selfish as ever. You need, you need.' His tone was taunting. She had even briefly contemplated asking him if he had an overnight bag. How could she have ever even thought the unthinkable? There was no choice. She would have to put her things in a plastic shopping bag. She felt both embarrassed and cross. Then she looked at her passport, newly arrived just two days before. It seemed to her it was a passport to freedom.

Half term had arrived. Fiona dressed in her best jeans, track shoes and tee shirt, with a sweat shirt tied around her waist. Her hair was brushed out and shining and her face aglow with excitement as she waited outside the back door for sight of the Harrisons' car. She saw it coming down the road and opened the door to say another goodbye to Claire and Stewie who had come into the kitchen to see her off. Then she ran down the drive to the waiting car. Just as she arrived at the car the front door opened. Down the drive strode the odious Mr Lennard. Fiona always thought of him these days as the O.M. – odious man. Today though, he was all smiles.

'Good morning, good morning,' he said as the Harrisons got out of their car to greet him. 'Take care of our little girl, won't you?'. He put his arm round Fiona's shoulders in a casual gesture of affection. Fiona squirmed away and climbed quickly into the back of the car. Amanda had opened the door when she saw Mr

Lennard approaching and somehow knew her friend would need to escape as quickly as possible.

As the car drove off, Mr Harrison muttered sotto voce to his wife 'Seems nice enough.' Mrs Harrison grimaced. She had caught the brief expression of complete loathing on Fiona's face.

Soon they were airborne. Everything was new and exciting for Fiona. She, unlike her friend, had never flown before, so everything from seatbelt to in-flight food was novel and enjoyable. The girls talked incessantly and the Harrisons smiled. Amanda would enjoy her birthday weekend so much more than she would have done had it just been the three of them.

The hotel was splendid, and although Paris in April was hot, the cool marble reception hall was welcoming. The girls shared a room with two double beds which they thought a complete hoot.

Amanda quickly unpacked her small holdall and Fiona noticed to her horror that she hung a dress in the wardrobe - quite a smart dress – and she only had the jeans she travelled in and a navy skirt and blouse in case she needed something slightly smarter. Amanda noticed her friend's expression.

'Don't worry Fee. Mummy always makes me bring a dress for dinner. Such a bore. Your skirt is fine.' As she spoke, a sudden thought flashed through her mind. After all, it would be Fee's birthday in two weeks.

There was a knock at the door. The Harrisons were ready to set off to Disneyland. It was only twelve noon so they could have lunch there and a long afternoon.

Of course, both girls had seen the advertisements for Disneyland, Paris, but even so, it was far better than they had imagined. Even Mr Harrison, who sometimes seemed rather solemn, entered into the spirit of the thing. They had lunch in a restaurant set in the New Orleans section and Mrs Harrison told the girls it was just like being in the real New Orleans.

'You've been to New Orleans?' Fiona sounded so surprised that they all burst out laughing.

'Years ago,' Mrs Harrison responded. 'I went coast to coast in a Greyhound bus. I must have been about eighteen at the time. It was my gap year before university.'

Fiona couldn't help contrasting Mrs Harrison's life to Mummy's and, indeed, Amanda's to her own. She loved watching the interaction between the parents and daughter and, for the first time in her life, she felt stirrings of envy.

They arrived back at the hotel around eight o'clock and all decided they needed showers and a change of clothes.

'In the lobby at eight thirty girls.' Mr Harrison spoke with mock sternness.

'Yes sir!' answered Amanda laughing.

The girls showered and giggled and chatted non-stop. Amanda put on her blue dress and Fiona her skirt and blouse. They both looked young, fresh and lovely thought the Harrisons as the girls came out of the lift, arm in arm and still laughing at some joke or other.

The doorman called a taxi and they were off to Montmartre. Mr Harrison said he knew just the place to take them.

'Oh goody, the Moulin Rouge,' said Amanda.

'No darling, not the Moulin Rouge.'

'Pity,' she replied with a grin.

It was a happy meal. The girls were allowed wine.

'After all,' said Mrs Harrison, 'it is France and it's your birthday tomorrow.'

She smiled happily at her daughter as she spoke and then glanced at Fiona. What a nice girl she is she was thinking as she looked, and what an odd life she seems to lead. It wasn't that Fiona said much, it was the little snippets of conversation which she obviously didn't realise gave away so much. Claire was doing the cooking this weekend, she learned, for herself and Stewart. How odd; what about the mother and that Mr Lennard chap? It was all very peculiar and, poor child, what a life. Thank God she seemed untouched by it and certainly she was such a good friend to Amanda.

The next morning was Amanda's fourteenth birthday. At eight o'clock, her parents rang her from their room and sang Happy Birthday down the phone. Breakfast and presents at nine they said. Fiona had thought long and hard about what to give her friend. After all, Amanda had most things and she, Fiona, didn't have much money to spend. Her savings were the five pounds that was the regular Christmas and birthday present from Mummy (and last year, Mr Lennard). She almost hated taking it, but it gave her a sense of security somehow and she had saved thirty five pounds to date. So, after much thought, she painted a picture of Amanda from memory. She had been quite surprised at how it had turned out. She'd always loved painting and drawing, but she'd never done a portrait before. She had bought a simple frame from Woolworths and now, with some trepidation, she handed it to her very special friend. Amanda, all bubbly and excited, took the package delightedly. Fiona nearly choked with embarrassment. It was obviously no good. Obviously, Amanda didn't like it.

'I'm sorry,' she began, apologetically.

'Whatever for? It's marvellous! It's the best present I've ever had in my life!' She put it down carefully on the bed and kissed her friend gently on the cheek.

'I mean it, Fee, I really do. I've never had anything, *anything*, I've liked more. Wait till M and D see it.'

Fiona loved the way she called her parents M and D, and they called her A.

'Look at the time!' screamed Amanda suddenly. The girls had five minutes to wash and dress and be downstairs. They just made it. At the last minute, Amanda dashed back into the room and collected the portrait.

'Oh no,' wailed Fiona.

'Oh yes!' laughed her friend, 'M and D will want to see this!'

Mr Harrison handed his daughter a small parcel. Again, Fiona watched as Amanda tore off the wrapping to reveal a small box. There, nestling inside on deep blue velvet, was a beautiful gold watch.

'Oh D, it's beautiful,' she breathed taking it out, handing it to him and extending her arm for him to put it on. Mrs Harrison glanced at Fiona, expecting perhaps to see a shade of envy on the girl's face. She was glad to be disappointed. Fiona looked as excited as her daughter, and it was then she decided that she was going to buy an advance birthday present for her.

'Now,' said Amanda, 'look at this.' She held out the small picture for her parents to look at. Fiona found she was squirming with embarrassment. She so wished Amanda had left it upstairs in the bedroom. The Harrisons looked at it casually. Then, when they saw the exquisite piece of work in front of them, they were both immensely surprised and delighted.

'But Fiona, it's beautiful. It really is exactly like Amanda. You've caught her exactly. I'd no idea you were such an artist – did you darling?' Mr Harrison turned to his wife as he spoke. She took the portrait carefully in her hands.

'I'm no expert Fiona, but I think this is really good. I've heard water colour is a difficult medium, but you've – well, it looks professional.'

Fiona felt her spirits soar. The art teacher had always been very encouraging, but this was the biggest accolade she had ever had.

'You should become a professional artist my dear. Go to Art College and perhaps, one day when you're famous, we shall be able to say we knew you.'

Fiona blushed. 'It's not that good.'

'It most certainly is.' Mrs Harrison spoke firmly. 'What a perfect present A,' she said.

'Isn't it M? It really is.'

After breakfast and all the excitement about the watch and the portrait, Mrs Harrison announced that now it was her turn to take Amanda shopping for a present from her. 'Also,' she said, glancing at Fiona, 'an advance birthday present from us; Mr Harrison and myself.'

'Oh, you shouldn't, really. Just coming to Paris with you and Amanda has been the best present I've ever had in the world.'

They all burst out laughing at her fervently expressed statement.

'Two hours, that's all girls,' Mr Harrison said, 'then it's off to see some more of Disneyland.'

'I think we can just about manage that, if we must.' Amanda's mother shepherded the girls in front of her like a mother hen with her chicks.

They went straight to Gallerie Lafayette.

'I want to buy you a really pretty dress A,' said her mother.

Amanda grimaced and Fiona grinned in response. Still, she thought, it must be lovely having someone who wants to buy you something, anything. A compromise was reached; silky wide trousers that finished at the hip, a brief top that exposed a bare midriff and a purple velvet unstructured jacket.

'Heaven knows what your father will think,' Mrs Harrison said somewhat ruefully.

'Now,' she said, briskly turning to Fiona, 'your turn.'

Amanda was obviously in on the plan and, with her mother, stopped Fiona's protests.

'It's an advance birthday present,' she said, 'and a thank you for that beautiful portrait Fiona dear.'

Mrs Harrison spoke as if she really meant it. Fiona felt almost overwhelmed at their kindness to her. There followed a most exciting half hour. Fiona tried on party slip dresses, suits, trousers, shirts and sweaters. But, like her friend, she finally finished with a trouser outfit. No silk though. When would she ever wear them again? Instead, she chose trousers of the softest, lightest wool that seemed to flow with her as she walked. To go with them, a pretty blue blouse that emphasised the colour of her eyes, plus a toning waistcoat with a hand woven design on the front panels.

'You look gorgeous,' Amanda and her mother chorused together.

Indeed, she felt pretty gorgeous too. Her eyes sparkled and her cheeks were flushed with excitement. It was obvious, thought Mrs Harrison, that this girl was going to be a stunning young woman one day.

The rest of the day continued to be sheer fun. They all four of them went on everything at Disneyland they hadn't been on the day before. Once again, totally fascinated, they watched the evening parade with its almost mesmerising music and twinkling lights. Later that evening, they went back to Montmartre.

'Another treat in store.'

Mr Harrison winked at his daughter. Fiona loved watching the family. Once again, she couldn't help but compare it with her own. A sudden worry about Claire and Stewart came into her mind. She felt guilty that she was having such a good time. She just hoped Claire was coping. She tried to banish her fears, but niggling in the back of her mind was the thought that Claire needed her.

The surprise, after wandering round the street artists for about ten minutes, was when Mr Harrison stopped by a young man in his early twenties.

'A portrait please,' and he pointed to Fiona.

'Oh no,' she protested, feeling somewhat overwhelmed.

'It's a little thank you for the portrait of Amanda, though it won't be as well executed as the one you did,' he whispered conspiratorially in her ear, followed by a little wink. A sign, Fiona realised, that was an acceptance somehow into their family group, if only for this weekend.

The young man, Paul, introduced himself quite formally. He told her to sit on the small stool and moved her head this way and that until he was satisfied he had her head in just the position he wanted.

Fiona sat very still while the three Harrisons stood behind the artist, watching his every stroke. He used pastels and charcoal, Fiona noticed; a messy medium, but very effective. She hoped he would spray it with hair spray to stop it rubbing off as she carried it home. It was weird really. The Harrisons' expressions, smiling, quizzical and interested, made Fiona wish that she, too, could see the development on the grey paper in front of them.

Finally, after about ten minutes, Paul sighed and smiled.

'C'est fini mademoiselle.'

Fiona stood up, a mix of shyness and excitement. What would she see? There before her was a slightly serious young woman, looking older than her nearly fourteen years; perhaps not older, but showing a maturity she hadn't been aware of. Her eyes looked bigger and bluer than they seemed to her when she peered at herself in the mirror. But he had captured something that she felt uncomfortable about, an air somehow of sadness hung around her. In ten minutes, it appeared that he had seen something of her soul. She felt quite unnerved. She watched as Mr Harrison paid her artist, who then sprayed the portrait, placed a piece of waxed paper on top of it and then carefully rolled it and handed it to Fiona.

'You are beautiful mademoiselle, a pleasure to do your portrait.'

Fiona smiled uneasily. She wasn't used to compliments.

'I bet he says that to everyone,' she whispered to Amanda.

'Well,' said Mrs Harrison as they walked away, 'it's very good but not,' she added, 'anything like as good as the one you did of Amanda and you didn't have her sitting for you.'

'Agreed,' said her husband. 'You have a career ahead of you young lady.'

'Perhaps I'll be an artist in Montmartre,' laughed Fiona, happy with the thought of a life like the artists of Paris.

They continued their walk, reaching the steps leading up to the Sacré Cœur. They climbed slowly up, turning at intervals to look down at the view.

The Sacré Cœur was like another world. Its peace and serenity hit them as they walked through the doors; the coolness, the smell of burning candles and a faint but discernible smell of incense. Fiona was overwhelmed. She hadn't been in a church since Dada's funeral. This was so different yet it brought back memories of him. She found she was crying.

'Oh my dear, are you alright?' A concerned Mrs Harrison put her arm around the girl, who was quietly sobbing and trying hard not to.

'I'm sorry.' She tried to smile through her tears. 'It's just so beautiful and it made me think of Dada – Daddy,' she corrected herself automatically.

'Shall we go?' said Mr Harrison, uncomfortable as ever with female tears.

'What are those candles for?' Amanda asked brightly, trying to lighten the atmosphere.

'People light a candle in memory of someone, or perhaps to think of someone especially.' Amanda's mother spoke softly.

Fiona smiled; a softness touched her face. Almost a spiritual look, thought Mrs Harrison to herself.

Fiona had changed the five pound note she had brought with her into francs. She had planned to buy something very small for

Claire and Stewart. Now she knew that she must light a candle in memory of Dada.

'May I light a candle – two candles actually – for my father and Claire and Stewart?

Mr Harrison put his hand in his pocket. With great dignity Fiona said, 'Thank you Mr Harrison, but I have some change.'

The candles were fifty centimes each. She carefully looked at the information and then put in one franc for two candles. Firstly, she lit one from one of the other candles for Dada. She watched as it flickered. She felt her spirits soar, as if, for a moment, Dada was there with her. She had never felt so comforted, never, that is, since that last hug from Dada seven years ago. Then she lit a candle for Claire and Stewart. Let them be alright, she found herself saying inwardly. Did God hear her prayers she wondered? Would he be keeping an eye on things? She'd never really thought about God before. Religious education lessons were a bit of a turn-off most of the time, but today, in the church, it was as if she was surrounded by God.

They were on the plane. The weekend, the wonderful weekend, thought Fiona, was over. Her mind re-lived it all. It has been so special, so very special. In a way it had been awful too. She knew for sure now that her life was different in every way to Amanda's, and probably from everyone else's in her class.

The Harrisons, too, were thinking about the weekend. It had gone better than they had hoped. Certainly, Amanda had enjoyed it far more than she would have done had not Fiona joined them.

'It was a good idea darling,' Mr Harrison said, squeezing his wife's hand affectionately. 'I wasn't sure when you first mooted it, but she's such a nice girl. I'm so pleased A has such a good friend.'

'I am too,' replied his wife, 'but I hate having to let her go back into that peculiar household.'

From odd snippets of conversation and occasional comments, Fiona had unknowingly let slip more than she realised, perhaps more than she would have wanted them to know.

The car stopped outside the house. Mr Harrison jumped out and opened the boot. The smart new holdall he had bought Fiona as an advance birthday present was handed over. He gave her a quick hug.

'Now you remember young lady, it's not just Amanda who is your friend, we all are.'

'Thank you.' Fiona felt choked with emotion. She had never known such kindness.

Chapter 5

The house was unusually silent as she let herself in through the back door. No television blaring from the kids' room, no Stewart chattering excitedly. A terrible fear touched Fiona. Almost too scared to look, she pushed open the door of the kids' room. It was in darkness and for a moment she thought it was empty.

A quiet moan and a faint 'Fee' made her hastily put the light on. Claire lay on the sofa. Fiona took in the whole picture at a glance. Claire's face was blotched and tear-stained, the bottom of her left leg red and blistered. She rushed to her sister's side; her worst fears had been realised. She should never have gone away!

'What happened Claire?' she said urgently, whilst her mind was racing ahead. She must get her to the hospital and fast.

'The soup,' sobbed Claire, 'Stewie wanted tomato soup. He knocked me, I spilt it on my leg. I remember sitting down, I suppose there was soup on the floor or something and I think I must have bumped my head. I don't remember much except my leg – it's hurting so much Fee.' She began crying again.

Fiona bent down and kissed her. As she touched Claire's head she felt something sticky; there was blood. She must have knocked herself out.

'Stay here Claire.' What a silly thing to say, she thought. 'I'm going to telephone for an ambulance.'

Her mind was full of questions. *What is Mr Lennard thinking of? Where is Stewie? What's Mummy thinking of?* All sorts of thoughts were rushing through her head as she dialled 999. Stewart had heard her voice and came running out of the lounge.

'Oh good, you're back,' he said happily 'I've had a nice time with Mummy and Uncle Len.' He obviously knew nothing of Claire's dilemma.

She put down the phone and started walking back down the hall to Claire.

'You're back then, from all your gadding about. I hope you're satisfied. We've had to look after Stewart.'

'It's a pity you didn't look after Claire too.' Her voice was so filled with fury that he turned abruptly and closed the lounge door firmly behind him.

Soon Claire was tucked up in a bed at the hospital. Mild concussion accounted for her coming in and out of consciousness which was why she hadn't been able to telephone for an ambulance herself. She remembered nothing after falling, then coming to on the sofa where she had lain for twenty four hours. The hospital social worker arrived and they concocted some story that seemed to satisfy everyone there. They must be so stupid, Fiona thought, believing everything we say.

Claire was in hospital for a week. Every day, Fiona and Stewart visited her. Every day, Claire asked the same question, 'Can Mummy come? I want to see Mummy Fiona.' How could she tell her that as far as she knew, Mummy didn't even know! Mr Lennard wouldn't let her into the lounge or bedroom. He now locked the door when he left her to go to the kitchen.

'Your mother is too tired.' 'Your mother is sleeping.' 'Your mother is not well.'

Finally, Fiona stopped trying. Perhaps Mummy really didn't care any more.

Amanda wanted to know what her mother had thought of the outfit and the picture. Fiona made up the usual fiction; it was easier that way. She even lied about Claire. She had had a fall, she said, when Fiona arrived home and was OK, but because of mild concussion, the hospital was keeping her in for a week. She hated lying to her dear friend, but how could she tell the truth? The Harrisons might well-meaningly report the incident and then the three of them could finish up in care, even split up. Never, she vowed to herself, never. She had developed into an agile liar where their home life was concerned. Sometimes, she almost believed it herself, but only momentarily. The realisation hit her all too soon.

A subdued Claire returned home, now very wary of Mr Lennard. She had called him Uncle Len. She had thought he liked her, but he had left her there alone for all those hours. Although at the time she hadn't realised she had lain there alone and unattended, she knew now, and she knew she would never trust him again. She couldn't call him Mr Lennard either. He had, after all, been in her life for the last seven years, so she avoided him and when she couldn't, she didn't call him anything.

Stewart, on the other hand, seemed to have built some rapport with the man. Fiona noticed that he hung around Mr Lennard in the kitchen and wasn't shooed away. He was also permitted to visit Mummy.

'Is Mummy ill?' Fiona asked.

'She's quiet, but she cuddles me sometimes,' the little boy answered happily, 'and Uncle Lennard plays with me. He's bought me a train set.'

Fiona was surprised to say the least, but she was happy for her little brother. At least he was having a slightly more normal life. But, for the girls, things went on as before.

Chapter 6

GCSE time was coming up. Fiona was thoroughly enjoying her art project. Since the Paris trip nearly two years ago, she had worked particularly hard. She had felt so encouraged and her art teacher was delighted with her.

'I think you have a real future in Art, Fiona, perhaps advertising. You must go to Art College after 'A' levels.'

Yes, thought Fiona, Art College. She knew though that portraiture would be what she wanted to work towards. She had bought herself a sketch pad which was now full of studies of Stewie and Claire; sometimes, just a few lines catching a moment of play, or rapt attention on a face watching television.

On her sixteenth birthday, Amanda gave her a beautiful set of paints and her parents sent her a selection of brushes. Fiona was over the moon, longing to start using her new presents. The usual five pounds had been handed over by Mr Lennard.

'From your mother,' he said sourly. No 'Happy Birthday' there!

Claire had wanted to make her a birthday cake, but didn't, she said, 'because I'm scared of the kitchen.' Instead, she had made a little purse covered with beads. She loved sewing and had been secretly sewing in her bedroom. Fiona was so touched. Claire had never given her anything like this before, but since the accident a closer bond had developed between the sisters, a closeness that was important to both of them. But although they were closer now, they never talked about their life. It was as if the subject was taboo.

Stewart had drawn her a special picture.

'The train set,' he said. It was his pride and joy and although Fiona could have wished for a different picture, she loved the fact that with Claire's encouragement he had both known it was her birthday and drawn her the picture.

The exams were over. Both Fiona and Amanda were quietly confident. They had both taken eight, slightly different subjects. They both knew they had done quite well. Even so, they pretended to themselves, and each other, that they were worried, 'particularly about maths,' they both said, laughing. They weren't all that bad at maths, but it was what they enjoyed the least.

The results when they came were better than they could have hoped for. Fiona had five 'A's and three 'B's, and Amanda four 'A's and four 'B's. They danced around, waving the slips of paper, hugging each other and their classmates who, with a few exceptions, were all pretty pleased with themselves.

Fiona couldn't wait to rush home. She was going to insist that she saw Mummy. Mr Lennard was in the kitchen. Fiona tried to still her fast beating heart. She knew she had to be forceful, not something that came easily to her.

'I've got my results.'

He looked at her sneeringly. She felt her ire rise.

'I'm going to see my Mother. She has a right to know that I've done well,' she added quietly, trying to keep the tremor out of her voice.

Something in her demeanour, her expression, made Mr Lennard look at her closely, as if really seeing her for the first time. She shivered slightly under his close scrutiny. How she hated the man. She forced herself to smile at him. He picked up the tea tray.

'Follow me,' he said.

For the first time in over a year, she went into the lounge. The curtains were partly drawn. Her mother lay as she had the last time Fiona had seen her, on the sofa. Thinner now and pale, as a result, Fiona supposed, of spending her life indoors.

'Fiona.' Her mother sounded surprised.

'Mummy.' She felt like a little girl again. 'Mummy,' she repeated, 'I've got my GCSE results.'

Her mother smiled faintly.

'How nice dear, did you do well?'

Fiona told her, explaining carefully what she had in each subject. She wondered if Mummy was even taking it in.

'You're a good girl Fiona, like your father.

She couldn't have said anything that would have pleased Fiona more. She kissed her mother on the cheek. It felt clammy to the touch and Fiona shivered slightly, as if a ghost had walked over her grave.

She lay in bed that night, thinking and planning her future. With 'A' levels two years away, which seemed an age, she nevertheless began to think of life after that. After 'A' levels, she decided she would try to get into Art College. Why London she didn't know, perhaps because it was so far away from Edinburgh. Claire would be sixteen by then and Stewie fourteen, quite old enough to manage without her; they would have to. She really would have to persuade Claire to do some cooking soon.

She was drifting off to sleep, that delicious moment before deep sleep, when she was aware of the door opening very slowly. She was immediately alert. Claire? Stewie? Was one of them ill? All the usual thoughts went through her mind in the split seconds before she realised it was Mr Lennard silhouetted in the doorway, the light on the landing providing a clear picture of him standing there in his dressing gown.

'What do you want?' Fiona sat bolt upright, her tone automatically cold and unwelcoming.

'My dear.' His voice was quiet and conciliatory. 'I felt I didn't really congratulate you on your exam results. You really did do very well. Your mother and I are immensely proud of you.'

For a moment, Fiona was thrown off balance. Then, to her horror, she noticed he was closing the door behind him.

'Please go.' Her voice, even to herself, sounded strained and not a little frightened.

'My dear,' he said again, this time sitting on the end of the bed.

Fiona opened her mouth to scream, but, as if anticipating her, he almost leapt to where she sat, his dressing gown falling open as he moved, to reveal the total nakedness beneath.

Fiona couldn't breathe. His one hand was clamped over her mouth as he forced her down. The other hand drew back the bed covers. She threw herself this way and that; she'd had no idea how strong he was and she felt as helpless as a small bird caught in a net.

He was on top of her, one hand still over her mouth, the other now pulling her nightdress up above her breasts. She heard him groan. Then, as his mouth replaced his hand and she smelt stale cigarettes and alcohol, she was filled with nausea as he forced her mouth open with his tongue. He forced his way inside her. Unprepared, she was dry and his every movement hurt and hurt again. His tongue was almost down her throat. She hoped the vomit that was threatening would pour all over him, but her body failed her. He uttered a tremendous sound between a groan and a sound like some primitive animal. *He's an animal!* Fiona's mind was crying out. He pulled out of her and this time kissed her quite gently on the cheek.

'Well, I knew you'd be a tasty one! Soon we'll know each other very well and I shall taste, lick and suck every tiny spot on your pretty body.'

He stood up and tied his dressing gown around him. She

40

couldn't scream now, she had no scream left, and anyway, it couldn't stop what had happened.

He bent down and whispered in her ear, 'It's no use telling your mother. She would believe me, not you.'

Fiona knew this was horribly true. He turned at the door and looked back at where she lay.

'Rape suits you my dear,' was his last remark as he closed her bedroom door quietly behind him.

She lay absolutely still, her body hurting. Every part of her felt violated; she couldn't bear even to touch herself. She could feel the tears sliding from her eyes and dropping silently onto the pillow. She felt a warm wetness oozing from between her legs and realised it was from him. She shuddered convulsively.

All she wanted was to scrub her body inside out. If she went to the bathroom she knew the sound of the running water would wake Claire. How could she share anything so awful with her younger sister? The washbasin; thank goodness she had a washbasin in her room. Very carefully, clutching her nightdress round her face, she staggered across the room and quickly filled the basin with warm water. She dropped her nightdress in a heap on the floor as she plunged her head fully into the water. The clean water washed over her face and hair. She took the soap and washed her body from her top, down her arms, her stomach. She paused. Somehow she had to get herself into the water. Drying her top half rapidly, she fetched her desk chair over and put it in front of the basin and, climbing up, she then lowered herself until her bottom rested in the, by now, tepid water. It was not enough, but it was better than nothing.

Standing on the chair, she soaped herself vigorously and then sat down again. She let out the water, refilled the bowl and repeated this process several times. At last she felt that she had washed him out of her. Her body may have been defiled, but her mind was crystal clear. There was no way she could stay. She must leave, and leave tonight before he was awake. Fiona knew she could never bear to see him again.

She dressed silently, then, taking the holdall from the bottom of the wardrobe – unused since the Harrisons had bought if for her in Paris – she opened drawers and collected undies, tee shirts and spare jeans and quickly filled the bag. Her toothbrush and paste were the last things she put in, having cleaned her teeth three times already. She still felt she could taste the grossness of his tongue.

Moving the chair back to the desk, she sat down and wrote a brief note to her mother, saying now that she had her GCSEs, she felt it was time to leave home. For Stewart also, she left a brief note and, of course, one for Amanda. She paused. She had to speak to Claire. She sat watching the clock. Five o'clock would be the latest she dared leave it, otherwise her movements might be heard downstairs. With her holdall in her hand, and no last, lingering look at the room she had, until this night, regarded as a sanctuary, she moved as quietly as possible along the landing to Claire's bedroom and let herself in.

Her sister looked so peaceful sleeping as she always did face down into the pillow, covers pushed back, an arm hanging loosely down on one side of the bed.

'Claire,' she whispered urgently, close to her sister's ear. 'Claire, please, please, wake up.'

As Claire stirred sleepily, Fiona added, 'Shush, shush.'

Claire rolled over onto her back. Her eyes flew to the illuminated clock on her side table.

'Fee, it's only five o'clock,' she began.

Fiona put her hand gently over her sister's mouth, then took if off again rapidly, remembering with horror that 'he' had started by putting his hand over her mouth. Claire was by now fully awake, her eyes wide with surprise.

42

Thank God she wakes up so quickly, thought Fiona. There followed an urgent whispered conversation. Claire tried to argue with her, but to no avail. For some reason, Fiona had decided to leave home and go to London; now, in the middle of the night.

'But why Fee, why?' she kept repeating.

'Darling Claire,' – how could she tell her the truth? Mr Lennard wouldn't touch her, as he hadn't touched her until she was sixteen – 'I've got to go, that's all there is to it.' Fiona spoke firmly.

Claire nodded as her sister handed her the note for Amanda and agreed to give it to her at school. She also agreed to give the note to their mother and to explain to Stewart, who would be impossible to wake as he would make so much noise he'd wake the household.

'You're in charge now Claire. I'll write as soon as I have an address.'

Claire started to cry and put her arms round Fiona's neck.

'Must you, must you?' but she already knew that Fiona was leaving her, leaving her and Stewart. Claire felt a pang of unease. Fiona had only left once before when she went to Paris and that had been disastrous. She wondered how she would cope.

There were two stairs that creaked. Fortunately, Fiona knew where they were and carefully avoided them. She crept down the hall, expecting at any minute to hear a shout as Mr Lennard threw open the bedroom door and caught her sneaking away.

She closed the back door; there was a slight click. She hesitated for a moment for the first time, wondering whether she was doing the right thing. It was a momentary doubt however. She almost ran down the short drive, turned right and headed for the main road and the nearest bus stop.

Chapter 7

The train for London arrived at six thirty. Fiona only had to wait twenty minutes. The bus had come as she arrived at the bus stop but she found herself glancing back, sure somehow that she would see Mr Lennard chasing after her.

It wasn't until she was on the train and it was pulling out of the station with no sign of pursuit that she heaved a sigh of relief that seemed to come from somewhere deep within. The woman sitting opposite, who had herself boarded the train only a few moments before Fiona, looked up from her magazine and smiled. But the girl opposite was gazing ahead unseeingly, her eyes fixed on some distant point, her face pale and, Mary Marshall noticed, her hands trembling.

Mary never knew quite what propelled her. She was not normally an impetuous person, but something about the girl facing her touched her heart. She knew, she just knew, something awful had happened. Without giving herself time to even think, she moved rapidly and sat down beside the girl, putting her square, capable hands on top of those trembling fingers.

Fiona sensed rather than saw the figure. The hands, warm and gentle, made her turn her head. She saw a woman of about thirty five to forty, mid-brown hair straight and shiny with a soft fringe. There was something in her eyes that made Fiona feel safe. Quite suddenly and unexpectedly, she found herself in this stranger's arms, sobbing and sobbing as if her heart would break.

'It's alright.' Mary held her closely, wondering what terror had befallen this child.

Fortunately, apart from them, the carriage was empty. It wasn't long before, slowly and with sobs cracking her voice, the story of the rape was told. Mary listened with mounting horror and anger.

'But who is this Mr Lennard?'.

Fiona hesitated. Her voice was calmer now. The lady had taken a handkerchief from her bag and gently wiped the tear-stained face. She thought of her own children waiting for her in London, so safe, so protected.

She repeated, 'Who is this Mr Lennard?'.

Fiona hesitated again. She had never told anyone about her home life, not her teachers, not even Amanda whom she trusted above everyone. She had always felt she would be betraying 'something family'. Yet now, feeling strangely calm, she started at the beginning.

'Dada died,' she said, this time not correcting herself. 'Dada died when I was seven'.

Time passed. Mary sat quite still as this child's life unfolded in front of her. The funeral; Mr Lennard moving in; her mother in a wheelchair; the separation of the children to their own quarters; the weekend in Paris, so happy but with such dire consequences for Claire. Finally, the GCSE results and the final straw, the rape, for that's what it was, of this innocent child by a monster.

Mary was moved to tears herself. She hugged the girl tenderly. The last time she had been hugged like that had been Dada. Fiona started crying anew. Mary was horrified. Perhaps she shouldn't have been so familiar. After all, Fiona – she now knew her name – probably didn't want to be touched by anyone. She tried to draw her arms from around the girl, but Fiona resisted and snuggled closer, feeling safe at last. She drifted into a dreamless sleep, exhausted from spent emotions and lack of sleep the night before.

It gave Mary a chance to think.

Fiona slept peacefully for over an hour, during which time, despite a now aching back from the uncomfortable position she was in, Mary had made a number of decisions. The first was that there was no way she was going to let Fiona loose in London. The girl had told her she had saved fifty five pounds, but hadn't actually planned what she was going to do when she got there. Mary and her husband had a largish house in Putney and, with no au pair these days, there was still what they referred to as 'the au pair's room'. It was at the top of the house and when they had moved there ten years earlier, it had been a large attic with a door reached by a ladder. They had had a short staircase put in and blocked off the sloping eves to make capacious cupboard space and a tiny bathroom, leaving a spacious central area large enough for a bed, sofa, desk, easy chair and bookcase. Mary had made new covers for an old kidney shaped dressing table, using the same pretty blue fabric as the blinds covering the two windows they had set into the roof.

The au pairs had always loved the room and now Mary could see no reason why Fiona shouldn't stay with them, as least for a short time while she got herself sorted out. James, her big teddy bear of a husband whom she adored, wouldn't mind. If Mary believed something was right he would generally go along with it. *Yes, that's it*, thought Mary positively, and looking down at the sleeping girl in her arms knew she had made the right decision.

Fiona woke quite suddenly, a tiny spot of moisture on her lips. She had dribbled a little while she was asleep, and to her consternation saw a damp patch on the lady's blouse. For a moment Fiona was confused, still perhaps a little asleep. She moved suddenly, sitting bolt upright. Had she really told this total stranger everything?

Mary moved, glad to ease her aching back and, as if sensing

Fiona's discomfort, she lightly touched the girl's hand.

'The sleep will have done you good, but I'm starving. How about some breakfast?'

Fiona realised she was ravenous. 'May I come with you?' She spoke a little hesitantly, still slightly overcome with embarrassment at having talked so much and, on top of that, having dribbled on Mrs Marshall's blouse.

'My dear, I would be most hurt if you didn't. Anyway, I hate eating alone, don't you?' She almost bit her tongue off. What a tactless thing to say! This child had, by the sound of it, not sat down to eat with an adult for years. It all seemed so unbelievable, yet she had no doubt that she had been told the complete truth.

'Mrs Marshall,' Fiona began hesitantly as they sat down at the table in the dining car.

'Please, call me Mary.'

Fiona smiled. 'Thank you Mary.' Again, she spoke rather hesitantly. Life had turned upside down in the last few hours. Her normal resilience and confidence had deserted her.

'I'm sorry that I unloaded myself like that – to a complete stranger too.'

'You know, it's often much easier to talk to a stranger.' Mary smiled. 'I feel honoured, Fiona, that you trusted me and I hope we can be friends?'

The waiter coughed to attract their attention.

'A cooked breakfast for me: bacon, eggs, toast, orange juice, coffee, the lot!' Mary laughed, *like a girl* Fiona thought. 'Please join me, or I'll feel more greedy than ever.'

Fiona thought about her fifty five pounds and a slight frown formed, but just as quickly, it went. One good meal, she deserved that. She nodded.

'I'd like exactly what you've ordered,' and, for the first time, she laughed. Mary saw a glimpse of a happier girl. All is not yet lost, she thought to herself.

It was over breakfast that she introduced the subject of where Fiona was going to stay and what she was going to do.

'I shall find a room and get a job.'

The wonderful confidence of youth Mary thought, a trifle wryly.

'I've a better idea,' she said. 'My husband and I live in Putney, only twenty minutes by tube from the centre of London. Why don't you come and stay with us for a few days, just until you've found your feet?'

She could see the doubtful expression crossing Fiona's face. She added hurriedly 'Actually, you'll be doing me quite a favour. Our au pair left some months ago and the children really miss having a teenager around.' Slight exaggeration she thought, but in a good cause.

'How many children do you have?'

'Three. Alison is ten, Lynn is eight and Sebastian is six.'

'Two girls and a boy, just like us. Oh, I didn't mean like us, I meant......'

'I know what you meant.' Mary smiled kindly. 'We would love to have you stay for a few days.' She added the last words as an afterthought. She felt sure James would understand and that the children would accept Fiona, but she supposed she must keep her options open, though her natural instinct was to invite Fiona to become part of their family forever.

The rest of the journey seemed to Fiona to speed by. Every sound of the train, every station, every tunnel took her further and further away from the recent nightmare. Mary Marshall was like a rock to a drowning sailor, Fiona thought dreamily in a half awake, half sleeping state that she was drifting in and out of.

'You are like a rock,' she said suddenly, apropos nothing.

Mary too had been in a reverie. She jerked back to the present with a jolt.

'What did you say dear?'

'A rock,' Fiona repeated, 'you're like a rock for a drowning sailor. In this case, I'm the sailor.'

Mary laughed, but quickly noticed the hurt look on Fiona's face.

'Darling, I wasn't laughing at you. It's just that I've never thought of myself as a rock, but in fact,' she went on, 'I think it's one of the nicest compliments I have ever been paid. I'm happy that I'm your rock and I hope you will always think of me that way.'

At the time, Fiona didn't notice the word 'always', but that night, as she lay in the comfy bed in the au pair's room, looking at the moon through the window, she remembered 'always'. Mary had said 'a few days', then she had said 'always'. Fiona felt confused. What did she want? Where did she want to go from here? She thought about their arrival – big, burly Mr Marshall hugging his wife affectionately; the children throwing themselves at their mother with delighted abandon. Fiona had hung back a little, feeling like an intruder, but Mary, ever watchful, had quickly changed all that. She had pulled Fiona into the family circle.

'My new friend,' she announced. 'Fiona will be staying with us for a few days.'

If Fiona had expected resistance, there was none, just an agreeable acceptance. They had enjoyed a pasta supper at the big kitchen table. Fiona listened and observed, only speaking when spoken to. She felt quite overwhelmed by this boisterous, happy mob.

Soon, Sebastian was packed off to bed, shortly followed by his sisters. Mary suggested Fiona might like to wallow in a bath 'after a long journey', she added, but meeting Fiona's eyes steadily. So Fiona had indeed wallowed. She had used the Badedas that stood on the shelf above the bath. She had felt the water cleansing her as she lay back. Never in her wildest imaginings had she thought of

49

finding herself in such a safe haven. Her last thoughts were of the moon shining through the window and of Mary and James. She slept deeply and untroubled, feeling safe at last.

Downstairs, Mary and James were having the usual catch-up.

'And how is Iona?'

Mary and Iona had been friends since Cheltenham Ladies College days, when they shared a dormitory. Iona, now a doctor married to another doctor and living in Edinburgh, had remained a close friend and the two women spent some time together most years – a week in London or a week in Scotland. This had been Mary's week away and, as usual, it had been full of reminiscences for both of them. But now Mary dismissed it with a quick 'Iona's fine, and of course she and Jack send their love.'

James knew his wife very well. He looked at her earnest expression and knew his beloved Mary was set on another mission.

'Tell me all about it,' he said gently, sitting back in his favourite armchair whilst Mary sat on the floor at his feet. She looked up at him, her face ablaze with love.

'I do love you James.'

'I know you do. Now stop trying to soften me up and tell me all about young Fiona.'

Mary took a deep breath to compose herself. She wanted to sound matter-of-fact. She did not want him to think she had been swept along on an emotional whim.

As the story unfolded, James face took on a grim look.

'My God!' he exploded, as the final episode of the rape came to an end and the escape from the house.

'My God,' he repeated, as if bereft of adequate words, 'hanging would be too good for him'. Then, as an afterthought and with a note of caution entering his voice, 'You do believe it all Mary, don't you?'

'If you had seen her James, you couldn't even ask me that.'

He nodded. 'I had to ask the question.'

He pulled her to her feet and she sank onto his lap, resting her head on his shoulder. They sat like that for some time.

'Time for bed I think,' he said finally. 'She'll stay of course,' he added, as an afterthought, not even a note of question in his voice. As a response, Mary stood on tiptoe and put her arms around his neck.

'I love you James Marshall,' she said, smiling into his eyes.

Chapter 8

Fiona opened her eyes. The surroundings were unfamiliar and she had a split second's moment of panic, then a slow, relaxed smile appeared on her face. She was safe with the Marshalls. She hitched herself onto an elbow and looked around. She had hardly taken it in last night. Her holdall was on the floor, still unopened. She looked down. She was wearing a pretty, short sleeved cotton nightdress, not her own. She remembered cleaning her teeth too. Mary must have put out a toothbrush and toothpaste. Fiona once again felt overwhelmed with such thoughtfulness. Apart from the Harrisons, who seemed a long way off now, no-one had ever, not since Dada, been so kind.

There was a light knock on the door. The eldest daughter came in slowly, carefully balancing a breakfast tray.

'Mummy thought you might like breakfast in bed this morning - as a special treat,' she added with a gamin grin. 'We only get breakfast in bed when we're ill. Are you ill?' she asked curiously.

'No, not ill, perhaps just a bit tired. How kind of Mary – your mummy,' she corrected herself.

'Don't worry about calling her Mary. I often call her that.' The little girl spoke with airy confidence. Fiona laughed. What a happy, uncomplicated family they seemed.

The breakfast was surprisingly welcome – orange juice, coffee, scrambled eggs on toast and a croissant, hot from the oven. Alison announced that she was staying and was soon joined by her brother and sister who squabbled and laughed and talked all together, or so it seemed. Fiona's head began to spin. As if on cue, Mary appeared.

'Shoo, all of you,' she said, pushing her children towards the door, 'it's my turn to talk to Fiona now!'

Several days passed, one drifting into another. A general lassitude seemed to have hit Fiona. She lay for hours on the hammock, her mind wandering over the years, but always taking a leap over her last night at home. She had to jump over the great black pit every time it threatened to surface. She couldn't, not yet anyway, bear to think about it.

Mary was worried; the girl seemed to be coming apart. She had been withdrawn and seemed to be dreaming her days away. This was not the girl on the train who, once she had told her story, had seemed to start fighting back. It was James who calmed her.

'Give her space darling, just for a few more days, until the weekend at least.'

So Mary, as ever trusting his judgement, let Fiona laze away her days.

Fiona looked at her paint box, her sketch book. She suddenly had an urge to do something. She sat at the desk and started to sketch. First James. Why him? she wondered as her pencil flew over the paper, deft lines creating the perfect image of her host. Then, one by one, the children; Alison with her straight black hair in a single plait; Lynn with her slightly curly short brown hair; Seb, as they called him, with his freckled face and merry grin; and finally, Mary. Her pencil was still, poised for a moment. This was the important one.

Slowly she started. Mary's face came alive on the page. The deep, still quality of her eyes, the perfect oval face. Somehow, even the beautiful quality of her almost alabaster skin shone from the paper, the slight fringe, the light brown hair forming a frame around her face. There was no colour, only pencil, but as Fiona sat back, she felt satisfied – complete again. Somehow, her drawing had acted as a catharsis. She felt cleansed and new.

With a new spring to her step, she ran downstairs and burst into the kitchen.

'What can I do for you Mary?' Mary, rolling pastry at the kitchen table, looked up with a smile. Fiona was better. Just looking at her smiling face, her eyes alight with energy, why, she is beautiful thought Mary. Alison came in from the garden. She'd found Fiona rather a disappointment. All she seemed to do was sleep in the hammock.

'Mummy, Lynn and I want to go to the Putney Exchange. I've seen a tee shirt in GAP that I simply have to have. I need it,' she added dramatically.

'You always need everything,' Mary laughed. 'Perhaps Fiona might like to go with you. You can show her around.'

'I'd love to go.' Fiona suddenly felt quite remiss. She had been here for days and done nothing. Whilst they were out, she could buy a paper and look for a room. They must want to be rid of her by now.

Mary put the pie in the oven and picked up a pile of ironing that her cleaning lady had done earlier. She climbed up the final flight of stairs to Fiona's room with a clean towel for the girl. The room was as neat as a pin, rather different from the au pair days; she grimaced inwardly.

Just about to leave the room, she noticed the sketch pad and paints on the desk. Curiosity getting the better of her, and feeling rather guilty, she almost tiptoed over to the desk. The first thing she saw was a picture of herself. It was like looking in a mirror. She gasped with pleasure and surprise. Silently, she turned back the pages; one after another, her family appeared before her. Finally,

James; it was James exactly. This girl was a brilliant artist.

Without meaning to, she continued turning back the pages. This must be Claire, she thought, looking at the picture of a girl painted in water colours, not unlike Fiona, but darker with smaller eyes. She smiled at Stewart. Looks a rascal, she thought. A very pretty girl was next. Amanda; it's Amanda. Mary felt as though she was intruding on Fiona's life, as she was, but it was like a magnet drawing her on. She kept turning the pages; a frail looking woman lying on a sofa, and on the first page of the book, a fine looking man, and alongside, a man who was obviously dying. Mary could feel the pain, both in the man's face and in the suffering of the artist. She quietly put the book back as she had found it and, without a backward glance, left the room.

The Putney Exchange was a bustling sort of place – two floors of shops, a supermarket, children's play area and glass lifts which, judging by the number of children in them, were of special interest. Alison headed straight for GAP; she knew exactly what she was looking for and found it quite quickly. Fiona browsed amongst the trousers and tee shirts, enjoying the opportunity to look with no pressure. That was short-lived however. The girls wanted to go upstairs to the coffee shop for some hot chocolate and to see if any of their friends were there. Fiona, breaking into her precious money, paid for three cups of steaming hot chocolate (in the middle of a heat wave she remarked to herself) but it was cool with the air-conditioning and the hot chocolate went down very well. Then it was up and down the lifts, Alison in one, and Lynn in the other.

On the way back, only a ten minute stroll, Fiona bought a local paper.

'Why do you want that?' asked the ever curious Lynn, 'we have a paper at home.'

'This is the local one. I need to find a room.'

Both girls looked surprised.

'Aren't you going to stay with us?' they chorused.

'No,' Fiona answered in a firmer tone that she meant to. 'No, I only came to stay for a few days.'

'Pity,' said Lynn, 'we like you, you know.'

'Thank you.' Fiona was touched. It would be hard to leave them all.

Of course, the girls couldn't keep it to themselves. Over lunch, they chattered about the Exchange and equally chattily, informed their surprised mother that Fiona was leaving. Mary raised a questioning eyebrow as she looked across the table at Fiona. Fiona lowered her head in brief acknowledgement. Mary couldn't wait for the meal to be over, and while she and Fiona were clearing up the kitchen and the children were once again in the garden, she broached the subject.

'Fiona, my dear, we wanted to give you some space, not to worry you, but James and I – well, we'll be so very disappointed if you leave. We would really like you stay with us indefinitely.'

There was a long silence. Mary stood up from loading the dishwasher and turned to face the girl. Tears were pouring down her cheeks.

'Why?' she said, 'why are you being so kind to me? I don't deserve it.'

'Nonsense.' Mary spoke quite brusquely, though she felt near to tears herself. 'We have grown very fond of you in the short time we've known you. Yes, James too,' as if reading the unspoken question hovering on Fiona's lips. Mary held out her arms and again Fiona felt their warm embrace. They cried quietly together.

'You are soppy.' Sebastian came in from the garden. 'Boys don't cry.'

'Oh yes they do Sebbie. It's good to cry sometimes whether you are a boy or a girl.' Mary picked up her little son and gave him a hug. He struggled manfully for a moment and then gave in, secretly enjoying the warmth and delicious smell of his mother.

Mary could hardly wait for the children to be in bed that night and, after supper, the three of them, James, Mary and Fiona went into the sitting room. They had got into the habit of watching the nine o'clock news together. Fiona generally watched for about fifteen minutes, as much to leave Mary and James some time on their own, and because she had been surprisingly tired of late, which she put down to the emotional stress that she had been through. She said her goodnights after a short while and went up to bed.

'James, turn the wretched thing off, I want to talk to you.'

James smiled good-naturedly. He'd caught the headlines; that was all that really mattered to him. He pressed the off button on the hand control.

'I'm all attention darling.'

'You'll never guess what I discovered today.' Mary's usually calm manner was gone. She could hardly contain herself for a moment longer.

'Fiona's a fine artist – not just good, but brilliant. You should see the drawings she's done of us all, from memory too! Really James, they're stunning. The one of you is more like you than you!' She laughed, catching his somewhat sceptical expression. 'I mean it James, she is good, very good. We must help her.'

'Let's see them then,' he said, 'put me out of my misery. I'd like to see what I really look like.' He laughed, half jokingly.

'I'm serious James, but she doesn't know I've seen them.'

'You've been snooping?' James' tone was not encouraging; he always believed individual privacy was very important.

'I know James. I have, I did but I didn't mean to. The pad was open on her desk and I was looking at myself. I simply couldn't resist looking at the rest of the book. Now you've made me feel terrible.' There was a slight catch in her throat.

'Come here you idiot,' he said affectionately, 'I know you wouldn't snoop, but if we're going to offer her a permanent home, she has to be able to trust us. Don't you agree?'

'Of course, James, you're quite right, but I can say I noticed the one of me and ask to see the rest.'

That sorted, they talked about the coming weekend. They were going to Rye. Mary and the children would stay for the rest of the holiday, and James would come down at the weekends.

'Tomorrow evening, after dinner,' said James, 'we'll talk to Fiona, ask her if she'd like to stay and tell her about Rye.'

Upstairs, and despite Mary's assurances in the day, Fiona was scanning the local newspaper for rooms to rent. Her money would last no time at all. For the first time she felt a sense of panic. She undressed quickly and was soon in bed, but slept fitfully, worrying about the future.

Chapter 9

It was after dinner the following evening. Fiona had mystifyingly come and gone once or twice during the day and it wasn't until Alison asked why Fiona bought a newspaper when they had already had one delivered that Mary twigged. Fiona was hunting for somewhere to live. Thank goodness they were going to talk to her that evening, but Mary was hard pressed not to speak out earlier and put the girl out of her misery. Several times she started to say something, then quickly changed her mind. It was important that she and James were together and spoke as one when they talked to Fiona about the future.

For the second day running, Mary couldn't wait for James to arrive home. She made a cheese soufflé and salad and rushed them through the meal, moving their plates as they put down their forks. If Fiona wondered why, she didn't show it. Indeed, her mind was mulling over the two grotty rooms she had seen. She had also been to the local job centre and they thought that with her GCSE results they would find her a job quite quickly. Meanwhile, they suggested she should sign on, though she wouldn't receive any money for several weeks.

Instead of turning on the television – indeed, it wasn't yet nine o'clock – James sat, not on his usual chair, but on one of the two sofas on either side of the fireplace. He indicated by a look and a gesture that Fiona should sit by him. Mary sat opposite, wanting to watch Fiona carefully, to see if she could read the girl's reaction to their plans.

'Fiona, have you thought about your future?' James began.

This is it thought Fiona, they want me to leave.

'I've looked at some rooms and signed on today.' She heard Mary gasp and looked at her in surprise.

'But we don't want …,' began Mary. James silenced her with a loving look.

'Fiona my dear,' he began again, 'we haven't known you for very long – indeed, a very short while, but in that time, we, Mary, myself and our children have become fond of you. My wife, Mary,' he corrected himself, trying to retain the informality in the conversation he wanted, 'Mary has begun to look upon you as another daughter.'

Fiona glanced at Mary, as for confirmation. Mary nodded and smiled warmly back. Fiona looked at James again.

'Your future is yours to do with as you choose, but we would feel quite honoured if you let us act as surrogate parents. I know your mother is in Scotland,' he added hastily. At the mention of her mother, Fiona shuddered because the image of Mr Lennard swam into vision.

'Oh my God,' James said helplessly, seeing tears threatening. 'I'm making a pig's ear of this Mary,' he said, appealing to his wife to say the right thing.

Mary smiled. 'Fiona, darling Fiona – all James, all we, are trying to say is that we want you here with us, to be part of our family for as long as you want. You can go to sixth form college, art college, whatever.'

At the mention of art school, Fiona glanced up sharply. She had been studying the pattern on the rug with great intensity.

'How do you know about art?', she asked, a question in her voice. Mary gulped, slightly guiltily.

'I couldn't help it Fiona. I took clean towels to your bathroom yesterday and saw your sketch pad on the desk, with an amazing drawing of me.' She gulped again. Time for honesty now, she thought. 'Actually, Fiona, I was so intrigued that I'm afraid I looked at all the other sketches and paintings too.'

Make or break time thought James to himself. He need not have worried.

'What do you think?' Fiona looked up eagerly.

'How could you even ask?' Mary said. 'Fiona, you are so gifted. I'm a complete novice but even I can tell you are an artist.'

Fiona sighed. That sigh said so much. *They really do want me to stay, they want to help me, they like me.* She looked slowly at one face and then the other. The silence was deafening.

Speaking slowly, as if measuring carefully every word she was saying, she said, 'You're both so kind, you've been so wonderful to me. How can I ever repay you?'

Her eyes were full of tears. James held out his arms to them both, with one either side of him. He kissed them both, first Fiona, gently brushing her hair with his lips and then Mary, full on the mouth.

'What a houseful of women I've got!' he said laughing. Suddenly, the tension was gone and they all laughed.

'This is cause for a celebration,' he added, getting up and leaving his wife and their new daughter alone, for that is how he had begun to think of her. Mary hugged Fiona. 'I'm so happy,' she said.

'So am I, so am I!' was the response.

Before going to bed, Fiona tasted her first champagne. The bubbles tickled her nose and made her laugh.

'I'll come and say goodnight before I go to bed,' Mary said, but by the time she climbed to the attic bedroom, Fiona was fast asleep.

Mary stood looking down at the sleeping form. Moonlight

flooded the room and Fiona lay on her back, her arms resting on the covers. She looked as if she was dreaming peaceful dreams, and, by the light of the moon, Mary thought that, in repose, her face seemed to have a slight smile.

'Sweet dreams darling,' she whispered, bending down and kissing her new daughter goodnight.

Chapter 10

The next morning the chatter over breakfast was all about Rye. Fiona listened. Ponies, gran, papa, donkeys, chickens, the cottage - her head spun.

'What are you all talking about?' she finally managed to break in.

'Shush, all of you. Seb, that means you too.' Seb gave an irrepressible grin to his mother.

'Important family announcement.' They all stopped eating and looked at their mother.

'It's the only way I can get their attention,' Mary added laughingly to Fiona.

'Important family announcement', she repeated. 'We have a new member of our family. Fiona is going to stay with us.'

'Like an au pair?' Alison asked.

'No, not like an au pair, like a member of our family.'

Fiona saw the eldest girl's lips trembling. Uncertainty swept over her; perhaps this was not right after all. Perhaps she shouldn't stay. Alison's comment added to her consternation.

'You mean, I won't be the eldest child of the family?'

Alison sounded hurt, deflated and even a little angry.

'Oh my darling, silly Ali – you will always be the eldest child of the family. Fiona is like my little sister.'

Alison's scowl faded as quickly as it had come.

'That's alright then,' she said, tucking in once more to her coco pops. And, as if in agreement, Lynn and Sebastian continued eating as well. Mary caught Fiona's eye and smiled. That's settled then, she seemed to be saying.

Their weekend cottage was in Rye. It wasn't much used during the winter months, but from Easter they went down most Friday evenings, and in the summer and Easter holidays, they spent as much time there as possible.

'It's got a funny name,' said Seb.

'You'll never guess it,' said Lynn, 'not in a thousand years,' she added dramatically. Lynn was inclined to the dramatic, as Fiona was finding out.

'It's in a cobbled street,' added Alison, not to be left out of the conversation. 'It's in Mermaid Street.'

'Are there mermaids there?'

'No, silly,' Sebastian answered in as superior a tone as a little boy can. 'It's because of the hotel – the Mermaid hotel.'

As the day progressed, Fiona heard more and more about Rye; its cobbled streets, its old church, the interesting people.

'It's quite an artists' and writers' community,' Mary told her, 'you must take your sketch pad and paints. It's an artist's paradise.'

Fiona became more and more intrigued. Still no-one would tell her the name of the cottage, and as the car drew up and she saw 'Round Window Cottage', she knew Seb had been right; she wouldn't have guessed the name in a million years.

Fiona was totally enchanted with Rye; the cobbled streets, the little cafes, the church with its beautiful windows and amazing pendulum hanging inside the church swinging to and fro, probably as it had done for centuries. She discovered the Ypres Tower, now a museum, but in former times a prison and fortress.

With the children, she went to various beaches and swam and walked, made great castles for Seb, Lynn and Alison, met Mary's mother and father who insisted she called them gran and papa as the children did. She loved their farmhouse just outside Rye in Playden, where, in the several paddocks attached to the farmhouse they had ponies and donkeys, all rescued through the local Blue Cross Rescue Centre. She swam in their pool and ate wonderful cakes and puddings. Gran was a fabulous cook and obviously enjoyed having the family popping in and out.

Papa – so called because as babies the children couldn't say granpapa, and gran because they hadn't been able to manage the full granmama either – found Fiona an old bike in one of the sheds. With her sketch pad and pencils, charcoals and pastels she would cycle off, enjoying the freedom she had never had before. She had never known life could be like this. It is a different kind of life, she thought, one that in her wildest dreams she couldn't have imagined. She looked brown and healthy, her hair shone, her skin glowed. Mary watched quietly, satisfied that Fiona had found her wings.

Sometimes Fiona felt she was being selfish and would stay and play with the children, but she soon realised that they were happy up at the farm where they spent most of their time. Mary was organising a party. Every summer she had a summer lunch party, she explained to Fiona, usually about forty or fifty of their local friends. They had been coming to Rye for the last fifteen years and were quite part of the local community now.

A number of Fiona's recent drawings and paintings began to appear, propped up on mantelpieces or lying around. Fiona had had to buy another sketch pad. She found a delightful art shop in Cinque Port Street, with its own gallery attached. The Reaves, who owned both the shop and the gallery, asked if they might look at some of Fiona's work. They now knew who she was and, as she had been in and out several times asking their opinion and advice on type and quality of paper and materials, they felt a curiosity and were hoping before long she would show them some of her work.

Fiona had never before sat out in a public place and drawn or painted. At first, she had felt shy and almost wanted to cover her work when a passer-by drew too close. After a while, she became so absorbed that she stopped noticing the interest she was generating as she sat and painted, using an old easel loaned to her by a local artist friend of Mary's.

Now the Reaves were looking at the pictures with delight. Fiona had sat in different parts of the churchyard, and the houses round the square had come alive under her brush: a woman with a Dalmation, walking through the square, made them smile as did the vicar's wife, walking her dog, both elegant in their own way; and then Rye Harbour with its fishing boats and yachts bobbing along the quayside.

'Where haven't you been?' they asked. 'They're all good Fiona. Do some more and perhaps we'll be able to offer you an exhibition before the end of the summer.'

Fiona almost ran home – for it was home now, the darling Round Window Cottage. Mary was delighted but not altogether surprised by the news.

'Why, darling,' she said, 'what a lovely end to the summer that will be.'

'Might,' countered Fiona, 'might be.'

Chapter 11

To Mary's great relief, the day of the party dawned bright and sunny. Now, as she had hoped, they could eat in the garden with the food set out on the oval dining room table.

The children were excited. They loved parties, each taking their roles very seriously in handing round nibbles and plates of smoked salmon on brown bread and butter that preceded the lunch. People turned up in merry mood and James served Pimms with champagne, his speciality. The children were allowed one Pimms-soaked strawberry. Alison liked the flavour but Seb and Lynn pulled faces.

'I prefer apple juice,' Lynn said, and Seb, for once, agreed with his sister.

Lunch was a great success. Mary's coronation chicken with fresh peaches and piquant rice, and her vegetable curry for those vegetarians among the guests, were heartily consumed followed by meringues filled with cream and profiteroles, both served with chocolate sauce, and a great bowl of strawberries and cream. Fiona had never seen so many people obviously enjoying themselves and, feeling a little overwhelmed, crept into the house with a plate of food to hide away in the beamed sitting room. There was someone there already. She almost turned to leave, but the man standing in front of the fireplace turned to look at her.

'You must be Fiona. I've been looking forward to meeting you.'

He was a tall man, with a kindly face, whitish hair, pink cheeks and, she thought, the twinkliest eyes she had ever seen. He introduced himself.

'I'm a bit of an artist myself,' he said modestly, 'I think you have an old easel of mine.'

'Oh yes, how kind. I mean, how do you do? Yes, I'm Fiona.' It all came out in an unseemly rush.

'Are these yours?' He turned to look at various of her pictures propped up on the mantelpiece. Fiona felt embarrassed that they were there, but Mary had insisted on putting them there for James to see the previous night, and in the rush of the party preparations Fiona had forgotten to move them.

'They're pretty good,' the kindly man continued. 'What are going to do about your art?'

'I'm not quite sure. All I know is that I want to draw and paint. I've only done portraits before, but I'm really enjoying Rye and all the wonderful things there are to paint.'

'Good,' he replied, his voice a little gruff, 'you do as much as you can. Paint anything, anywhere, any time. Don't get stuck into one particular medium or style at this stage in your life. How old are you?'

'Sixteen.'

'Good.' And with a friendly smile and a pat on her shoulder, he left her in the peace of the sitting room. It wasn't until evening that she learned she had been talking to a famous artist and writer of children's books. She felt a thrill. A real artist and he had been encouraging – at least she believed so.

And so the summer slipped by, but Fiona hadn't forgotten everything she had left behind. She wrote regularly to Claire, always with a little note for Stewie included, and always at least a message for her mother. From Claire she only had intermittent rather scrappy notes, often including a drawing of a train, or a line at the bottom from Stewie.

Things had changed, apparently for the better, though mummy was now more frail than ever. Uncle Len, it appeared, was becoming Claire's hero. They ate, the three of them, with mummy, on a table in the lounge.

'Uncle Len's being a sport,' wrote Claire, 'he doesn't want me to cook, Fee, so you needn't have worried so.'

Apparently he had been furious when he found she had run away. 'Some boy' he'd suggested to Claire and her mother. 'Was it Fee, was it?' Claire asked in several of her notes, 'or why did you leave us?'

Fiona soon realised that she was being painted black in her sister's eyes by that 'odious man' as she still thought of him. She talked her worries through with Mary and James and showed them Claire's letters.

'Leave well alone', they advised, 'just let her know what you are doing now.'

'She seems alright, doesn't she?' Fiona openly voiced her fears for the first time, hardly daring to think of what had happened to her sister.

James was all for going to the police. He had been from the start, but despite their pleas, on this Fiona was adamant. However much she hated him, her mother needed Mr Lennard and she believed Claire would be safe, at least for the next two years until she was sixteen. Mr Lennard was not a fool.

By summer's end, she had amassed more pictures than she had ever done in her life: the children riding their ponies, a portrait of gran and papa on the swing seat under the apple trees, more pictures of Mary and James, and little hidden corners of Rye – Hucksteps Row, Traders Passage and several houses around the square - the churchyard full of sunshine, men cutting the grass and scything around the gravestones, and of course, the 'Rye Collection' would not have been complete without Round Window

Cottage nestling comfortably half way up Mermaid Street.

With some trepidation she put all her work into the portfolio that James had brought with him from London. 'A little present for our hardworking artist,' he had said, kissing her lightly on the forehead. She was getting used to the regular displays of affection shown her by the family. It still felt slightly strange, but she loved them all dearly.

The Reaves were expecting her. Patricia put the closed sign on the door. They had asked Fiona to come at the end of the day so they could give her plenty of time to show them her work. Daniel cleared one of the counters and Fiona, heart thudding in her chest, put the portfolio on its surface and with slightly trembling fingers undid the tapes that held it together.

One by one, she lifted them out and handed them to either Patricia or Daniel. Gradually, first one counter was covered, then another. Finally, having kept what she thought her best one until last, she passed them the portrait in water colours that she had done of Alison, Lynn and Sebastian. She hadn't shown this one to either Mary or James. She wanted to surprise them with it. She almost hadn't included it, but at the last moment had put it carefully at the bottom of the pile. She knew it was probably the best work she had ever done.

For a few moments there was total silence as Patricia and Daniel looked critically at each picture, finally looking at the last one of the three children. Fiona thought her heart had stopped beating; she thought she was going to suffocate. The suspense was frightful. What if they didn't like anything? They were, after all, professionals; they held regular exhibitions.

It was Daniel who broke the silence.

'Fiona, we would be very happy to exhibit your work, all of it.'

Fiona took a deep refreshing breath.

'This one,' Patricia spoke now, 'is outstanding. What are you hoping to get for it Fiona?'

Fiona was taken aback. How stupid of her, she thought. Selling them hadn't occurred to her. She stumbled over her words, unsure of herself.

'I hadn't thought to sell them.' *But why not?* a voice in her head said. 'Definitely not the one of the children.' Her voice sounded calm enough, but her heart was lurching about in a most peculiar fashion.

'Of course,' they said, nodding, immediately understanding.

For the next hour they went through picture after picture. Fiona was amazed at the prices they were proposing.

'Nobody will pay that,' she said, thinking how awful it would be if they were for sale and nobody wanted them. Finally they agreed on all the prices. They wanted to exhibit the picture of the children, but promised to put a 'reserved' sticker on it. Fiona left them to decide on the frames. She felt it would be better for them to select them, they knew what they were doing.

That evening at supper, amidst the general chatter, Fiona told the family what had happened at the gallery. Mary hadn't even realised that it was today that Fiona was going.

'You kept that pretty quiet. I'd have been worrying about you – not,' she added hastily, 'about the pictures, but at how you were feeling.'

'That's why I didn't tell you,' laughed Fiona. 'I was terrified actually, but they were so kind. They want to see if they can sell them.'

'All of them?' Mary was surprised.

'Not quite all,' Fiona answered with a secret sort of smile.

Chapter 12

It was one of the most successful exhibitions the little gallery had ever had. The Reaves had sent out invitations to a private view, followed by a general invitation in the local press, with flyers posted around the town.

The private view proved quite an ordeal for Fiona. In hindsight, it need not have been. Everyone was so charming and friendly. The wine flowed and little canapés were handed round by the Reaves' two assistants. Surprisingly quickly, 'sold' stickers appeared on a number of the pictures. Local people found pictures of their homes, or favourite corners of Rye. Mary's parents wanted to buy the one of them under the apple trees.

'It's not for sale,' Fiona quickly told Patricia and a reserved notice went on it, much to the Reynolds' disappointment.

The highlight of the evening for Fiona had to be the moment Mary and James saw the painting of their children. It had pride of place in the exhibition and attracted a lot of attention. Mary and James were speechless with delight, and watching their faces was all that Fiona hoped for.

'We'll certainly buy that one,' said James.

'It's reserved,' Mary said sadly.

'For you,' said Fiona, coming up behind them. 'It's for you, with all my love.' She had hoped they would be pleased; even she had been surprised at how good it looked now it was framed and Mr and Mrs Reaves wouldn't even let her pay for the framing.

Mary turned, tears in her eyes.

'Dearest Fiona, you couldn't have given us anything that would have given us more pleasure.' James nodded.

'I agree,' he said, hugging her warmly.

Slowly they walked around the rest of the exhibition. James has seen several of the pictures before, but he was amazed at the variety he saw and the different effects she had managed to create.

'She really has got talent, hasn't she?' he said quietly to Mary.

'I told you.' Mary sounded triumphant. What a delight in every way darling Fiona was proving to be.

By the end of the private view, nearly half the pictures had 'sold' stickers. Fiona did some mental arithmetic as she walked round. Several hundred pounds ….. she would, she decided, give it straight to Mary and James as a thank you and towards the cost of keeping her.

Later that evening she cycled up the hill to see gran and papa as she now called them quite comfortably. They had left the exhibition before she had had time to tell them that the reserved sticker on 'their' picture was a 'reserved for them' sticker.

'For no-one else, for sure,' she told them.

They sat at the table in the lovely old farmhouse kitchen, both beaming at her in sheer delight.

'We've never had a picture of us painted before, it's so exciting.' Gran was very bubbly tonight. Papa, always slightly more serious, was beaming too.

'We shall treasure it Fiona, and one day, when you're famous, we shall say, very casually, 'we have a Fiona McInnes' and everyone will be very jealous!'

They had returned to London. School was due back the following week. Mary noticed that Fiona had been off her breakfast recently. This morning, she looked at the wan and rather subdued little face and unwittingly a terrible thought entered her head. She quickly banished the thought but, despite herself, a lingering doubt remained. Had she known, Fiona too was having the same thought. For several weeks she had felt nauseous in the mornings. At first she had dismissed it as a tummy upset and as she always felt better during the day, if somewhat more tired than usual, she put it down to the totally different life she was leading. But she realised to her horror that she had not had a period since she left Edinburgh. She couldn't even say to herself 'home', for it was no home to her anymore. It was, she calculated as she lay in bed that morning, nearly six weeks ago. It seemed so much longer. So much had happened, but now this: a baby, with 'him' as the father. She had lain in bed and wept copiously. Just when her life was so wonderful. Fiona knew she would have to tell Mary, now, today. She loved Mary and James and felt she belonged, but what would they say? Would they want her to leave? Her heart sank at the prospect. They had talked so much about the sixth form college in Putney, then the College of Art. They had raised her hopes beyond her wildest dreams.

Her face still bore evidence of shed tears, despite the cold water she splashed on her face. She saw Mary looking at her as she played with a piece of toast. She knows, Fiona thought, somehow she knows. There was no putting it off. After breakfast she would talk to Mary, tell her what she feared. There was no point in trying to conceal something that would all too soon become patently obvious.

As usual, after some cursory help from the children, Mary and Fiona were left in the kitchen with the residue of the clearing up. Somewhere in the house the hoover buzzed as the daily started on the bedrooms.

'Fiona'. 'Mary.' They both spoke at once, but neither laughed.

'Let's go into James' study. We shan't be disturbed.' Mary led the way as she spoke.

Fiona followed, every footstep leaden with despair; all hopes were dashed, all expectations crashing around her ears. Visions of living in dark, squalid rooms with a crying baby that she knew she would hate – could only hate – loomed.

They sat down, each in one of the extremely comfortable chairs that James insisted on having in the study, 'so that when I interview prospective suitors for the girls, we can sit her with a glass of sherry in comfort'. He would laugh heartily at the thought of even interviewing prospective sons-in-law; he still remembered how nervous he had felt with Mr Reynolds, Mary's father.

Mary began the conversation.

'You're pregnant, aren't you Fiona?'

Fiona looked down at her long, slender artist's hands.

'I think so,' she almost whispered. 'I'm sorry Mary, I'm very sorry. Of course I'll leave.' She was crying uncontrollably and Mary could only just catch what she said. Mary gasped in horror. Could Fiona really believe they would want her to leave? She got up and in one moment was hugging the child; she was still a child.

'There, there, little one, don't cry. You are certainly not leaving.'

She took one of the pretty handkerchiefs she always carried with her out of her pocket and tenderly wiped the girl's tears.

'Fiona, we love you. We'll work something out, I promise you.'

As she told James when they lay in bed that night, 'what else could I do, James? Turn her out on the streets?' James held her tightly in his arms.

'I guess this is what it's like having a daughter,' he said soberly. 'Pray God ours will never be raped.'

'Amen to that,' she said.

The next day, Mary spoke to her doctor and through him, a clinic. She then suggested going out for a coffee.

'No, children, this morning is for Fiona and me. But how about going swimming this afternoon?'

'Hurrah,' all three shouted and happily went off to play.

Over coffee, Mary broached the subject as carefully as she could; she wasn't sure what the reaction would be.

'Fiona darling, please don't be upset. I'll quite understand if you don't agree, but I thought you ought to at least think about an abortion.' *I can't believe I'm saying this,* she thought to herself; *me, totally anti-abortion. Amazing how one's views can change!*

As she'd been speaking, she'd been watching the girl's face intently and saw a look like 'a startled fawn' was the way she described it to James later, followed by a look of utter relief.

'Mary, oh Mary, yes,' Fiona breathed, 'I couldn't bear to have his child, but I've been so mixed up. I love children. I'd always hoped one day for a baby of my own, but not, not like this….'

It was settled; a visit to the doctor, an appointment at the clinic, mandatory counselling which Mary sat through with Fiona. The counsellor outlined the options.

'You've obviously got your mother's support,' she said, glancing at Mary.

Fiona looked at Mary, who discreetly winked back.

'Yes.' Fiona nodded. 'I have her support, but I have decided.'

'The baby's father?'

The woman continued in a soothing, counsellor style voice.

'It was rape,' Mary broke in.

The counsellor looked slightly uncomfortable.

'I see. Then you've made up your mind?'

Once again, she looked steadily at Fiona.

'Yes.'

The appointment book was brought out and Fiona was 'fitted in' for the following week. Both Mary and Fiona knew it would be a very long week.

Chapter 13

The children had settled quickly back into the routine of the school day, Sebastian at his nursery in the mornings, and the two girls at the private school they had attended since the age of five.

Decisions lay ahead. Mary had so enjoyed her boarding school years but was reluctant for the children to be too far away from home. She rather liked the idea of weekly boarding and was thinking about Benenden which was quite close to Rye, over the border in Kent. She had agreed, with much soul searching, that Seb should go to prep school, the same one James had so happily attended, before moving onto Eton, following again in his father's and grandfather's footsteps.

Fiona decided she also wanted to start at the sixth form college. To miss the first week would mean she would feel very strange when she did start. So, feeling a little nervous, she set off to walk to her new school, or college, as she had to think of it now.

Although a number of the students knew each other from their previous schools, there were also a number that didn't. James had been to see the Principal and given a version of Fiona's story that he and Mary had agreed, so Fiona found her entry smoothed for her.

Whether it was because she no longer had her previous responsibilities of looking after home and siblings, or whether she had changed more than she knew, Fiona found herself settling in easily and happily. The atmosphere was so different to her old school. Here, being a sixth form college, they were treated as young adults. They had the responsibility of turning up to classes, or not as the case may be.

Fiona was to study Art (of course) and Maths plus French. She still remembered with delight her happy weekend in Paris which had really encouraged her to take her art seriously. Who knows, she often thought, perhaps one day I will return there.

A week later, the day of the appointment, Fiona woke up feeling perfectly happy. Then she remembered. Her hand rested on her stomach, still flat, yet in there was a foetus. She wouldn't allow herself to think beyond that. It was too painful. They had said just to think of it as having a minor operation and Fiona tried hard to hang onto that thought.

Mary, of course, took her in and kissed her warmly on both cheeks.

'I'll be here when you come back from theatre,' she said softly.

Fiona was in the short-stay unit of the large London hospital. The consultant had said he would just want her in for twenty-four hours.

A nurse gave her a pre-med, and Fiona found herself drifting on clouds somewhere above her bed. She knew she was being wheeled down a corridor. She heard a distant voice say 'very light anaesthetic'. A face in a mask bent over her.

'Alright young lady, soon be over.'

She was back in bed, Mary by her side.

'Hello Mary.'

'Fiona darling, it's all over.'

Fiona felt a shudder go through her. It was all over, the last drop of that man was expelled from her body. She felt new, herself, her body, her own. Not a pang of regret did she feel.

'Should I feel sad Mary? I don't.'

'No darling, it's done and over. Life begins from here!'

Three days later, Fiona was back at college. The whole episode had a dream-like quality about it. As far as the college was concerned, she had had a tummy upset, and it was as if she had never been away. She slipped easily back into her classes and was already making friends, something that had never come easily to her before. Amanda however, even though so far away, would always be her best and closest friend. The girls corresponded regularly since Fiona's rapid departure from Edinburgh and although the Harrisons were delighted that Fiona seemed to have found happiness, they had nevertheless written to the Marshalls themselves, and felt very relieved to receive a telephone call in response when they spoke to both Mary and James.

The conversation had gone so well that Mary, knowing how fond Fiona was of Amanda, had suggested that she should come down for a few days during the Christmas holidays. The girls were delighted at the prospect of seeing each other again and Fiona had all sorts of ideas and plans already in hand for the visit.

Amanda stayed a few days before Christmas and was a great success. Mary, perhaps unsubtly, pumped Amanda quite carefully to see if she could glean any more information about Mr Lennard. Amanda had little to say except that she had only seen him a few times and had never been invited into the house. She did say that Claire seemed happier these days and had quite come out of her shell. Mary was relieved on that score, but something still worried her about the strange set-up, for strange it really seemed.

Christmas was, as family tradition demanded, spent in Rye. The cottage in Mermaid Street, with its oak beams and inglenook fireplaces, lent itself to the Christmas atmosphere. The midnight service by candlelight on Christmas Eve and the walk home afterwards over the cobbled streets, seemed to Fiona to have a certain mystical quality. No Christmas had ever been like this: Christmas morning, with its bustle and wonderful smells emanating from the kitchen, gran and papa arriving mid-morning, laughing happily as they struggled in, their arms full of brightly wrapped packages.

Parcel opening took place straight after lunch that was the most delicious Christmas lunch Fiona had ever imagined. Three excited and happy children and only once was a black shadow cast as Fiona thought of Claire and Stewart. She knew it was no use telephoning; she wouldn't be allowed to speak to them, that had become obvious from Claire's letters, but she did so hope they liked the gifts she had sent, chosen as they had been with much loving care. For her Mother, she had chosen a very pretty bed jacket in a shade of blue that, as far as she remembered, was her mother's favourite.

'Come back, Fiona!' James' voice seemed to boom. 'You were day-dreaming.'

Fiona jerked back to Rye, the glowing fire, the spitting sound made by new logs on the fire, the children's laughter and the beaming smiles of the adults.

'I'm back,' she responded quietly, looking at them all with a love and gratitude that surprised even her.

Chapter 14

The first year at college sped by. Fiona had never had so many friends; the telephone rang constantly for her. James said, half jokingly, 'perhaps we should put in a private line for you Fee.' They had heard Amanda call her that and adopted the nickname too. The second year began as the first year had, but the pressure was building as 'A' levels loomed.

The telephone rang one evening.

'For you, Fee,' James said, his big voice booming jovially, 'as if we didn't know!'

Fiona took the receiver from him with a smile. There was a pause.

'Who is it?' Fiona asked, a trifle impatiently, wanting to return to her art project which had reached a rather critical mid-way stage.

'Fiona?' The voice was questioning.

'Claire, is that you?' In all the time she had been away, Claire had never phoned. The worst possible thoughts flooded her mind. Dear God, she prayed involuntarily, please let Claire be alright. She couldn't bear Claire to suffer as she had. She would never ever forget how she felt after the abortion, a sense of emptiness and guilt that she hadn't anticipated, a baby's life taken. Her first feelings of relief and elation that there was nothing left inside her of Mr Lennard had soon been overtaken by some very black moments and it was only later, looking at her sketch book of the weeks following the abortion, that she recognised the mental anguish and sense of guilt that showed on its pages.

'Claire, are you alright?' Her voice was urgent with worry. How could she have left her sister? Claire was crying now, she could hear her. 'Claire, please tell me, what is it?' What's happened?'

'It's mummy,' said Claire through her sobs, 'she's dead'.

Fiona felt a terrible pang of guilt. She hadn't thought about mummy for ages. Her mother had never replied to the letters Fiona had written and gradually Fiona had put her somewhere in the recesses of her mind.

'I'll come home straight away.' *Home?* her mind was saying, *this is my home, here with Mary, James and the children.*

'It's too late,' Claire's voice broke with tears, 'she was cremated yesterday. Uncle Len didn't think you'd be interested. He said you didn't love us any more, you were part of another family now.'

Fiona was silent. It was true, she was part of another family now. Claire and Stewart seemed a world away. Mummy too had seemed - had been - a remote figure for so long that Fiona had forgotten how to care about her. But now, faced with her death, it brought back all too vividly that grey, misty day, the day that Dada had been lowered into the grave, the day she had realised that her childhood was over. Fiona heard a man's voice in the background.

'Goodbye Fiona,' Claire said suddenly. There was a click and Fiona was left holding the telephone with the dialling tone echoing in her ear.

She hung the telephone back on the wall and walked slowly back upstairs to her bedroom. She lay on her bed, looking at the sky, remembering the first time she had looked out of this window, her first night in London. She lay quite still and dry-eyed. She couldn't cry. She hadn't known her mother for so long. She felt sad about that, but she also felt betrayed, for had mummy really cared, surely she would have protected her during those awful years? Now she was dead and Claire and Stewart were at the mercy of Mr Lennard.

She didn't know what she could do, what she should do. She turned her head into the pillow and drifted off to sleep.

Mary found her like that a few hours later when she came up to bed. Fiona had unusually not come and said goodnight. These days, she had so much studying that she often spent hours in her room, but always came down after a bath or shower for a chat and a cuddle before she went to bed.

'Fee darling, Fee.' Fiona heard a far away voice.

'Mummy,' she said, still half asleep.

For a moment, Mary was startled, then she realised that Fiona was thinking about her real mother. Her eyes opened suddenly; she saw Mary, her face full of concern.

'I'm not undressed,' she said in a surprised voice. 'Mummy's dead,' she continued, 'and I don't know what to do.'

Mary sat down on the bed and held Fiona's hand.

'I'm so sorry darling, about your mother. You'll want to go up to the funeral. We could stay with my friend Iona if you like. I'll come with you of course.'

'It's too late,' Fiona's tone was flat, 'mummy was cremated yesterday.'

Now it was Mary's turn to gasp and, as she said to James later, 'That awful man wouldn't let Claire even phone her sister until after the cremation. Can you believe it?' Mary's voice was filled with righteous indignation. 'Of course Fee's worried about Claire and Stewart now. What do you think we should do James?'

James was quiet for a moment, taking it all in before making a decision. Then he said, very firmly, 'I'll take a day or two off. The three of us will fly up to Edinburgh. Fiona has to know her brother and sister are alright.'

'Should we phone and let them know we're coming?'

'I think not. It might be wise just to turn up.'

Mary nodded.

'I'll ring Ma in the morning. I'm sure she and Pa will be happy to come and stay with the children for a few days.'

'Today's Tuesday,' James was thinking aloud. 'I'll go into the city in the morning, few things I have to deal with and I'll organise tickets for Thursday. Will that give Ma enough notice?'

'Don't worry about that James. I'm sure she'll drop everything under the circumstances, even if Pa can't come too.'

Before Fiona left for college the next morning, Mary told her what she and James had agreed, providing, that is, the plans met with Fiona's approval. They did, and it was a happier Fiona who left for college.

They arrived in Scotland at lunchtime on Thursday. On this occasion, James had felt that rather than stay with Iona, they would be better in a hotel. He had booked adjoining rooms at the Great Western as it would give them greater flexibility.

'Heaven knows what we'll find', he said.

James was worried and he knew Mary was as well, but they both tried to hide the fact from Fiona, who seemed almost too calm by half, though they both felt much of this was a brave façade.

They were more right than they knew. Fiona felt as though her knees were knocking, as though she were to meet the devil incarnate. It was decided to get to the house about four in the afternoon when the children would be home from school. The taxi was booked for half past three. Time had never moved so slowly. All of them kept glancing surreptitiously at their watches whilst apparently intent on reading magazines they had bought at Heathrow.

Three thirty finally arrived and they climbed into the taxi with a sense of anticipation, laced with foreboding. None of them, particularly Mary and James, had any idea what to expect. James tried to be light-hearted, but even he failed to lighten the mood of gloom that had overtaken them.

The taxi drive followed Fiona's directions and pulled up in front of a quite substantial double-fronted house. The three of them got out and Mary grasped Fiona's hand and squeezed it tightly. Don't worry the squeeze seemed to say, we are here for you.

For the first time in what seemed like many years, Fiona stood by the front door. Her hands hung limply by her side, and it was James who rang the bell. There was silence for a moment, then the sound of running footsteps and ten year old Stewart opened the door. For a moment he seemed not to recognise his big sister, but with a sudden whoop of delight he yelled 'Fiona!' at the top of his voice. Fiona stepped forward to hug her little brother, but before she could even get across the threshold Mr Lennard stood there, glowering at her.

'What are you doing here?' His voice was cold and his tone unfriendly. Then he saw Mary and James who had stepped back to allow Fiona to greet her brother.

'Ah, you must be Fiona's friends from London.' He suddenly sounded very smooth and friendlier. Fiona thought he sounded like the oily snake he was, but Mary and James seemed charmed by him. All three of them were ushered into the lounge.

'So sad, my dear Fiona, your mother's death. What a pity you didn't manage to get up for the funeral. She so would have wanted you to be here. She loved and missed you so.'

Fiona nearly choked, her anger almost at boiling point.

'Of course,' he continued smoothly, 'it was such a shock to your dear mother when you left. She never could come to terms with it. I must say, I was more than a little hurt – after all I'd done for you since your father died – that you went off without a word.'

Fiona exploded. 'How *dare* you!' she began, her voice both angry and bitter. 'How dare you,' she said again. Just then, the door opened and Claire burst in.

'Fiona, how lovely! I didn't expect you.'

Fiona saw a look pass between Claire and the 'odious' man. It had a kind of intimacy that troubled her, but she didn't know why.

'A cup of tea?' Mr Lennard broke the silence. 'Come Stewie boy, give me hand' and they were gone.

'Hello Claire,' Mary broke the ice quickly, 'I'm Mary. This is my husband James. We've heard so much about you from Fiona. We just wanted to bring your sister to visit you and make sure everything is alright.'

Claire looked puzzled.

'Of course everything's alright. Why shouldn't it be? Len takes very good care of us. He says he's our daddy now and he's so kind.' Claire paused and then said 'Why did you leave Fiona? I never did understand. Stewie cried and cried and Len was very cross that you had upset us all so much.'

'But,' Mary, with rapidly mounting anger, started to speak when the door opened and in came Mr Lennard with a tray of tea and biscuits.

'If I'd known you were coming I'd have baked a cake,' he sang in a sing-song voice. Fiona cringed. She still hated him, but she had never seen him like this. Mary and James wouldn't believe a word she'd told them.

They all sat down. The silence as Mr Lennard poured the tea was not a comfortable one. Whatever he had said to Stewart in the kitchen had subdued his high spirits and he now sat with head bowed, only glancing from time to time at his eldest sister.

Claire, on the other hand, was in great spirits, almost being coquettish with James and obviously very attached to Mr Lennard, who informed Mary and James almost casually that he was now the children's guardian.

'Indeed, my dear sweet lady, the children's mother left me the house of course, knowing I would care for her two children.'

'Three,' Mary corrected him quietly.

'I'm afraid as far as she was concerned, she only had two children. Fiona was always difficult, though I did my best all those years to look after all of them.'

James stood up suddenly. He had been watching Fiona intently and seen distress and anger alternate on her expressive face.

'I'm afraid we have a plane to catch. Fiona, say your goodbyes my dear.'

With a sense of relief, Fiona, her tea untouched – how could she even touch anything he had made – stood up abruptly and went over to Claire. She kissed her on both cheeks, then tried to do the same to Stewart, but he turned his head away and wouldn't even look at her.

'What a pity you can't stay longer,' the oily, ingratiating voice broke in, 'such a pity.'

As he spoke, he was ushering them towards the front door and they were outside with the door closed firmly behind them before they realised. Fortunately, James, ever the practical man, had asked the taxi to wait. Thankfully, and wordlessly, the three climbed in.

'The hotel please,' James told the driver.

Fiona, sitting between them, started to cry. 'It's not true, it's not true.'

Mary and James answered as one.

'We know,' they said, putting their arms around her and looking over her bent head at each other, with raised eyebrows indicating their feelings to each other.

Later that evening in their room, and with James' approval, Mary telephoned the Harrisons.

'We've got a terrible nerve I know,' she told Mrs Harrison, but we wondered if you could possibly keep a bit of an eye on Claire? Fiona was very distressed today when we visited. It all seems rather a peculiar situation.'

Mrs Harrison said she would do her best, but with Fiona in London and Claire two years junior to Amanda, it would be difficult to keep any sort of eye on the girl. But she did say she would try and create opportunities for Amanda and herself to speak to Claire regularly.

'It'd be better than nothing I suppose,' Mary said, telling James what had been arranged. 'It certainly is a rather strange atmosphere there.'

James ruminated.

'I have a feeling young Claire is a lot more worldly than she should be.'

Mary didn't answer, but inwardly acknowledged that she felt the same. For once though, she didn't share her thoughts with him. Somehow, she felt if she voiced them, they might actually come true.

'What an extraordinary reception,' she said instead. 'Did you hear the tone he used to Fee until he saw we were there too?'

'He's acquired a nice property, and did you note, with no mention of Fiona receiving anything? What does he do for money?' James mused.

'Probably living for years off Fiona's mother's savings.'

For the first time ever, James heard a cynical tone enter his wife's voice.

'Enough,' he said, 'Fee is with us now, safe, and will always be part of our family. In fact,' he continued, 'this has confirmed for me that we did the right thing twelve months ago. Where would the poor child be otherwise?'

They talked late into the night, finally realising there was nothing they could do, or even should do, for Claire and Stewart. They would return home in the morning, taking their beloved Fiona with them.

Chapter 15

'A' levels were over. The whole class celebrated with a wonderful party in the garden at Putney, Fiona's home. As far as her new friends were concerned, these were her parents. She certainly felt more their daughter than she had ever felt her mother's. She was quietly confident about her 'A' levels. She had adored French literature. Satre was challenging, Racine even more so, but she had enjoyed the contrasts and felt she had acquired a broad understanding of the French and their philosophies.

Art had, of course, been wonderful, although she hadn't particularly enjoyed all the project work. It was not quite what she wanted to do, but she had the sense to realise that this was good discipline; an artist can't always do exactly what he or she wants. Maths was good too because it hadn't involved all the reading and preparation of the other two subjects and she seldom had a problem with it. On one or two occasions, she had talked maths with James who had read maths before going on to qualify as a chartered accountant.

'If our three are half as conscientious as Fee,' James said to Mary, more than once during the year, 'I'll be delighted.'

Now talk was all of the future. Fiona had set her heart on Slade, but had been warned there were always around two thousand applicants for about two hundred places. Her Head of Art had advised her to do a year's foundation course at the local Art College first, but Fiona set her hopes high and Mary and James, although commending caution, felt that Fee had to be in with an excellent chance of one of two hundred places.

The results were more than Fiona could have hoped for – three straight As. The college felt that they had had a 'good year'. Many of the students had two As and a B, but only three of them the three straight As. The Principal spoke warmly to Fiona, trying to encourage her to go for Oxbridge and read Maths or French.

'Keep Art as a wonderful hobby,' she said, 'it's so difficult to make a living from it. There are so many struggling artists.'

'I have no choice,' Fiona responded quietly, but firmly. 'I'm an artist inside. How can I be anything else? I would be lying to myself.'

There was no answer to that and the Principal shrugged sadly.

'Well, you might change your mind at a later date and become a mature student.'

Fiona burst out laughing, finding it impossible to imagine herself as a mature anything, let alone a mature student. With a smile, the Principal joined in the laughter.

James was delighted. A colleague had offered him the use of his villa in Nauzan on the west coast of France. Peter was spending a year in the States in a consulting role, with the blessing of the Bank. At supper that evening, James broke the news to Mary and Fiona.

'How about a holiday in France this year?'

Mary paused, with a forkful of food halfway to her mouth.

'France, why France?'

James explained.

'It sounds lovely, but what about Ma and Pa? They'll be so disappointed. They really look forward to our summers in Rye.'

'Well, they shall come too,' said James magnanimously.

'For goodness' sake James, how big is this place?'

'Apparently it has seven bedrooms, plenty for us all. You could take a friend if you want to Fee.' James was enjoying himself.

'Could I really? I'd love Amanda to come with us.'

'I'll take a month off; we'll go for a month'.

'Oh James, how lovely!' Mary was delighted. All the people she loved best in the world, together for one month.

Plans were quickly made. Fiona telephoned Amanda that evening and after an excited conversation, she handed the telephone to Mary for her to talk to Mrs Harrison and confirm arrangements. Amanda would travel to London by train and join up with them to go by car through the Channel Tunnel for the drive south.

'We can take seven without luggage,' James said thoughtfully later that evening.

'Ma and Pa can take the luggage in their Volvo. They'll have loads of room.'

Mary had already spoken to her parents who had accepted with alacrity. Their gardener come handyman would look after the animals and keep an eye on things generally. It was all set. On the day of departure, a letter arrived from the Slade.

Dear Miss McInnes,

Thank you for submitting your portfolio and A level project work. We would be pleased if you would come for a first interview on 30th September at 11:30 a.m.'

It was signed by the Administrative Secretary.

Amanda had just arrived.

'Fee, that's brilliant! If I get into London University we'll be together again! Well, in the same city anyway.'

The holiday started on a wonderfully happy note. Apart from the occasional moan from Sebastian about the journey lasting forever, it all passed smoothly enough. He had loved going through the Chunnel, though Alison had mild hysterics about being under the sea, and Lynn didn't help matters by asking all sorts of questions about cracks appearing in the concrete and if the sea came in, would the train float? Fortunately, that part of the journey only took about thirty five minutes and soon they were travelling south, heading for the proposed breakfast break and then an overnight stay in Chartres, giving them an opportunity to explore the attractive town and cathedral.

Luckily the hotel had a small swimming pool, much to Mary's relief, as the three children needed to let off some excess energy. Poor Alison looked pale; the tunnel experience had really upset her. Ma and Pa arrived in time for lunch, having had a slightly later start, and with the car heavy with all the suitcases which they had driven to London to collect.

Breakfast next morning was a cheery affair, the children refreshed after a good night's sleep. Despite having talked for most of the night, Amanda and Fiona looked bright and were still chattering non-stop. Ma and Pa sat glowing with pride at their extended family and Mary and James, who had an idyllic night of lovemaking, feeling like honeymooners.

The day sped by, passing remote country areas where simple methods of farming were still employed, then to the more prosperous towns such as Angoulême where they stopped to look up a French friend of Mary's. Sadly, the Suze family were away, but they had lunch in the lovely square before setting out on the last part of their journey, arriving at Nauzan as the sun was setting.

The maid, as promised, was there to let them in, and a simple supper was set out on the large table in the combined dining room and sitting area, cool with marble floors and scattered with simple rugs. They were all surprisingly hungry, and once Mary and Ma had sorted out who was sleeping where, they sat down for a meal of salads, cold meats and fruit, with wine, 'which Monsieur asked me to serve you from the cellar,' Maria reassured a worried James.

One by one they yawned and James carried a sleeping Sebastian upstairs to bed, followed by Mary, shepherding her two tired daughters to the room they were to share. Ma and Pa were delighted with the coolness of their room, which, on opening the shutters, they found overlooked the garden - a sandy oasis with cedars and with a strategically placed bench or two.

'Perfect darling,' Ma said, 'just the place for you to sit and read.'

At breakfast, James told them about the beach tent that went with the villa, and armed with buckets, spades, fruit and water, they made a procession over the road, down the steps to the beach looking at the brightly coloured pavilion style tents for number thirty one.

'Here it is.' Alison, now recovered, was the first to spot it. It was only about six feet by four feet, but provided the perfect base. Mary covered her children in sun cream and they ran off happily towards the sea and the wide, sandy beach, a lovely safe play area.

Mary pulled off her tee shirt and shorts.

'Umm, what a lovely figure,' James said appreciatively, eyeing his wife's lithe form and savouring warm memories of lovemaking.

Ma and Pa, having surveyed the tent, announced they were going on a meander.

'Do we have to do anything in the way of shopping?' Ma wanted to know.

'It's all taken care of. Apparently Maria does three meals a day and cleans, right James?'

'Right,' said James, 'what a deal!'

Blissful day followed blissful day. The children were all glowing and tanned, despite loads of sun cream and constant putting-on of tee shirts. Fiona, with her long legs that seemed to go on forever (James' description), her hair bleached even fairer by the sun and a golden tan with a light sprinkle of freckles over her nose made her look lovelier than ever, but of which she seemed delightfully unaware. Amanda, shorter, curvier and dark-haired, had acquired an amazing tan and looked very Italian James told her, much to her delight.

It wasn't long before a clutch of young men started appearing at tent number thirty one. Bernard and Jean Pierre were the most faithful, appearing daily and bringing with them different friends at different times. Fiona and Amanda, though looking so different, were equally attractive to the boys, and it wasn't long before evening outings were suggested, and table tennis matches under the trees at the back of the beach were a regular, daily event.

For Fiona particularly, it was a magical time. She and Amanda were enjoying each other's company and having harmless fun with the boys. Every night they would lay awake talking. Fiona had her first kiss that summer. She had always avoided getting close to the boys at college, but now in the hot sunshine and relaxed way of life, she didn't push Jean Pierre away when he brushed his lips against hers as they stood under the stars on the way home after dancing on the platform that had been erected under the cedars at the back of the beach.

That night, Fiona and Amanda talked as always, but this time she found herself holding back a little

She could still feel the sensation of the kiss and it was too precious to gossip about. Amanda, however, was full of Bernard's kisses.

'He touched my breasts,' she confided, 'it was lovely.'

Both girls had a fit of the giggles. Although Amanda was eighteen, she was quite innocent thought Fiona who suddenly felt very worldly. Although she shared so much with her friend she had never told her about the abortion; no-one knew apart from Mary and James. Now, for some unaccountable reason, she found herself telling Amanda about the rape and the consequences. For the first time she found herself able to talk quite matter-of-factly about the degradation after the rape and the guilt and pain after the abortion. It all seemed to have happened to someone else. That life seemed to belong to another girl, not Fiona Marshall McInnes, as she often thought of herself now. Somehow, Jean Pierre's chaste kisses on her cheeks had provided a healing balm.

Amanda listened, horror struck. She had imagined all sorts of reasons why Fiona ran away. She had even contemplated Mr Lennard making a pass at her friend, but rape! A baby!

'God, how awful Fee. I can hardly believe anything so terrible happened to you.'

Tonight, their talk was not idle chit-chat, and when Fiona clicked off the bedside light, both girls lay in the darkness wrapped in their own thoughts.

The cars were loaded. Maria stood at the door waving them goodbye. Ma and Pa led the 'off', whilst Mary and James lingered to allow the older girls to say goodbye to their special friends. Bernard and Amanda were entwined together, whilst James was glad to see that Fee and Jean Pierre, although holding hands, were talking quietly.

'Yes,' Fiona was saying, 'of course I'll write.' And she would, but she knew that, dear as he had become, it was a holiday friendship and she had no desire for romance. She had so much ahead to look forward to. At least she hoped she had, mentally correcting herself, when I make it to Slade. Positive thinking, she thought, was one of Mary's favourite phrases.

Jean Pierre said he would come and see her; he lived and studied in Paris.

'That would be nice,' Fiona said, trying hard to let him know that friendship, not romance, was all she had in mind.

The toot of the horn was almost a relief.

'I must go Jean Pierre,' she said, lightly brushing her lips against his, and sped over to where Mary, James and the children were waiting. Another toot.

'Amanda, come NOW!' Amanda extricated herself from Bernard's embrace and, hand-in-hand, they walked very slowly towards the waiting car.

It was a rather subdued journey. Amanda was lost in thoughts of Bernard. She was, she had told Fee the night before, 'madly in love with Bernard. Madly, Fee, really madly.' Fiona had wisely kept her own counsel, but now she could see how upset Amanda was at leaving Bernard behind.

For herself, her mind was winging forward. The interview was only two days away. By the time they had reached Chartres for their overnight stay, they had all cheered up. A swim in the pool and a lovely meal was all that was needed.

'A lovely way to end the holiday,' Ma said, and Pa, now looking bronzed and fit, his mouth full of lamb provençale, nodded his head in agreement.

By the time they reached the Channel Tunnel, all three children were sleeping. Alison woke up just as they reached the motorway.

'Have we got to the tunnel yet?' she asked, still a bit upset at the thought of going through it again.

'We're in England,' James replied.

'We went through when you were asleep darling,' Mary said, turning round and blowing her eldest daughter a kiss. Alison beamed.

'I'm glad we're going home.'

'That's the sign of a good holiday,' said her father. 'I think we're all glad to be going home after such a lovely summer holiday.'

Seb and Lynn were awake now.

'Can we go next summer?' Lynn wanted to know.

'What about the Round Window Cottage?' replied her father.

'Um.' Lynn was stumped. She loved it there, and Gran and Papa's farm.

'It's very difficult,' she said, so solemnly that it made them all laugh.

Chapter 16

The day of the interview dawned. Fiona couldn't eat any breakfast despite Mary's best endeavours.

'I can't, I simply can't. I feel so sick.' Indeed, thought Mary, she even looks sick.

But once on the tube, her fears seemed to disappear. This was her great opportunity, the opportunity of a lifetime. She was earlier than she intended to be, so decided to walk down the Embankment to Gower Street. It would take about twenty minutes and would be better than sitting in a waiting room at Slade. Her arrival was well timed. The previous candidate had just left, the secretary informed Fiona, and the panel were consulting. She offered Fiona some coffee, which was surprisingly welcome, and for the next ten minutes she sat gathering her thoughts. Her whole life, she decided dramatically, hinged on the next half hour.

The Panel, three of them, stood up as she was shown in. Their chairs were in a semi-circle, with a chair for Fiona opposite. The Dean of the Faculty was the Chair, then there was an external independent assessor whom Fiona recognised as an Art Critic of world renown, and then the Art Tutor for the first year intake.

The first few moments were very relaxed. They talked generously about her work. They told her she had done well to get as far as an interview and that she mustn't feel badly if she didn't get a place first time round. She could, they suggested, always do a foundation course and try again next year. Fiona began to feel her hackles rising. They were writing her off before they had even given her a chance.

'What, If any, art form do you wish to specialise in?'

If any? Fiona was incensed.

'I have no doubt,' she responded firmly. 'I plan to be a portrait artist.'

The Dean and the Tutor frowned in unison.

'It's a very specialised field, very competitive.' The Art Critic spoke for the first time. 'So many artists – one could even say too many chasing the same work.'

'I shall be the best.' This time, Fiona's voice was stronger and surer even than before. 'I know I've a lot to learn, but I also know that I'm good. I was born an artist. It will be my life and although I enjoy all forms of art, I'm going to be a portrait artist, whether you help me or not,' she added defiantly, burning her boats and probably losing her potential place at Slade as a result.

They conferred briefly. One piece of work from her portfolio passed from hand to hand.

'How old were you when you did this?' In his hand the Dean held the portrait of the three Marshall children. It had been taken out of its frame and placed in the portfolio at the insistence of Mary and James and it was the one all their attention was focused on.

'I was sixteen.' Fiona answered quietly, knowing that if they didn't like this, one of the best portraits that she had ever painted, then she was doomed to failure. She saw the slightest of smiles pass between them.

'That will be all for now Fiona. You may be called back for a second interview, or you may just receive a letter in which we will tell you that we are unable to accept you at the moment.'

Fiona stood up. She heard herself saying, and couldn't believe what she heard.

'If you don't accept me, it will be your loss, not mine, because I know I'm a good artist.'

'Thank you.' The Dean spoke curtly and Fiona's heart sank.

I've blown it, damn, damn, damn! But, as she told Mary and James that evening at dinner, 'They were patronising. At least I felt they were, but I've blown it. I know I have.'

'You know,' said James, 'after I'd had a simply foul interview at Cambridge, my father told me it was a good sign. His argument was that if they weren't interested in a candidate, what was the point of giving him or her a tough time? But conversely, if they thought a candidate was worth having, they tested their metal, stretched them to extremes. It seems to me,' he continued, 'that your interviewers were doing this today.'

Fiona shook her head sadly. 'I wish you were right James. I wish I could believe you, but I honestly think I've blown my chances.'

If only she could have been a fly on the wall! After she had left the room, the Panel had looked at each other and laughed.

'A feisty one that,' the Art Critic spoke first.

'She is good though, no doubt of that,' the Tutor responded.

The Dean picked up the proforma.

'Only eighteen. You don't think a foundation course first?' He answered his own question. 'No, she should come to us, because if she doesn't we'll certainly lose her to someone else.'

Honour was satisfied. They had studied her portfolio in depth. They had questioned her ambition. Of her talent, slightly undisciplined though it might be, there was no doubt.

Three days later, the letter arrived. Mary collected the post and saw the white, typewritten envelope addressed to Miss Fiona Marshall McInnes. Mary smiled. She and James loved the way Fiona had incorporated their name. She turned the envelope over and over, wondering whether to run upstairs with it, but deciding instead to put it on the hall table, where all incoming letters were put. Fiona could then open it privately or not as she chose.

Fiona woke feeling slightly grey. She often thought of feelings in colours these days and despite the sunshine streaming through the open windows, she knew the greyness was caused by the feeling in the pit of her stomach. Perhaps a letter today.

She washed hurriedly and pulled on a pair of jeans and tee shirt, quickly brushed her hair and ran down the stairs to help Mary with the breakfast. The kids were always ravenous. Alison at twelve was all lean and legs and forever hungry longing to start at Benenden in January.

As she came down the last few stairs, her eyes automatically looked at the hall table. The post had arrived. There, on the top, was a large, white envelope addressed to her. She picked it up. This is worse than 'A' levels, she thought, walking into the drawing room. She had to be alone; this was a momentous time in her life. She eased open the envelope and pulled out a single piece of paper.

Dear Miss Marshall McInnes,

The Slade School of Art is happy to offer you a place to study for a BA Arts Degree. The new course begins on 24th October. Please complete the enclosed forms, indicating accommodation needs etc. On your first day...........'

Fiona didn't read anymore. With a whoop of joy, she ran along the hall and down the three steps to the kitchen.

'They'll take me Mary!' Fiona's voice sang as she grabbed Mary and they danced round and round the kitchen table, laughing and crying in equal measure.

'I never doubted it darling, not for one moment.' Mary stopped dancing. 'We must phone James – no, you must phone James.'

Fiona had never rung James at his office, and as she stood in his study and spoke rather hesitantly to his secretary, she wondered if she really should be bothering him.

'Your daughter, Mr Marshall,' Fiona heard the secretary say, and felt a quick thrill of delight to hear herself addressed in this fashion.

'Hello.' James sound very businesslike.

'James, it's Fiona. I've been accepted by Slade.' She spoke hurriedly, hating to interrupt his busy day.

'That's the best news Fee darling.' She heard him speak to his secretary, 'Fiona's made the Slade.' He spoke into the telephone again. 'We'll celebrate tonight, the whole family, even Seb. Just wait until I get home. And,' he added as an afterthought, 'ask Mary to put some champagne in the fridge.'

'She already has,' was Fiona's happy reply.

Chapter 17

Alison had settled down happily at Benenden. Lynn could hardly wait to join her there. Sebastian was due to start at prep school soon and Mary had decided she would go back to teaching, at least part time.

Fiona, now in her second year at Slade, was in seventh heaven, though it irked her at times to have to conform and do the work she didn't want to, but she knew it was all a big learning curve, not only learning from her tutors, but from her fellow students.

Amanda too was in London, studying Physics at South Bank University, with a two-bedroom garden flat just off the Kings Road, bought for her by her doting parents. Fiona spent much of her time there. Lectures and parties almost in equal measure meant it was often not practical to go home to Putney, but she made sure she spent at least two nights a week with Mary and James. She knew they felt quite lonely in the big house with everyone away at school for so much of the time.

During lunch one wintry day, Fiona's tutor came looking for her with a message to telephone home urgently. There was a queue at the first college telephone, so, with a sense of panic, she went to the secretary's office and, breaking all the rules, persuaded Mrs Evans to let her use the office telephone.

'Just this once,' admonished Mrs Evans when she heard the reason for the request.

It was James who answered the telephone. Why is he home at

this time of day? What has happened to Mary? But it was not Mary, it was Pa. He'd had a stroke and died on the way to hospital. Mary had already left to be with her mother, but she knew that Fiona, who had grown so fond of Pa during the past three years, would want to come to Rye with James for the funeral.

Fiona was crying when she came off the phone. It was odd really, her mind was saying. I didn't cry when I heard Mummy was dead. Dear Pa, he'd made her part of his family, 'my adopted grand-daughter' he used to tell everyone.

Pa's death precipitated changes. Ma decided she didn't want to stay in the farmhouse. It was too big and rambling for her on her own. So, after the funeral, when all the friends and relatives had left, Mary and James sat down with Ma and Fiona. Alison, Lynn and Sebastian had been at the funeral but they were now out in the stables brushing down the ponies.

'Good therapy,' said James wisely. It had been Fiona's idea really, though perhaps they would have come round to it anyway.

'Why don't you move into Round Window Cottage Gran, then the farm could become the weekend place instead?' suggested Fiona.

'Hang on a minute.' James was suddenly struck with a thought. 'If you like that idea Ma, why don't we move down here?'

Mary looked thunder struck. 'But James, your work?'

'I can commute for a while, and anyway, perhaps we could buy some more land and have some sheep!'

Despite herself, Ma burst out laughing. 'You don't know one end of a sheep from the other,' she said.

'Then I'll learn.' To Mary's surprise, James sounded quite serious.

'You know, it's not a bad idea and,' she said, warming to the thought that the children could be weekly boarders. 'Well, it would be lovely to have them home every weekend.'

'Steady old thing. What do you think Ma?' James looked at her in concern. 'Are we rushing you?'

'Far from it. I can't stay here, I've already said, and Fiona's idea of the cottage is such a good one.' She smiled affectionately at Fiona. 'Let's do it!'

Things moved quickly from then. The children were thrilled at the thought of living in the country in the farm that had been a second home to them ever since they could remember. They also liked the idea of coming home every Friday.

'Can I come next Friday?' Alison wanted to know.

'Just wait a few weeks darling, while we sell the house.'

In fact, it all happened more quickly than they could have imagined. James contacted Savilles who found a buyer for the Putney house within two days. The couple wanted the carpets and curtains and even negotiated to purchase some pieces of furniture that were not suitable for the farm. Meanwhile, Ma decided on the few items of furniture she wanted at the cottage, and she and Mary spent several hours deciding what to sell and what to keep. Because she was only working part time, Mary had only to give a month's notice and James was already making enquiries about doing an intensive sheep rearing course in Gloucestershire.

In London meanwhile, Amanda's love life was rather bothering Fiona. Bernard had become a regular visitor to London. He would drive from Reims, his home town, and spend every possible weekend with Amanda. The trouble was they now slept together, and if Fiona was staying over for the weekend, she found their noisy, irrepressible lovemaking quite disconcerting. She would put her head under the pillow in order to block out Amanda's delighted squeals and Bernard's grunts of pleasure. It was not really a surprise when Amanda announced her engagement. The Harrisons came down from Edinburgh to meet their prospective son-in-law and throw an engagement party at the Cavalry and Guards Club. Mr Harrison had been in the regular army and a member of the

Household Cavalry. Mary and James were, of course, included in the dinner and Fiona was asked to bring a young man. She had a lot of friends of both sexes, but no particular 'one'.

'She really puts art before anything these days,' Amanda complained to her parents, half jokingly, half seriously. She had never quite understood what went wrong between Fiona and Michael. Fiona had, for once, not confided in her. Michael was really just one of the Slade crowd that Fiona went round with. True, they often paired off together; he made her laugh with his mimicry of their tutors and fellow students, never cruel, but amazingly accurate.

'If you don't make it as an artist,' Fiona teased, 'you could always take up acting.' He would thump her playfully.

He had been to the cottage one weekend and Mary thought they were like puppies romping around together. She wondered if anything serious would come of it. Michael had given her the occasional kiss on the cheek. He would aim for her mouth but she always managed to move just at the right moment. Nothing daunted, he thought she was overly shy and he determined to move slowly.

Romance was the last thing on Fiona's mind. Her total focus was on the art course. When Michael hugged her, it was like James or a member of the family. When he kissed her, she avoided it. She wasn't ready and doubted she would ever want a relationship 'like that'.

Michael asked her down to his family's place for the weekend. She accepted gladly. She had heard about his family, his young siblings, his horse-mad mother and his stockbroker father. They sounded a jolly lot, and one Friday in April, they drove down to Surrey in his somewhat battered Renault.

The house was a complete surprise. It was more of a mansion really, surrounded by sweeping lawns and a lake with fountains playing. When they arrived, the housekeeper ('Our old nanny,' Michael whispered) showed her to her room. As she told Mary afterwards, 'The bathroom adjoining my bedroom was bigger than the sitting room in Round Window Cottage!' The bath stood in splendid isolation in the middle of the room. On one side, there was a big comfortable sofa covered in a pretty pink, white and green fabric that matched the curtains. On the other side of the room, cupboards stretched from the floor to the high ceiling and covered the length of the room. Guiltily, Fiona opened one door after another. Each cupboard was empty, but each had linen inner 'doors', tied with tapes, presumably, she thought, to protect the non-existent clothes hanging within. A large double bed looked positively small in the enormous bedroom where, on a low table, a big bowl of freshly picked daffodils added a splash of colour to the pale greens and golds of the room.

Fiona thought about the few clothes she had brought with her for the weekend. Michael had said 'casual'. Did he mean evening dress? Soon they were walking in the walled kitchen garden where one of the gardeners showed them around. In the greenhouses were melons, figs and grapes in the early stages of growth. The smell of damp earth and the warmth of the pale sun streaming through the windows was a delight but Fiona felt more and more overwhelmed.

By the side of the lake, from where the house seemed a long way off, Michael tried once again to kiss her. Once again, she turned away, a sense of revulsion being her only emotion.

Michael sighed. 'I thought you liked me?'

'I do, but not like that.'

He sighed again and they turned and walked towards the house, keeping a space very carefully between them.

This time she met his mother who had just returned from working with her new horse. She was tall and aristocratic looking, very friendly and welcoming, talking constantly and putting Fiona completely at ease. She didn't ask any questions about her home or family. Perhaps she wasn't interested, but as far as Fiona was concerned, that was a good thing. Explanations could become rather complicated.

Gradually the whole family were assembled, and at half past eight, when Michael's father arrived from London, they sat down to dinner. Fiona was starving. She was not used to eating quite so late and it was difficult not to go through several bread rolls with the gazpacho.

Everyone talked at once, reminiscent of life at home thought Fiona. Once or twice she caught Michael looking at her a bit too seriously for comfort and she felt perhaps she had been unfair to encourage him. As far as she was concerned though, she had only encouraged friendship, nothing more. She shuddered. The thought of anything more made her feel physically sick.

Michael's mother noticed the shiver.

'Are you cold my dear? We don't have the heating on, but I've plenty of sweaters you can borrow.'

Fiona smiled. 'I'm fine thank you, just someone walking over my grave.'

'Who?' asked Michael.

'What a question Michael,' his mother said quickly. She had seen a shadow cross the girl's face. A complicated girl this; seems nice, but not for Michael. She changed the subject, asking Fiona if she rode, and delighted to find that Fiona had been learning to ride for a while, arranged for them both to go out for an early ride the following morning.

Fiona wondered if the weekend would ever end. She loved the riding. The countryside was beautiful and the land they had ridden on belonged to the house. She avoided Michael as much as she could but on the last night he came to her room.

She heard the knock just as she was about to get into bed. Wrapping her cotton dressing gown around her, she went to the door. Michael stood there and pushed his way in. Her right hand came up in front of her mouth, her eyes showing fright, even horror. Whatever Michael's intentions had been, she never knew, for he saw an expression that he could no longer deny. To save face, he said 'I just came to say goodnight and to say I hope you enjoyed the weekend.'

The look of relief that spread over her face confirmed his thoughts. Perhaps she was one of those frigid girls, even a lesbian. Pity, he liked her a lot. Whatever, he was certainly not going to take advantage, particularly in his parents' home.

'Good night then.' He paused. 'Good night,' he repeated.

After he had gone she sat on the window seat looking out into the darkness of the gardens, seeing outlines of trees in the moonlight.

'Never,' she whispered to the trees, 'never will I let a man touch me.'

Thoughts of Mr Lennard came unbidden and unwelcome into her head. 'He has ruined my life forever,' she whispered again.

Finally, she went to bed, longing to get back to London, to the family and away from the pressures of personal relationships.

Chapter 18

Bernard charmed his future in-laws and was happy to see the familiar faces of Mary and James whom he had got to know quite well during their memorable first family holiday in France.

As ever, the Cavalry Club provided a perfect dinner and the smoothness of the service and the delightful atmosphere of the dining room made for a happy and informal occasion.

Bernard's parents spoke little English, so most of the conversation was conducted in French. They discussed wedding plans, and somewhat to the Harrisons' disappointment, Amanda wanted a London wedding.

'I think you'll have to get a special licence,' James mused, 'unless you get married in the church nearest you.'

Fiona happily agreed to be a bridesmaid and the wedding date was set for immediately after finals.

'That's ages away,' moaned Amanda, totally besotted with her Bernard.

'Ten months will speed by. It's hardly long enough.' Amanda's mother spoke with some fervour, her mind already full of lists and more lists.

Time did indeed speed by. Amanda graduated with a 2:1 Physics degree at the end of her third year, leaving Fiona with one more year at Slade for her Masters.

The wedding, it was finally agreed, would take place in the Italian church in Clerkenwell. Bernard was a Roman Catholic and

Amanda decided she would like to follow his faith and after several months of instruction she was accepted into the Roman Catholic Church.

The church was one of the most lavish Fiona had ever been in. There was none of the beautiful simplicity of the Sacré Cœur but gold columns and ornate furnishings provided a setting that Amanda revelled in. She made a lovely bride, her dark hair against the white of her veil, and the dress moulded to her prettily curved figure. By contrast, Fiona, slim and fair, was in a dress of palest gold that seemed to emphasise the golden flecks in her hair that the sunshine always brought out.

Afterwards, about one hundred and fifty guests went into the Café Royal for a pleasant wedding dinner, followed by dancing until the early hours. The principal guests were staying in the hotel, so they repaired to their rooms at intervals for a welcome break.

James bought the flat from the Harrisons, it seemed such an obvious thing to do. Fiona revelled in the peace. Occasionally, James would stay overnight or Mary would come up to London to see old friends or do some shopping and take the opportunity to stay over and be with Fiona.

True to his word, James had given his notice and was at agricultural college in Gloucestershire. After much consideration he had decided to do a one year course. The Bank had been very generous, and with the money from the Putney house carefully invested and Mary's now almost full time teaching job at the local primary school in Rye providing useful income, in addition to the children's school fees being paid for by the Trust Fund set up for the grandchildren by James' now very elderly parents, they didn't feel they had any financial worries.

They had been able to buy back a lot of the original land that had belonged to the farm, so with the two paddocks they already had for the ponies and rescue donkeys, the apple orchard and the returned acreage, they now had about fifty acres. Mary continued looking after chickens and ducks her mother had reared for years and it all began to come together.

Fiona and James realised they would finish studying at the same time. It caused great family hilarity when Mary said she hoped James' diploma was as good as Fiona's degree would be.

Alison, Lynn and Sebastian loved their new life. Returning home at the weekends gave them the freedom to ride and swim and generally run wild, usually bringing a friend or two with them whose parents lived too far away, or even abroad, so only had the opportunity for term-time holiday visits.

A letter arrived at the flat with a French postmark. As ever, Fiona and Amanda kept in close contact. Amanda was loving life in Reims and wrote to say that she and Bernard were expecting their first child. Fiona felt a pang, remembering the first time for years the baby that never was. Unbelievably, Claire had written to her out of the blue a few months ago. They had had virtually no contact since the awful Edinburgh visit after their mother died. Claire had written:

Dear Fiona,

I thought you might be interested to know that Len and I were married last week. I think I have always loved him, though you tried so hard to poison me against him. Anyway, we are married and that is that. Stewart is being a pain. He never comes in at night and the police have been round several times. He loves joy riding you see, and as Len says, who can blame him?

Your sister
Claire

Fiona had been horrified at the thought of Claire married to that man. At least he had married her, not raped her, but she could hardly believe Claire was happy, married to 'him' and still only seventeen. As for Stewart, Fiona's heart sank. He had been such a dear little boy, but she had noticed a change on that visit. He had appeared – apart from the excitement when he first saw her – to have become sullen and wouldn't look at her. Fiona had often pondered on that, reflecting that his attitude had changed after he had gone into the kitchen with the 'odious man' to make the tea. She wondered what had been said to make him behave so differently on his return.

After showing Mary and James the letter, and doing a great deal of soul searching, she realised there was little she could do for Claire. As far as she was concerned, Claire was lost, and Stewart going rapidly downhill. However, Dada had always asked her to protect 'the bairns' and she felt she had failed them. It was only the wise counsel of the Marshalls that prevented her from leaping onto the first train north. Finally, after much discussion, she wrote separate letters to her sister and brother. She could hardly bear to mention the marriage, but felt she had no option.

*My dear Clair*e, she wrote.

Your letter obviously took me by surprise. Seventeen seems very young to get married, but I do hope you will find happiness and contentment.

Your loving sister
Fiona

Dear Stewie

It seems a long time since I had any news of you. I know Daddy had great hopes that you would, like him, go to Edinburgh University and then on into the Army. Do write and tell me how you are getting on. I hope one day you will come and visit me, either in London or Rye.

Your loving sister
Fiona

She had no reply from either of her siblings, and after a while, tried very hard not to think about them although there were times when she felt she had not kept her promise to Dada which made her unhappy.

Amanda's letter was different. A baby! And she knew exactly from the scan that it was a boy. They were to call him Henri Michel, Amanda wrote, Henri after Bernard's father and Michel after her own father, Michael.

It all seemed so beautifully ordered and Fiona couldn't wait to get pen and paper and write a joyous letter back. It's almost as good as having a baby myself, she wrote, only I won't have to have it and get up in the middle of the night!

Henri Michel arrived safely on Christmas Eve. After a happy family Christmas at the farm, with some lovely church services taken by the new young vicar who was throwing himself into everything with extra enthusiasm, Fiona felt spiritually uplifted. The day after Boxing Day she was off in Mary's car through the Channel Tunnel and a few hours later, was outside Amanda's dear little house in the suburbs.

Fiona would never forget the sight of Amanda and Henri Michel as they called him in full.

'It's too much name for such a tiny scrap,' said Fiona looking in wonder at the tiny perfection of fingers and toes.

Amanda was looking radiant, more beautiful than on her wedding day. Bernard was the doting father, fussing attentively over his wife and son, his mother bustling away in the kitchen, in her element, cooking delicious meals to keep up all their strengths.

It was then that Fiona started to paint what was probably her favourite portrait of all time. She called it, unsurprisingly, 'Mother and Child'. It showed a glowing Amanda, her dark eyes pools of pride and happiness. It started as usual with a few sketches and a few photographs to make sure she had the positioning exactly as she wanted and then, during the week she stayed with them, she started the basic outline of the portrait.

'My christening present for Henri Michel,' she said.

'One day, when you are very rich and famous and don't deign to speak to us any more, I shall say, 'that's a McInnes you know, THE famous artist.'

Fiona smiled. Pa had said that what seemed years ago about the portrait she had done of him and Ma.

'We'll always be friends Amanda.'

'I know,' she said smiling. A comfortable silence followed whilst Fiona used her skills.

'I'll bring it to you when it's finished.'

'Perfect! Another visit to look forward to!'

Chapter 19

Fiona was in her last year. Where had the time gone? At almost twenty-two, she felt she had already lived 'so much life'. After experimenting in all aspects of oil, water colour, acrylic and pastels, she had decided that, depending on the subject matter, her preferred mediums were oil and water colours. Despite much pressure, she had stuck to her guns and knew without a shadow of a doubt that portraiture was what she wanted to do most. It didn't stop her enjoying the occasional landscape. In fact, she found that restful compared with the tensions she sometimes felt with a sitter. But as the people who sat for her on the whole were friends and family she felt nothing but totally alive when she had a blank canvas in front of her.

The portrait of Amanda and Henri Michel had been duly delivered amid many screams of delight from Amanda, who was already pregnant with baby number two. Fiona had almost been loath to part with it. There was something about the expression of love so pure, so perfect on her friend's face as she gazed at her son that Fiona realised this was indeed the most selfless and perfect love there could ever be in human life.

She had taken a selection of photographs at different stages in the development of the painting and she kept them in a pocket of her portfolio as both a reminder of her friend and godson, as well as finding them helpful if she hit a difficult moment and needed some artistic inspiration.

The final term was coming to a close. The exhibition, which was the highlight of the year's end, was almost ready. Fiona had already had the accolade of winning the Princes Trust prize for the Young Artist of the Year presented by the Prince himself, who had first promulgated the idea.

Now, with the exhibition almost ready for the press review, the students were both nervous and excited. For many of them, it was one of the first opportunities for outsiders, including the press, to see their work. Fiona and a few other students were very much in the minority having either sold or exhibited something, somewhere at some time.

The final results were out. Fiona could hardly believe she had a First. She could barely wait for Mary, James and the children to arrive for the preview. She kept them in suspense, knowing full well they knew that she must have her results by now. But even they were overwhelmed though, as James said, 'We always knew that you could do it Fee.'

'A First!' Mary cried, 'darling Fee, what a clever girl you are!'

After the preview was over, it was a case of waiting for the press reviews. The students knew that the right words could boost their careers and equally, the wrong ones could do damage, maybe permanently.

At Fiona's request, the meal that night was at the Hard Rock Café. Sebastian had whispered into Fiona's ear earlier that he wanted to go there more than anything in the world. 'Then we shall,' Fiona whispered back.

It was a happy evening. It was not too often these days that all six of them could be together. Alison was now sixteen; *the age I was when I ran away* Fiona thought to herself, looking at the assured young lady that Alison had grown into. Alison had grown so like Mary that at times it was uncanny. Though their colouring was different, their expressions and even the way they moved their hands was strikingly similar. Lynn, now fourteen, was more robust, but had James' wonderful charm and ease of manner. As for Sebastian, he was always up to something, falling out of an apple tree, or off a pony. He had decided he wanted to be pirate he announced, and the family solemnly listened to his plans, all desperately trying to hide their smiles.

'I'm serious,' he said that evening as he caught a giggle and look between his sisters.

'We know darling.' Mary smoothed troubled waters as usual, and James distracted his son with a question about the number of sails and would he fly a Jolly Roger?

The papers next morning didn't do the Slade any harm.

As ever, wrote the Evening Standard reviewer, *the Slade Exhibition was a resounding success, perhaps this year showing more variety and depth than ever.* They mentioned several of the young artists by name.

'And of course,' remarked Alison happily, 'they noticed Fee.'

'Of course,' the family joined as one.

Fiona felt she had never belonged more. Every day she blessed the day she had met Mary on the train. She hugged each one of them in turn, even Sebastian, who turned bright red. 'Get off silly cow,' he said.

'Sebastian!' Mary said in a tone she seldom used, but she smiled as she spoke. It was such a happy day for them all.

Fiona was to spend part of her summer in France with Amanda and her growing family, and the remainder of the holiday at the farm. James told her that she must not rush into anything, but take her time in deciding what she wanted to do. She had been left a bequest by Pa, who had generously included her in a codicil of his will, treating her the same as his other grandchildren. So far she hadn't touched a penny of the ten thousand pounds which she knew would cushion her for quite a while, particularly as the farm was her home and Mary and James wouldn't hear of making any contribution to her keep.

As ever, time with Amanda, Bernard, Henri Michel and Hélène Fiona was fun. The two friends talked non-stop though Fiona noticed changes in Amanda. Her life was now orientated towards her family; she had little thought of anything else. Physics seemed a world away and when Fiona talked about the children growing and Amanda going into research – which had always been her dream – Amanda shook her head dreamily.

'I can't even think of that now Fee. The babies – and I'd like at least two more - are all I want; and Bernard,' she added with a laugh.

Fiona was happy for her, but resolved then and there that children would be way down at the bottom of her list. She adored Amanda's babies, loved cuddling them, but was equally happy to hand them back to their doting maman when they squealed.

The only thing they argued about was language. Amanda spoke French with Bernard and French with the babies.

'You should speak to the babies in English,' Fiona scolded her. She'd even observed Amanda speaking French to her and she had responded automatically in French until she realised what she'd done. From then on, she made a point of only speaking in English, even with Bernard which she knew was a bit mean. Bernard's English was poor, whilst Fiona's French was excellent but as she said to Amanda, 'I'm making a point. You don't want your children not hearing your mother tongue from you do you?'

Amanda smiled, the dreamy smile of the 'now' Amanda. 'I love speaking French. I feel like a French maman, so why shouldn't I speak French with my babies?'

Fiona realised that for once they weren't on the same wavelength and decided to drop the conversation, but she felt the opportunity of a bi-lingual household was being lost and that dear

Amanda was becoming more French than the French.

Back at the farm, and with quite a sense of relief, Fiona settled into the family holiday routine of the Marshalls. Their usual summer lunch party had been arranged and Fiona, now both well known and knowing most of their friends, moved and conversed comfortably amongst their guests.

Mary and James were particularly pleased this year because their dear American friend Baynton Rivers would coincidentally be visiting Rye, staying at the house in the Square that he had bought several years previously.

'It's so sad,' Mary told Fiona as they were preparing the food the day before the lunch. 'Baynton married this very pretty woman, Marietta. She was, is, a doll-like creature and Baynton was totally smitten. It was because of Marietta that he bought the house, which was one good thing.

'Anyway,' Mary continued, 'at the end of the first year, she calmly announced she was leaving him for someone else. And imagine it Fee, it was she who wanted the house in England. Thank goodness Baynton stood firm on this and instead, she took over their house in New York.'

Fiona listened in silence. She vaguely remembered Baynton. She thought she had seen him once or twice during her first summer in Rye, but she wasn't sure. Anyway, he was an older man, so she wouldn't be so likely to have really noticed him.

The lunch party was another success, with fifty people arriving out of the sixty who had been invited. It was lovely having the party at the farm because in the event of rain, they could always move into the barn, as had happened the first summer after they moved in.

But this year, the sun shone. It was one of those balmy English summer days with blue skies and a gentle breeze. Fiona, Alison, Lynn and even Sebastian were handing around the food and drinks.

Fiona had been promoted the last year or two and now helped James pour the Pimms. She'd been shown how he made his secret recipe. So Fiona made and poured whilst Ali and Lynn handed around the pre-lunch canapés made the previous evening by the 'older women' as Mary described them. Fiona loved it. She felt less like a child and more a sister to Mary than ever, the age difference disappearing as each of Fiona's birthdays arrived.

They had wanted to have a party for her on her twenty first birthday but Fiona just wanted to celebrate with 'her' family, for that is what they were and had been for a long time.

It was ages now since she'd heard from Claire, though she had received a card announcing the birth of a son, Lennard John.

'How unimaginative,' Mary had said, 'he'll be Len Lennard won't he?'

Fiona felt numbed at the thought of her sister bearing that man's child and wondered if Claire had ever learned the truth from her husband about her running away. Somehow she rather doubted it. She had received one telephone call from Stewart. He had joined the Army. Fiona had felt a great sense of relief. He was at least away from that household and judging by what he had said in their brief conversation, he had come to his senses at last. He confided that appearing in juvenile court had been a shock and the probation officer who had been assigned to him had become more of a friend and steered him towards the Army as soon as he was old enough. To his amazement, he was enjoying it and was already a Lance Corporal.

Fiona thought of her father. Dear Dada, he'd taken early retirement as a Major. He would perhaps be sad that Stewart was in the ranks, but then perhaps not. If Stewie was happy, what did it matter? From time to time she received a postcard from him, but from Claire, after the birth announcement, she heard not a word.

Chapter 20

Baynton noticed Fiona. How could he fail to? She filled his glass several times. He found himself drinking more than he should just so he could seek her out for a top-up. Every time she filled his glass she would glance shyly up at him as she finished pouring. There was something in the way he looked at her that made her stomach do somersaults. But in all the bustle of the party, she soon forgot and it wasn't until after getting supper with Mary and then falling tiredly into bed that she found her mind wandering in his direction.

He must be old she thought, thirty-fiveish she surmised. He was, she conceded, quite good looking, probably about six foot two. His face had that healthy American look, as if he had just been on holiday somewhere sunny; not bronzed, but healthy looking. His teeth were white and perfect. Why, Fiona wondered, do all Americans have perfect teeth?

Before she knew it, she had drifted off into a deep sleep and found herself on the top of an apartment block. She had never been to New York but she knew that's where she was. She knew for some reason she had to jump; she was in terrible danger. She glanced around. There, walking towards her with an odious smile on his face, was Mr Lennard. He seemed bigger than ever, getting closer and closer. She had no choice, she had to jump.

Just at her deepest moment of despair, she heard a voice calling, 'Jump Fiona, jump! I'll catch you, don't be frightened. Jump Fiona, jump!' She took another look behind her. He was only a few steps away now. Taking a deep breath, she jumped. She was falling, falling, falling, blackness all around her. She heard, as if from someone else, a scream, and knew it must be her screaming. Then suddenly, arms were around her, holding her, cradling her.

'It's alright darling Fiona, it's alright.'

She opened her eyes. It was Baynton holding her tightly in his arms.

Someone was shaking her.

'Fiona, Fiona, wake up! Wake up Fee, you're dreaming.' With a start, Fiona opened her eyes. She was in her bedroom at the farm. Mary was standing by her bed.

'Fee, you were screaming. I thought something terrible was happening. I had such a job to wake you up. Are you alright?'

Fiona sat up slowly. The dream/nightmare was still very clear in her mind. She shuddered, remembering the menace in Mr Lennard's face as he approached her and then the safety she had felt as she fell out of the sky into Baynton Rivers' arms. She felt her cheeks go hot. Mary noticed and put a hand on the girl's forehead.

'Perhaps you have a fever darling. Are you alright?' she repeated.

By now, Fiona had regained her composure.

'It was just a bad dream,' she said, 'thank you for waking me up.'

But something in her head asked what would have happened next, and why Baynton Rivers?

At breakfast, Fiona announced she was going to spend the morning painting a view she had admired for years, over the valley with the church of St Mary's in the distance. She always thought that if only the gradient had been greater, St Mary's would not be unlike Mont St Michel, but even so, the slight gradient from all the streets in Rye leading up to the church gave St Mary's a wonderfully dominant position in the town.

Armed with her easel, water colours, large sheeted sketch pad and artist stool (a present from James one Christmas), Fiona set off to identify the perfect location. It took her over half an hour and finally, with a sigh of relief, she knew she had found it and settled herself comfortably. Several hours passed; she was totally unaware of the time.

Baynton arrived with a bouquet of flowers for Mary. 'A thank you for a wonderful party yesterday. Hope we didn't overstay our welcome.' The last guests, Baynton included, had left after six o'clock.

'Some lunch,' James had said, but he said it with a laugh, knowing what a successful party it had been. Baynton looked around as Mary made a cup of coffee.

'Really, there's no need,' he protested. Then, seemingly casually, he wondered aloud 'Where's Fiona this morning?' Mary looked at him sharply. Something in his tone alerted her. He is interested in Fee she thought, and found herself thinking it would be rather a good match.

'I'll tell you what Baynton, you could do me a big favour actually.'

'Anything for you Mary, you know I adore you!' They both laughed, completely comfortable with the light-hearted flirtation that existed between them.

'Fiona's been out since the crack of dawn.' She permitted herself some exaggeration in a good cause. 'When you've had your coffee,' she continued, 'would you be very kind and take her some coffee and a sandwich or two? She'll be starving and not know it, she gets so engrossed.'

Baynton nodded. Perfect he thought to himself.

'I'd be delighted,' he said, trying not to betray the pleasure he felt at the request.

Mary, however, was no fool. She had seen his eyes light up and, as she said to James in bed that night as they had their usual cosy chat before settling down or making love, 'he's interested in her.' James almost growled. Mary had laughed, for James' response had been a typical father's for, along with his growl, he had muttered, 'but he's too old for her.'

'What's a year or two, when you're in love?'

'Steady on old thing, aren't you jumping the gun a bit?'

'I just have a feeling,' said Mary, snuggling closer.

'So do I,' James laughed, 'but it's you I'm thinking of,' and he drew her tighter into his embrace.

It took Baynton several minutes to locate Fiona. She had settled herself partly in the shade of an old tree in the meadow that was now given over to James' sheep. He stood looking at her back; she was sitting so still. His eyes took in the view for himself and he longed to see what she was painting. He was no slouch himself when it came to art. He had no artistic skills himself but he knew what he liked and had acquired a number of very fine paintings over the years.

Quietly he drew near until he was only a few feet away. Fiona was completely absorbed in her work, so much so that Baynton suddenly felt like an intruder. He gave a slight cough to alert Fiona to his presence and at the same time said 'Hi there Fiona, remember me? Baynton Rivers.'

Fiona stopped and looked up as he came alongside. She felt suddenly shy as the memory of the dream/nightmare came into her mind. She felt her face colour and Baynton thought, *God, she's so innocent, so young and lovely*. He sat down on the grass beside her.

'I come bearing gifts,' he said, 'but I'm not a Greek, I promise.'

Fiona laughed, aware of the quotation.

'Umm, coffee and sandwiches, I'm starving,' she said, eyeing the basket that Baynton had brought with him.

'Mary said you would be, but I'm afraid she's put enough lunch in for both of us.'

'That's nice. I should probably pause for a while anyway.'

'May I?' Baynton stood up and moved back whilst Fiona got off her stool and stood up, stretching her arms above her head.

'It's very good.' Baynton spoke quietly. He had heard of course how talented she was. He had indeed seen some of her work at the farmhouse, but he loved the gentleness of the scene in front of him. It wasn't finished of course, but the church stood in the back ground, a slightly early morning mist giving it an ethereal quality.

'Fiona, do you take commissions?' It was more a statement than a question.

'Of course,' Fiona laughed, 'I have to make a living now. I'm no longer a student.'

'Will you give me an option to buy this?' He indicated the picture. 'It will be a wonderful reminder of Rye, and of you,' he added quickly, 'when I'm in New York.'

Fiona looked at him for a moment.

'Let's eat,' she said, breaking the silence. It was not an awkward silence, but Fiona felt confused about her emotions.

As if reading her mind, and as they ate the delicious sandwiches, Baynton said, in a matter-of-fact tone, 'I'm thirty-five Fiona. Does that seem terribly old to you?'

Fiona was silent for a moment.

'Well,' she began, 'I thought so, but somehow…….well,' she began again after another pause, 'you don't seem old,' she added in a rush.

Baynton burst out laughing.

'Well, that's a relief,' he said, and for some unaccountable reason, they were both laughing.

Baynton came every day after that. He was only in England for a week. Fiona put her painting to one side, and every day the two of them walked and talked. Baynton told her about his childhood in Colorado, how he had learned to ski as a small boy, his time at Harvard, his training to be a lawyer, his move to New York and his marriage.

'That,' he said, 'officially lasted a year, but in fact it was over in months. My judgement was all wrong. I was the wrong man for Marietta. She wanted to party and dance every night away and I was – I am – just a sober sides.'

'You don't seem that to me,' said Fiona. He was quiet at times, yes, but she found that restful. He was full of humour and made her laugh more than she had ever laughed before. By now, they were holding hands as they walked.

'And you Fiona? You're a bit of a mystery woman you know. People in Rye tell of how you suddenly appeared with the Marshalls. Some gossips say you were a child Mary had before she married James, but that doesn't ring true. Anyway, you're not a bit like Mary.'

'Oh Rye and the gossip.' Fiona sighed. 'It's harmless really, but sometimes what people don't know they make up you know.'

'So tell me Fiona, where did you spring from? No,' he added, 'that's unfair of me. Why should you tell me anything you don't want to?'

'But I do.' To her surprise, she really did want to tell him, everything.

He listened attentively, not interrupting her once, just squeezing her hand from time to time and once, stopping her and looking at her silently. It was, for Fiona, the most healing experience. When she had told Mary all those years ago, she had been a frightened child. Now, with the perspective of a young woman and the loving environment with Mary and James, she felt suddenly at peace.

'I've only ever told Mary and James. I'm not quite sure why I've told you,' she finished rather lamely.

'Perhaps because you realise I care. You do, don't you Fee?' he said, slipping into the diminutive he had heard her family use. 'Fee, would you ever consider marrying an elderly chap like me?'

Fiona was stunned. It was the last thing she had expected. Before she could speak, he added, 'I know you hardly know me, but I feel I've always known you.'

How strange thought Fiona, I feel like that too, but marriage? All I want to be is an artist.

Baynton interrupted her silence.

'I'm sorry, I've shocked you,' he said. 'I just couldn't help myself. Just forget what I said. We'll be special friends eh?' He knew that if he didn't back off, he might lose this dear girl. He would have to be very patient.

He left for New York the next morning. Fiona hadn't realised how much she would miss him, but as ever when faced with anything disagreeable, she turned to painting. She spent the next few days in the meadow, working on the picture he had admired and wondering all the time if, by her reaction, she had spoiled a beautiful friendship.

Mary couldn't help but notice that Fiona was being rather quieter than usual.

'She's missing Baynton I'm sure,' she told James serenely. James was unconvinced.

'He's too old. Fiona needs a chap her own age.'

The letter from New York arrived about a week later. Fiona saw it lying on the floor with the other post. Pocketing it, she put the other mail on the kitchen table: a letter in Seb's handwriting – that would be fun. He wrote the most amusing letters, invariably saying he was broke. He was enjoying Eton though Mary missed him coming home at the weekends as he had from prep school. Fiona didn't mention the letter, though it was burning a hole in her pocket. She waited until breakfast was cleared away and Mary assured her there was nothing to do.

'Go away and paint Fee, you know that's what you want to do!'

For once, Mary was wrong. Fiona walked to the meadow and sat under the tree, the tree where Baynton had found her.

My dear Fee, began the letter. *Life in New York seems very mundane after the fun in Rye – the party and especially having the opportunity of getting to know you. I only hope I didn't frighten you with my wild suggestion. I was wondering how the painting I was admiring is coming along? What enormous price will you put on it, because whatever it is I want to buy it and add it to my collection. A real McInnes.* Fiona smiled at this. *I'd love you to see my collection one day. I think you might enjoy it. I'm very fortunate to have acquired one or two rather special pieces and some from artists who were once like yourself, at the beginning of their careers and who are now established artists in their own right as I'm sure you will be one day in the not too distant future. Perhaps one day I shall be able to persuade you to visit New York. How I would love to show you the city I have adopted as my home. But then, perhaps, you don't like cities?*

I am in the process of putting together a rather difficult defence at the moment, a young woman who allegedly killed a man who was trying to rape her. I must admit Fee, I thought about you and your terrible experience and it helped me to understand what the poor young woman (though several years older than you were) went through. Sorry, not the most cheerful thing to write about!

Please give my love to Mary and James and the rest of the family. Perhaps you will write back? I would really enjoy that.

Your affectionate friend,
Baynton

Fiona read the letter through several times. There was much to digest. Yet there was no hint of pressure to pursue a relationship other than friendship. For a moment, Fiona felt a pang of disappointment, but quickly pulled herself together. She didn't want, wasn't ready for, anything else yet, if ever.

After a walk through the meadow and a visit to the ponies, she headed indoors to write a reply. If Mary was surprised to see her so soon, she didn't show it, but she did notice, with a feeling of satisfaction, the airmail letter sticking out of Fiona's pocket.

Fiona sat for a long time with her pen poised over the paper. It was not that it was difficult to write to Baynton, but she just wanted to put what she had in her head rather carefully.

Dear Baynton, thank you so much for your letter.

What a boring beginning she thought.

I was interested to hear about the case you're defending. It must be so difficult to defend someone if you don't believe them, so I'm glad to learn that you feel sympathetic towards your client. She hoped that was the correct terminology. *From all I have ever heard and read, New York sounds like a fabulous city and I'd certainly love to visit it one day, and maybe see your collection at the same time.*

I haven't finished 'your' painting yet. The light hasn't been quite right. We've had some thunderstorms since you left. I'm writing about the weather for God's sake! she thought. Anyway, by the time you return to England it will certainly be finished and I will reserve it for you.

Kind regards
Fiona Marshall McInnes

She wished she hadn't put her surname, but to cross it out would look terrible, so she left it as it was.

Baynton smiled when he read the letter. At least she had written, and although he wanted to write back straight away, he forced himself to wait for several weeks.

Fiona found herself looking at the post with particular interest. Mary noticed of course, but again, keeping her own counsel, she said nothing. When Fiona was ready to talk about it, she would.

Several weeks went by. Baynton's picture, as Fiona now thought of it, was finished. James particularly liked it.

'That'll sell in Rye for sure,' he said.

'It's not for sale,' had been Fiona's response.

'I have a feeling it's for Baynton,' Mary told James out of earshot of the artist.

'Really? How odd,' said James.

Mary smiled a knowing smile. 'Not really,' she said.

Chapter 21

In New York, Baynton Rivers was feeling pretty pleased with himself. His assistant had tracked down another woman who had been attacked by the alleged rapist and who was prepared to testify to that effect. The case became something of a cause célèbre, as the attacker turned out to be a rather well-known actor. Despite a brilliant performance on his part – and an equally brilliant defence by his counsel – Baynton's case proved watertight and the actor was convicted and jailed.

Baynton wrote to Fiona.

My dear Fiona, thank you for your letter.

Boring beginning he thought.

You may be interested to know that the case I was working on is over and we were able to get a conviction. What a pity I wasn't around to get your chap a heavy sentence too. Anyway, because I'm feeling so pleased with myself, I've decided to treat myself to another little holiday and am going to be in Rye in around ten days time when all the loose ends are tied up here, for about five days. I do hope you'll be in Rye and we can take some more of those very pleasurable walks and perhaps you'll allow me to buy you dinner at Le Bistro, one of my favourite little Rye restaurants. How is the picture?

Your friend

Baynton

Dear Baynton, Fiona replied by return.

Congratulations on the trial result. How nice you're returning to Rye so soon. The picture is finished by the way.

We all look forward to seeing you soon.

Kind regards

Fiona

p.s. I'd love to have dinner at Le Bistro. It's one of my favourite restaurants too.

Alison announced that she wanted to be a doctor. She was at home for the autumn half term holiday. Her GCSE results had been good and, unlike Lynn who really loved only English and Drama, Alison was like James and enjoyed the sciences. Biology and Physics were her particular favourites but she rather suffered Chemistry. Mary and James were delighted.

'Well,' said Sebastian, 'I'm actually going to be a vet.'

'I thought you wanted to be a pirate,' James said with a grin.

'Oh,' said Sebastian grandly, 'only when I was a child.'

'Well Seb, it'll be jolly useful having a vet in the family, with all the sheep let alone the ponies and donkeys that seem to cost me a fortune.'

'I won't charge you anything Daddy.'

'That's what I like to hear,' James laughed heartily, 'we must be doing something right Mary; a doctor *and* a vet!'

'What about you Lynn?' Fiona wanted to know. Lynn looked thoughtful.

'Actually,' she said in a very serious voice for her, 'I'm going to RADA.'

'What's that?' Seb asked.

'It's a special acting school,' Lynn replied, somewhat impatiently, 'everyone but everyone knows that.'

'Not so sure about acting,' James began, but Mary quelled him with a look that said we'll talk about this later.

As much to change the subject as anything else, Fiona said that she'd had a letter from Baynton and that he would be coming to Rye again quite soon.

'Great!' said Sebastian, 'I like Baynton. He knows magic you know,' he said, turning to Fiona. 'He can make things appear and disappear.'

They all laughed as Alison got up to clear the table whilst Fiona got the fruit salad she had made earlier from the fridge.

'What does Baynton write to you for?' Sebastian asked.

'Sebastian, you should call him Mr Rivers.' Mary frowned slightly.

'Why?' said the boy, 'he told me I could call him Baynton and anyway, I still don't know why he writes to you and not to me or Ali or Lynn.'

'Curiosity killed the cat,' said Lynn.

'Satisfaction brought it back,' answered Sebastian automatically.

They all laughed and any awkwardness there might have been in answering the question disappeared because the question was never answered.

Baynton duly arrived ten days later. In a way, it was good that the children were back at school. They had sensed something about Fiona they couldn't really identify and they certainly would have teased her although Alison secretly told her sister 'I think they're madly, passionately in love.'

'Oh,' said Lynn, dramatically repeating what her sister had said. 'Madly, passionately in love! How romantic!'

Perhaps they would have been disappointed if they had been able to listen into the conversations between the two in question. They talked the talk of good friends. There was never an awkward pause; conversation flowed, punctuated by comfortable silences.

Baynton had been delighted when he saw the painting and it was over the painting they had their first disagreement. He wanted to buy it and he offered her what she felt was a ridiculously high price. She, on the other hand, had already decided she wanted to give it to him.

'You can't Fee. That's so unbusinesslike, so un-professional. How can you give it away? I want to buy it from you.'

'And I want to give it you,' she retorted. 'James and Mary accepted paintings, and so did Ma and Pa. Why can't you be more gracious?'

He realised suddenly that he was included in a very elite band of people. Paintings of the family and Amanda were the only ones she had given away.

'I'm sorry Fee,' he said, suitably contrite, 'I shall be honoured to accept such a beautiful painting as a gift.'

For a few moments, Fiona was unmollified.

'I'm not sure I want to give it to you now,' she muttered.

'What's that! What did you say!' He went to grab her playfully. She ducked under his arm. He chased her, she ran, he caught her. He kissed her.

She had never been kissed like this before. The gentle summer kisses she had shared with Jean Pierre were never more than a breath on her cheeks or a kiss on the palm of her hand, and she had tried too hard to avoid the casual kisses from the boys at Slade and from Michael, of course.

This was different. For a split second, Fiona felt almost afraid of the emotion welling up inside her. Then she abandoned herself to his lips, their bodies close. They clung together, feeling something neither of them had known before.

It was Baynton who eased away, suddenly afraid he might get carried away with passion and only too aware that he must move slowly. He needn't have worried. At that moment, under the tree in the meadow, she would have given herself to him body and soul. As it was, she felt a slight sense of disappointment when he said 'Let's walk back.'

They walked hand in hand as they had many times before, but this time both feeling an enormous step had been taken in their relationship. Baynton had the sense not to talk of marriage again, but they did touch on her visiting New York at some unspecified time in the future. As James said to Mary during their bedtime chat, 'Baynton seems to be spending most of his time here these days.'

Baynton returned to New York. Fiona was amazed at how much she missed him. They were now corresponding regularly and the letters continued to move their relationship forward. All of the stiff formality of Fiona's first letter had completely disappeared. She wrote as she felt and her pen flew over the pages, telling Baynton the minutiae of her daily life. For his part, Baynton read and re-read her lively letters that conjured up so vividly the farm, the family and her own sweet self.

Chapter 22

Mary and James were working very hard. It was lambing season. Fiona too was up many nights keeping them supplied with hot drinks and watching with them as a particular ewe had problems producing twins, feet coming first. Fiona marvelled at the ewe's stoicism and the way that the minute the ordeal was over, she was licking the lambs as if their entrance into the world had been an easy affair, as it was thankfully for most of the flock.

James was by now very much the farmer. City days seemed long away and he and Mary revelled in their lives together on the farm. The only sadness was that Ma was quite poorly these days and despite their efforts, refused to come back to the farm so that Mary could take care of her.

'You know how much I value my independence,' she would say, not realising that the daily visits and shopping that Mary did for her were actually considerably more wearing than had she lived with them. Mary had arranged for a daily to start early enough to make Ma's breakfast, then Mary would arrive around twelve every day to prepare a light lunch. Ma's appetite was small these days and she seemed to be visibly shrinking.

So, it wasn't really a surprise when there was an early telephone call one morning from the daily, crying as she spoke.

'She's dead Mrs Marshall, lying there ever so peaceful in her bed. I thought she was asleep,' she continued, 'so I went and made her breakfast and the Earl Grey, but I couldn't wake her.'

Mrs Clifton was crying so much that Mary had to try comforting her before hanging up the phone and sinking into a chair, knees tucked under her chin as she always sat when hit by an emotional shock. James found her like that a few moments later.

'My darling, whatever is it? Is it Ma?' Some instinct told him.

'She's dead James. Ma is dead.' Now with James with her, she could cry. 'I'll miss her so much.'

'I know darling.' James sat on the edge of the chair with his arm around her shaking shoulders.

The funeral was, as Pa's had been, very well attended. Ma and Pa had lived in the area for all their married life and had had a large circle of friends, many of whom were now deceased. Even so, the old village church was full and the grandchildren sat with their parents and Fiona, feeling immense sadness that the grandmother who had always had unlimited time and love for them as children, who had been a listening ear, who had always been there to talk to if they had had a problem, she was no longer with them. Alison in particular felt bereft. She had memories of stories Ma used to tell about her childhood and also the wonderful stories she would make up for herself and Lynn about a secret world that only children of a certain age could find.

Mary felt numb. Pa's death had been a shock, but losing a second parent seemed even harder, and if it hadn't been for James' comforting hand holding hers, she would not have got through the service without being in paroxysms of tears.

Sebastian, as the grandson and youngest of the three grandchildren, read the lesson. His clear voice only faltered once and they all felt so proud of him. The new vicar had taken the trouble to find out from Mary and James some details and stories about Ma's life, and a number of people in the congregation were surprised to learn that she had written numerous children's books using a pseudonym. It had been a very well kept family secret, at her insistence.

Fiona wrote to Baynton that evening.

Dearest Baynton she began, *it has been such a sad week for us all. Gran died in her sleep five days ago and the funeral was today at the village church. It was packed and everyone was surprised to learn of Gran's secret life of writing. Did you know she had written about fifteen children's books? It was such a well kept secret. I'm sorry, I don't feel like writing any more, but I knew you would want to know, and I wanted to write to you anyway.*

Much love
Fiona

My dearest Fiona, I was so sad to learn about your adopted grandmother's death, and I have written to Mary and James separately. It's always sad to lose someone you love. That's why I believe we should spend as much time as possible with those we do love.

I love you.
Baynton.

Time slipped by. The spring blossom was on the trees and the Easter holidays brought the whole family together again. Fiona had started riding the ponies, very tentatively at first. James had encouraged her by saying that they should be ridden regularly and that the weekends with the children were not enough.

Mary rode alongside her on Hinge, while Fiona generally rode Bracket. Silly names, but that was what the rescue centre had named them for some unaccountable reason, and the names seemed to suit them. After a few weeks of gentle hacking and gradually learning the rising trot, Fiona found her confidence and was soon starting every day with an hour on Bracket. Hinge was trickier, slightly temperamental, and Fiona didn't feel confident enough to ride him yet.

Apart from that, her days were spent painting or presenting portfolios of her work to various small galleries in the small and large towns on the Sussex/Kent border. But what was most exciting was that she was getting occasional commissions.

A friend of Mary's wanted a portrait of her parents as a fiftieth wedding anniversary present. They had seen Fiona's work at the farm – the portrait of the three children and several studies separately of the children and of Mary and James that were dotted around.

Fiona drove to Wittersham, only a few miles away, to meet the parents who were visiting their daughter and son-in-law. They were a rather daunting couple, very highbrow and not particularly friendly towards Fiona. However, she did a few preliminary sketches, took some photographs of them in several different poses, both together and separately, and arranged to visit their house in a week's time. They suggested that she stay with them for a few days, and although she was not enamoured with the idea, she realised it made good sense. In fact, the whole experience nearly put her off portraiture forever. She was served her meals in her room and somehow they managed to convey by their conversation and attitude that an artist was really no more than a menial artisan. Despite their attitude, indeed perhaps because of it, Fiona was determined that this would be the best portrait she had ever done. After four days of sittings, she announced that she would do a period of work in her studio and come back for perhaps another two days in a few weeks.

Her studio was now part of one of the barns that James had himself sectioned off, and then had a window put in so that Fiona could get the northern light she required. Fortunately, the barn was well screened from the road and James had had the work done very discreetly using a local builder. He had an awful feeling that if he'd applied for planning permission, the local council would be against it and the local conservation society would be up in arms. In fact, in his view it improved the barn, and Mary had planted some shrubs and creepers which were quickly blending in and providing screening. James admitted to Mary that he felt a trifle guilty, but nevertheless, he was equally determined that Fiona should have her studio.

The portrait was proving a challenge. Without meaning to, Fiona had captured all too exactly the rather superior and supercilious expression on the face of the wife.

'In all honesty,' as she said to Mary and James, 'she looks just like that, but I feel bad about it because, after all, it's a gift from her family and they're paying good money!'

She was so concerned that Mary and James followed her to the studio one morning to see for themselves.

'You're worrying needlessly,' James said, 'they won't even see that. They'll see a skilled portrait that looks exactly like them and they'll be thrilled.'

Mary nodded in agreement.

'He's right Fee. You're seeing something that they look at every day in the mirror and don't even notice!'

Fiona felt slightly better, but on the day when she was returning to Green Court, she felt distinctly nervous. She needn't have worried. For once, they seemed genuinely pleased.

'It's not quite finished,' Fiona interjected as they admired themselves.

It only took two more weeks. Fiona breathed a sigh of relief when she put the final touch of colour on the large oil painting, and when it was thoroughly dry, the varnish. She agreed that she would arrange for the framing after consulting with the daughter who had commissioned the portrait in the first place.

It was a great relief to her when the whole episode was over and a cheque for three thousand pounds was in her pocket. She felt like celebrating. The thought of visiting New York and Baynton had been popping into her head at regular intervals. On the spur of the moment, she telephoned him on his home number. A sleepy voice answered.

'Baynton, it's Fiona.'

'Fiona, what's wrong?'

Fiona glanced at the kitchen clock – it was nine o'clock.

'Baynton, what time's it there?'

'God Fee, you didn't ring me to ask me the time did you?' but he was laughing now and completely awake. 'It's four a.m. here.'

Now it was Fiona's turn to be confused.

'Oh Baynton, I'm so sorry. It's just that I've received a big cheque this morning. Big for me anyway, and I thought, if you didn't mind, I'd like to come to New York to see you,' she ended in a rush.

Baynton, now thoroughly awake, leapt out of bed as naked as the day he was born.

'Fee, that's wonderful, when are you arriving?'

They talked for half an hour, though it only seemed minutes to both of them. It was arranged that she would arrive the following Saturday, allowing four days for her to sort herself out and for Baynton to re-arrange his diary.

Chapter 23

Mary and James drove her to the airport. She felt as excited as she had when she had gone to Paris with Amanda and Mr and Mrs Harrison all those years ago. That thought brought back unpleasant memories, so she concentrated on the thought of seeing Baynton again.

Her small suitcase with just a few changes of clothes and one rather pretty cocktail/dinner dress was all she had brought with her – apart from, of course, her sketch pad and a few pencils and pastels just in case. She hardly imagined though that she would be allowed much time to be creative; she had a feeling that Baynton was going to really show her 'his' town as he called it.

The plane touched down at Kennedy exactly on time and before she knew it, she was through customs and in Baynton's arms.

'Oh honey, it's so good to see you.'

She had never been called honey before and decided she rather liked it.

'Is that all you've brought with you Fee?' Baynton looked at the modest sized bag with a raised eyebrow, remembering how much his former wife would take for a weekend.

Fiona nodded happily. 'I think I've everything I need, but if I haven't, I'll buy it here. I feel quite rich at the moment.'

'What a pretty pin.' Baynton looked at the delicate diamond and ruby brooch Fiona was wearing on her lapel.

'Isn't it lovely? Gran left it to me in her will. That whole family, my whole family, have been so wonderful to me.'

Baynton squeezed her hand. 'Well deserved darling, well deserved.'

The apartment was immense. Fiona couldn't believe the big, airy, spacious rooms high up (fourteen floors Baynton told her), above the hurly burly of people and traffic below. It was a penthouse apartment, so the windows looked out on all sides.

'Wonderful light,' the artist in Fiona mused aloud. Baynton smiled; just the reaction he had hoped for.

There were three bedrooms and a dressing room, all with ensuite bathrooms, a large sitting area and a raised dining area where a dining table and chairs were conveniently adjacent to the kitchen. Baynton's study – a book-lined room with a big desk and chair, computer and leather sofa and matching chair – was very much a man's study. There was one more room that Baynton said he planned at some stage to put in a pool table for evenings with his friends.

Fiona walked from room to room, delighting in all she saw. The walls were covered with an interesting selection of paintings, and in one of the bedrooms she found the painting she had given Baynton the previous summer.

'This is my bedroom,' Baynton said quietly, 'and every morning when I wake up, the first thing I see is your painting.'

Fiona felt very touched and not a little overwhelmed. His tone spoke volumes.

'I thought you might like to sleep in here.'

Baynton led the way out of his room into a room with an old four-poster bed.

'What a wonderful bed!' Fiona was admiring the beautiful carvings on the posts and the patchwork quilt that was so obviously handmade.

'My great grandparents brought it with them from England. It was all taken apart for the journey on board and then put back together again. It's been in my family for longer than that though I believe.'

'You have English roots? How fascinating.' Fiona wanted to hear more, but Baynton had other ideas. He fetched her case into the room.

'Now, be a good girl and wash and brush up and do whatever you have to do, then I'm taking you out on the town.' He closed the door behind him, leaving her alone with her thoughts.

They had a wonderful evening, wandering whilst it was still light through Central Park where Baynton told her he jogged most mornings. Afterwards, he took her to a favourite Italian restaurant where the owner – the most Italian owner with the most Irish of names, Mick McLochery – welcomed Baynton enthusiastically.

'Ah, Signor Baynton, it's good to see you again. Signorita!' He smiled at the tall slim girl who was with Baynton tonight. Surely this one would be the one that Signor Baynton would find happiness with?

The meal was a great success, the food simple but 'oh so good!' Fiona said as the last morsel of a delicious home-made cassata slipped down.

'Let's have coffee back at the apartment,' Baynton suggested and Fiona, happy to do anything he suggested, agreed.

Baynton seemed completely at home in his very American kitchen, so different from the farmhouse kitchen. Soon the coffee was ready.

'Proper coffee,' said Baynton, 'the only way to finish a good dinner.

Fiona slipped off her shoes and tucked her feet under her as she sat on the sofa. Baynton sat opposite, letting her conversation wash over him. The pleasure of seeing her here in New York, in his apartment, made him the happiest man in New York tonight. He grinned inwardly, wondering what Fiona would say if she could read his mind. As if on cue, she yawned suddenly.

'Poor Fee, I've dragged you out when you must be exhausted. The time difference is a killer.'

He stood up and she struggled to her feet, sudden waves of exhaustion washing over her. They walked together towards her bedroom door. Fiona had a slight moment of panic. She was so tired she couldn't deal with emotion at the moment. As if reading her mind, Baynton leaned across and opened the door, kissing her lightly on the cheek before giving her a gentle shove into the room.

'Good night Fee. See you in the morning,' and, for the second time that evening, he pulled the door closed.

For a moment, Fiona leaned against the door, almost too tired to move. Then, shedding her clothes as she moved, she headed for the bathroom, where earlier she had put her toiletries. She stood under the shower, the water pressure so great that it was almost as if she was having a massage. Feeling a little refreshed, she put on her short cotton nightdress and climbed into the enormous four-poster. For a moment, she wondered if Baynton would come back. She even thought briefly about going to his room, but even as the thought crossed her mind, she was drifting off into a deep and dreamless sleep.

When she awoke, she felt momentarily disorientated, then, gradually as her mind came into focus, she looked around her with delight. It really was a most wonderful bed and the bedroom has been furnished to complement its centrepiece. She glanced at her watch and found to her horror that, by American time, it was already ten thirty. Leaping out of bed, she had a hasty wash and threw on a pair of jeans and a tee shirt. There was no sign of Baynton, but the smell of coffee lured her to the kitchen where she found it perking away and the table laid for one – her, she supposed. Propped up against the cornflakes was a note from Baynton.

Dearest Fiona, do hope you slept well. I've gone out for my jog and will be back soon. Help yourself to juice and anything else you want from the fridge. There's some cinnamon toast in the toaster, just pop it down.

See you soon, love B

Fiona smiled. What a thoughtful man. She opened the fridge, the most enormous one she'd ever seen. Two doors and an ice-making machine, what fun! She helped herself to juice and found a pack of milk to have with her cornflakes. She poured herself some coffee and, as instructed, popped the toast down. With a satisfied smile, she sat down and ate the cereal, hearing the pop of the toaster after she'd had a few mouthfuls. The toast was lovely. She'd never had cinnamon toast before and thought it was a delicious way to start the day.

'Hi Fee.' Baynton arrived back, looking fit and hot. 'I'll grab a shower and be with you in five minutes.'

'Alright B,' she said, but he didn't hear her. Fee and Bee she mused, how silly!

He took her on a tour of New York. Firstly, they went on a tour bus so she could see the main sights. Then they took the Staten Island ferry and crossed to Manhattan to see the Statue of Liberty. They even climbed up inside it which seemed quite bizarre to Fiona who had never imagined it was hollow. They ate a very late lunch in Times Square at another of Baynton's favourite restaurants, but this time they just had salad and dessert, Fiona feeling still rather replete from the late breakfast.

That evening, Baynton told her he had invited a few of his closest friends round for drinks and after that they could have a quiet dinner at home when, Baynton assured the surprised Fiona, he would show off his culinary skills.

Fiona couldn't help feeling rather nervous about the evening;

well, the early part of it anyway. She wondered what Baynton's friends would think of her and indeed what she would think of them.

Lally, Baynton's daily housekeeper, had been in during their absence. She would also stay on for the first part of the evening and hand round drinks and the canapés she had prepared most beautifully.

Lally looked at the young Englishwoman with interest. Now this one, she thought, was more like it. Her black face was wreathed in smiles.

'Now, Miss Fiona, Mr Rivers told me all about you. It's sure good to have you stay here with us.'

Fiona was fascinated by her accent. Lally seemed to guess this. 'Now, ahm not from Noo York honey, ahm a real southerner, but I married a Noo Yorker and then he done left me in this big city all alone. Mr Rivers, he done found me in Central Park one day when he was doin' one of his jogs. Ahs crying mah eyes out and he brought me breakfus and before ah noo it, ahs workin' here and found me a little room close by.'

This was a side of Baynton that Fiona hadn't known but somehow it didn't surprise her at all and she felt her feelings warming to him even more.

The evening was a great success. Five couples arrived, all close friends of Baynton's, and all curious to see his English friend. One or two of the wives were a bit taken aback by her youth. 'She's so young,' one of them confided to her closest friend.

Fiona found them all extremely friendly. Indeed, her only problem was that she was almost overwhelmed by the apparent instant, genuine friendship they offered. For their part, they all knew she was an artist. They had all seen the painting that hung in Baynton's bedroom and she had at least two people ask to see some more of her work and ask if she did portraits of animals.

'We have such a sweet dog,' one man confided. Fiona had hard work keeping her face straight.

Finally they left.

'Phew, that's better. Now I have you all to myself at last. Perhaps having them round tonight wasn't such a good idea after all.'

Lally had cleared the glasses and tidied up generally and now the two of them sat side by side, one of Baynton's arms resting casually along the back of the sofa. Inwardly, Fiona still felt rather overwhelmed, but she knew they were his friends and they had all been extremely kind.

'I thought they were very nice,' she said tactfully.

'Liar,' Baynton laughed, 'they were a pain going on at you about painting portraits of their pets.'

'Only one.' This time it was Fiona's turn to laugh.

'Supper.' Baynton got up suddenly and pulled her to her feet. 'Come on slave!'

'Yes master!' she replied, trying and failing to sound suitably servile.

Baynton cooked them a steak. He pointed to the fridge.

'The salad's in there wench – do your worst.'

'I'll never find anything, your fridge is so huge.' Her horrified tone made Baynton laugh again, but soon there was just the sound of the steak sizzling in its butter and the sound of Fiona chopping up the salad which she had eventually found. It was, they both thought independently, a lovely way to end the evening.

Chapter 24

Once again, Baynton kissed her gently outside her bedroom door, and then turned abruptly towards his own room. Fiona showered and put her nightdress on and climbed into bed. She lay there for several minutes, the bedside lamp providing a pool of light. Then, before she could change her mind, she got out of bed, momentarily wishing she had a dressing gown, and crossed the room to the door.

Like a thief in the night, she crept along the corridor and stopped outside Baynton's bedroom. The corridor was in darkness, but she could see a crack of light under his door. She lifted her hand to knock, then changed her mind and slowly turned the handle.

Baynton was sitting up in bed, reading. She had never seen him with glasses on before, but thought in some strange way it made him look more handsome than ever.

'Fiona,' his voice registering surprise, 'are you alright, is there anything you need?'

Fiona paused by the open door, and then turned and closed it behind her, leaning back on it for support.

'Yes Baynton, actually there is.'

He took off his glasses and looked at her steadily. Their eyes held for what seemed like minutes to Fiona. She had a split second when she thought, I shouldn't have come. Then Baynton held out his arms and said 'Come here darling Fee, I've been waiting for you.'

Their night of lovemaking was more than Fiona could have ever imagined. Her fears evaporated. Baynton was a tender and considerate lover, and he transported Fiona to somewhere she hadn't known existed. He slowly let his hands caress every part of her body as he kissed her with his lips. Finally, when she thought she could bear no more exquisite emotions and feelings, he entered her. She greeted him eagerly and they came together in a great explosion of passion.

Afterwards, she lay in his arms, her fingers touching his face as if she was seeing him for the first time.

'I hoped you'd come to my bedroom Fee my sweet.'

'But why didn't you ask me?'

'You had to choose your own time and place – and now I'll never let you go!'

'And I'll never want to go,' she replied, 'this is where I belong, forever, with you.'

It was over breakfast the following morning that he raised the subject of marriage. Fiona was horrified.

'But I can't possibly marry you Baynton,' she said.

He was taken aback by the strength of feeling in her voice.

'But you said you'd never leave me.'

Fiona smiled, a slow, happy smile.

'Dearest Baynton, I meant it, I mean it, but I don't want to get married. I want – I need,' she hesitated, 'I need to be free. It doesn't stop me loving you or living with you – if you'll have me,' she finished.

There was quite a long silence, then 'If the only way I can have you in my life is to have you living with me, than that's what it will have to be. But,' he continued, 'if you ever change your mind, you must promise me here and now that you'll tell me.' He looked quite stern.

That's how he must look in court sometimes she thought.

'I promise you,' she said.

Fiona arrived back in London, her mind full of thoughts of Baynton. So much had happened in one week. Now she had the task of telling Mary and James, not that she imagined it would be that much of a surprise to them.

They were at Gatwick to meet her.

'America obviously suits you,' James said, hugging her warmly.

Mary looked at the girl closely. She had never seen her look so radiant. Despite the long flight she was full of energy and her eyes were alight with – Mary strove in her mind for a word – joy, she thought, she's full of joy.

On the journey home, they chattered about her first impressions of New York. She described Baynton's flat and told them of the places they had visited.

'He even had me out jogging in Central Park every morning, and you know how I love getting up early,' she added wryly. They all laughed.

In New York, Baynton was having dinner-à-deux with one of his favourite people. Suzanne Rowe was a newspaper columnist who, eight years earlier, had interviewed him during a particularly difficult court case. It had been one of his first appearances in a New York court at the age of twenty seven, having just become a junior partner in a law firm following a short period in Denver after qualifying. Suzanne had arrived to interview him unannounced and with a fairly intractable point of view over the case. Something about his obvious sincerity and determination to help his client made Suzanne review her thinking and her article, as a consequence, had been written with a very different slant from the one she had anticipated.

Once the trial was over she contacted him again to commiserate on the outcome. To her surprise, he was not in the least cast down, 'Merely,' he said, 're-grouping for the appeal.'

To his surprise, this attractive woman then proceeded to ask him out for dinner. They had a great evening and Baynton found Suzanne totally fascinating. Her dark hair and eyes, she told him, she had inherited from her Italian grandmother. This perhaps, Baynton thought, explained, in part, her outgoing personality and wonderfully expressive gestures and way of speaking.

The Maitre'D at the restaurant of her choice obviously knew her well.

'Good evening Duchess, Sir,' was his warm greeting when they arrived.

'Duchess?' Baynton had said enquiringly.

'It's just a nickname,' she had said, laughing.

'But it suits you,' he had replied, and from that evening had never called her anything else.

Their friendship had developed quickly and for a short time they had become lovers. One morning, waking up in her luxurious apartment, he looked at her sleeping form and knew he had made a mistake. He wasn't in love with her; he loved her dearly as a friend. He had to tell her, it wouldn't be fair not to, but it would probably mean he would lose her friendship.

At that moment, she woke up.

'Baynton,' she had said sleepily, 'I want you as a friend, not a lover.'

He had burst out laughing and she had sat up in bed, looking indignant and not a little angry and, he thought, very Italian.

'That's not the right response,' she had said crossly.

Baynton somehow got a grip on himself.

'It's just that,' he finally got out, 'I was thinking exactly the same thing. I was thinking what a wonderful friend you are and I don't want to lose your friendship.' He paused. 'It's such a special friendship.'

'Oh Baynton darling, what a relief!' she had said, smiling.

Baynton often thought how funny it was really, how close they were. If either of them were at a loose end or needed a partner, they always rang each other. They had occasional ski holidays together in Colorado, and everyone assumed they were 'an item'. When Baynton bought his new and rather splendid apartment about eighteen months after they had first met, he decided to throw a big party and it was then that Suzanne met the man she was to marry.

'You arranged it all perfectly Baynton,' she had said afterwards. 'You knew I wouldn't be able to resist him.'

The 'him' in this case had been William Rowe, a cosmetic surgeon who had consulted Baynton about a client of his. The two men had hit it off instantly and Baynton included him automatically. It was obvious that Suzanne was not alone in being smitten, and the two of them left early which was unusual for a party girl like Suzanne.

Apart from her bi-weekly column, Baynton heard not a word for two weeks and then, out of the blue, he received a telephone call from Las Vegas.

'Darling Baynton, we are married,' it had announced.

'Who are you married to?' but he knew the answer as he asked the question.

'Why, William of course, who else?'

Now William was in Canada on a lecture tour. Suzanne had been with him but had come back a few days early to finish her column and had, of course, phoned Baynton straight away.

'Darling Baynton, what's all this I'm hearing about a sweet, young English girl? You dark horse you.'

'Come and have dinner with me tonight and I'll tell you all dear Duchess,' he had replied.

'She's an artist,' he began, 'twenty two.'

'Twenty two? Baby snatcher,' Suzanne teased, 'when are you getting married?'

'We're not.' For a moment, Baynton looked downcast. Then he visibly cheered. 'But she's gone to England to get all her things and her art gear and tell her family – well, adopted family – and then she'll be coming back here to live with me.'

'It sounds intriguing. What's this about an adopted family and what sort of artist is she and how did you meet and when am I going to have the pleasure?'

'Duchess, stop being a columnist for a moment! I can't tell you everything, that would be betraying her trust. Suffice to say, she had an unusual and unhappy childhood and then was more or less adopted by very dear English friends of mine. As an artist – to answer your next question – she is, I believe, quite outstanding. Hold on,' he continued, 'I'll show you a sketch she did of me the other evening.'

He went to the den and picked up her sketch pad which was still lying open as she had left it. The top picture was a study of Baynton engrossed in a law book and, unbeknown to him, Fiona had been sketching him.

'Look at this,' he said, walking back to Suzanne, 'and it was done in just a few moments.'

Suzanne took the book from him.

'It's good Baynton, isn't it?' She idly turned the pages to see what else there was.

'Oh Baynton, they are so good.'

'Let's have a look Duchess,' he said, 'I hadn't realised there was more.'

'Indeed there is,' his friend replied, 'and some of it particularly accurate.'

Fiona had managed to draw from memory every one of

Baynton's guests at the drinks party. She had, as she always had done, drawn from what she saw and what she saw with her artist's eyes was not always a flattering view, but an accurate one.

'Baynton, I'll interview her for my column. I'll introduce Fiona to the New Yorker. There'll be people knocking at her door, demanding a portrait from your artist friend.'

Baynton looked a shade worried.

'Duchess, this is charming of you, but Fiona may not want your sort of fame.'

'Then she can be the judge my dear,' she countered. 'Don't worry dear friend,' she said with a smile, 'I won't harm a hair on the head of your little English rose.'

Chapter 25

'That was a wonderful welcome home supper!'

Fiona sat back and smiled at the two dearest people in her life, *apart from Baynton of course*, her mind said.

'When are you going to tell us Fee?' Mary asked.

James looked at her in surprise.

'Tell us what my love? She hasn't stopped telling us since we collected her from the airport!' He winked at Fiona as if to say 'and we've enjoyed every word!'

'Fee has something else to say. I'm right aren't I darling?'

'Yes Mary, of course you're right. It's Baynton.'

Mary sighed happily.

'I thought so.'

'It's just that … well, Baynton and I … well, we love each other.'

'That's marvellous!' said James. 'Let's break out the champers and have a toast!' He got up from the table.

'We're not actually getting married.'

'Why not?' James turned, for once frowning and concerned.

It took her some time to convince them that it was her and not Baynton who didn't want to get married.

'I don't quite know why,' she said, 'I love him so much it almost hurts. In fact, saying goodbye to him this morning, or rather last night, was awful. But I don't want to get married, ever.'

'Ever is a very long time Fee,' Mary said quietly.

'I mean it, and I'm going back to New York next week when

157

I've packed all my things and arranged for all my paints and materials to be crated.'

'You're leaving, just like that?' asked James.

'No James, not 'just like that', it's going to be a terrible wrench and I'm going to be horribly homesick at times, but what would you do if Mary was at the other side of the world?'

He looked thoughtful.

'You're quite right Fee. I would do exactly what you're doing. I'd pack up pronto. But,' he added, 'we shall really miss you, so will the children.'

'But we'll come and see you,' Mary said, as much to cheer herself up as anything. 'You know Fee, this is good practice for us. Perhaps it won't be quite so hard when one of our other fledglings flies the nest.'

James produced the champagne.

'Let's phone New York.'

They phoned, but the answer phone asked the caller to leave a message.

'Congratulations!' James said to the machine, 'you're a lucky chap to have won the heart of the beautiful Fiona!'

'Oh James,' Fiona groaned in embarrassment, 'what a corny thing to say,' and she threw a bread roll at him in mock anger.

It was one of the busiest weeks of Fiona's life. Mary found an old trunk that she'd had for boarding school. It took most of Fiona's clothes and some of the treasures she had been given or acquired over the past six years. The packers arrived to crate all her art materials and a number of half-finished pictures, canvasses, brushes and oils. It took them an afternoon to clear the studio.

Fiona stood in the empty room. A momentary panic assailed her; then she thought about Baynton and her heart started to pound. She had no regrets. All she wanted was to be with him wherever he was in the world and to do the best work she had ever done.

It was terribly hard saying goodbye. She spoke to each of the children on the telephone and all three of them said they wanted to come and see her, and would she please take them to Disneyland. The hardest part of leaving was the actual goodbye to Mary and James. Finally, Fiona decided to write a note for them to find after she had left.

Once again, they drove her to the airport, and amidst tears and hugs they said their goodbyes. It was only when they returned home that they found the letter propped up on the mantelpiece in her bedroom. It read:

Dearest Mary and James,

I'm not saying goodbye, because although New York seems a long way away, we all know it isn't. I shall be across to visit you regularly and look forward to showing you and the children New York.

How can I ever begin to thank you both for the happiest six years of my life? You gave me a home and security that I had never known before and because of that I have become the person I am today – which would never have been possible without your continued love and support. I love you both in a way I am not able to express coherently, but I hope you know me well enough to read between every word and every line.

Your loving 'extra' daughter
Fiona Marshall McInnes xxx

Mary read the letter silently, then handed it to James. He looked up and saw the tears on her cheeks. He took her gently into his arms.

'Mary Marshall,' he said, 'you are a wonderful woman.'

'You're not so bad yourself,' she said through her tears as he held and comforted her.

The plane was fifteen minutes late landing. Fiona looked eagerly at the crowds waiting at the barriers as she came through customs. She scoured the crowds again. No Baynton. Then she noticed a very attractive dark haired woman holding a placard with 'Miss McInnes' written on it in bold letters.

Must be his secretary she thought as she walked over pulling her wheeled suitcase behind her.

'I'm Miss McInnes,' she said to the woman.

'I thought so the minute you walked through. You're exactly as Baynton described you, a real English rose. I'm Suzanne Rowe,' the woman continued, 'Baynton and I are best friends,' she said with a warm smile.

For a moment, Fiona felt slightly disconcerted. Where was Baynton? And she wasn't sure that she liked him having such a beautiful woman as a best friend.

Suzanne had everything in hand. She went to the freight desk and arranged for the trunk and crate to be delivered. Then she ushered Fiona outside to a waiting limousine, complete with chauffeur. All the while she talked charmingly to the girl, trying to put her at ease while realising that she was not the person that Fiona had wanted to meet on such a momentous occasion.

The car drew up in front of the apartment block. Fiona started to thank Suzanne and say goodbye, but Suzanne was having none of it.

'Darling,' she said – as Americans often do – 'I've got the key and instructions to stay with you until Baynton get back from court. I've even been in and prepared a salad lunch for us, which, if you knew me and my lack of culinary skills, is fairly remarkable.'

Fiona couldn't help feeling a sense of unease. Suzanne was so at home in the apartment, even saying that Baynton had already moved his things into the four-poster room for them to share and that he'd cleared the fourth room for her to use as a studio.

Suzanne showed her what Baynton had had done in the week she had been in England. Cupboards and shelves were now built into one complete wall of the room, ready for her to store all her paints and papers. A brand new and expensive looking easel stood in the middle of the room.

'This will be a fabulous studio my dear, won't it?' Suzanne continued blithely, apparently unaware of the slow anger that was beginning to smoulder in Fiona. How dare this woman, this 'dear friend', have so much to do with the apartment and know so much about Baynton and herself.

After a quick shower and a change of clothes, she felt strong enough to tackle Suzanne. She determined to ask her to leave. She wanted the apartment to herself until Baynton arrived. She heard a telephone ring and went to pick up the one on the bedside table, but Suzanne reached another telephone first. Feeling rather ashamed of herself, she didn't put down the one she now had in her hand.

'Baynton darling,' she heard, 'for Heaven's sake, when will you be home? I have a feeling I'm not going down too well with your English rose.'

'Duchess,' Fiona heard him reply, 'haven't you told her we're just best friends?'

'Perhaps a woman doesn't like to hear that when she's flown halfway across the world to be with you. For God's sake, hurry the case through and get here p d q.'

Fiona heard Baynton laugh.

'My dear Duchess,' she heard him say, 'just be your adorable self and Fiona will love you as much as I do.'

There was a click as Baynton hung up and Fiona, feeling frightfully guilty, put down the receiver too.

What do I really know about Baynton? What am I doing here? She began to feel she had made a terrible mistake and the thought of Mary and James and the security of the farm suddenly seemed very attractive.

Suzanne was no fool. She had heard the second click and knew Fiona had listened to the conversation. Somehow she must build bridges, and fast. Fiona must trust her. She busied herself in the kitchen, tossing the salad and putting the salmon steaks (cooked earlier by Lally) onto the plates. A large bowl of fruit would have to do as dessert, and from the refrigerator, she took out the bottle of a crisp, white Chardonnay she had put in earlier to chill.

'Hello,' she said in the friendliest of tones as Fiona appeared in the kitchen. Suzanne noticed that the girl had changed into a skirt and blouse and her fair hair was brushed and shining, but her face was serious and Suzanne knew she was going to have to level with her if there was to be any chance of a friendship between them. She waved to one of the seats and took the one opposite.

She seems so at home here Fiona couldn't help thinking, and despite everything, she found herself wondering where Suzanne fitted into the scheme of things.

Anticipating Fiona's thoughts, Suzanne told her the story of how she had met William at Baynton's apartment warming party.

'I'm afraid,' she said with a cheerful grin, 'we were frightfully rude. We left the party early and two weeks later we were married in Las Vegas. I adore William! He's a cosmetic surgeon by profession – a good one too, though,' she added, 'on principle I won't let him 'improve' me! There are too many spouses of cosmetic surgeons who have been so 'done over' that they're barely recognisable now!'

In spite of herself, Fiona found she was laughing and equally, she was relieved to hear that this attractive, dynamic woman was married.

'How long have you known Baynton?' she finally plucked up the courage to ask.

'Umm, about eight years I suppose. Listen Fiona, I'm going to level with you because if I don't, someone else will fill you in.'

Fiona's heart missed a beat, but she looked steadily at Suzanne.

'Were you lovers?' she asked in a rather strained voice.

'We were,' came the reply, 'but only very briefly. We both realised that we really wanted to be good friends and not spoil a great friendship by complicating it with sex. Do you understand my dear?' Her voice was sympathetic. Here was this young, almost virginal creature having to accept the fact that Baynton had had lovers before her. He was, after all, thirty five.

Fiona's mind was running along the same lines. *He's thirty five*, she was thinking, *why, he was even married briefly but it's me he wants now*. She sat back in her chair and looked Suzanne straight in the eyes.

'I'm glad you've told me. Of course, Baynton has had other women in his life, including a wife, but now – well, he and I …' Before she could finish, Suzanne broke in.

'He loves you. I've never seen him so happy. I couldn't be more pleased and I think he's a very lucky man to have found you.'

Suddenly, the atmosphere lightened. Fiona could see why Baynton liked Suzanne. She was straightforward and fun and would be a good friend. She held out her hand.

'Hello Suzanne,' she said, smiling, 'shall we start again?'

By the time Baynton arrived home, his dearest friend and the woman he loved were, to his delight, getting on like a house on fire. Fiona threw herself into his arms and he whirled her round and round, hardly able to believe that she was here to stay. Over the top of her head, he smiled warmly at the Duchess, delighted that two of his favourite women were to be friends.

A few days later, Fiona's trunk and crate were delivered and she began to set up her studio. It had been quite a hectic week as so many of Baynton's friends wanted to meet her and they hardly seemed to have much time alone.

Every night though, they climbed into the four-poster bed in the bedroom that was now 'their' room and most nights they made love, delighting in learning more and more about each other and each other's needs and pleasures.

Fiona could hardly believe how happy she was and how her rather cautious nature was taken over by a passionate woman she hardly recognised as herself.

As for Baynton, he had never been happier in his life, and if he regretted that she wouldn't marry him, he didn't let his disappointment show; he just revelled in the delight of his beautiful and talented lover, who made him happier than he had believed possible.

Chapter 26

With the arrival of her materials from England Fiona set to to put her new studio in order. She knew exactly how she wanted everything and her orderly nature meant that all the cupboards and shelving Baynton had had put in were filled and labelled so that she could put her hand on anything she needed.

The Duchess was a frequent visitor and watched with interest as Fiona sorted out the studio. She found herself looking at a number of portraits that Fiona had done for pleasure and that were, for the most part, stored in her large portfolio or propped up against the walls. One day Suzanne arrived with a pad and pencil, poised to do an interview with this up and coming young artist – as she described Fiona to her Editor. The sketch of Baynton that Fiona had started before she returned to England was now framed and on the studio wall.

'My inspiration,' Fiona had said when the Duchess commented on it.

So on this day, pre-arranged with a rather dubious Fiona, she arrived to do the interview. Suzanne was accompanied by a photographer who took a number of photographs of Fiona and her work before leaving the two women to talk. Suzanne, at her most professional, was almost daunting. She managed to find out about Fiona winning the prize in the Prince's Trust 'Young Artist of the Year' when she was only nineteen; about the exhibition at the Slade and how she was one of the artists who had received much acclaim; about her degree and how, when only sixteen, she had had her first exhibition at the Reave Gallery in Rye and had sold a large number of her paintings; and then of the commissions for portraits by an increasing number of people in England where she was recognised as a portrait painter of singular talent.

'Now,' she said, somewhat downhearted, 'I shall have to start all over again.'

'Not a bit of it,' retorted Suzanne. 'By the time my article's been read you'll have people knocking at your door. You have no idea of how conceited people are in the United States. They rather fancy having a portrait done of themselves or their children.'

'I've had one request,' laughed Fiona, a trifle ruefully.

Suzanne glanced up with interest. 'Really? Who from?'

'It's to do a portrait of a much loved dog.' Her tone was almost apologetic, but both women started laughing and couldn't stop. Finally, Suzanne caught her breath.

'Actually honey, that's perfect. What a perfect end to my article.'

They both started laughing again, helplessly.

The article was in fact a turning point, or rather, a wonderful beginning. Written with Suzanne's usual flair, she managed to paint the picture of a distinguished young artist who New Yorkers were fortunate enough to have in their midst. By implication, she made it sound as if only a McInnes portrait was worth having and, with exaggeration, she managed in her wonderfully fluid article to imply that anyone would be lucky and indeed honoured to be able to book this rising star. Suzanne also announced that, by the end of the year, Miss McInnes would be holding an exhibition and much of the work done during the next twelve months would, of course, be on display.

Fiona read the article with a certain amount of alarm. It made her sound important, even famous, but as Baynton pointed out, the Duchess had not lied but told the truth in her own particular style.

The article was accompanied by several photographs of Fiona's work, including the pencil portrait of Baynton, the picture painted in the meadow and several sketches of Baynton's friends from the first party.

As a result of the article, the telephone started to ring and potential commissions began pouring in. At first, Fiona found it all rather overwhelming. The pace of life at the farm had been so different; here, everyone seemed so eager and enthusiastic, and the energy level of New York was quite difficult for her to adjust to. It was only Baynton's calm and their early morning jogs that kept a sort of perspective in her life, but she soon adjusted to the different pace and expectations of New York living.

Clients came regularly to her studio and she began to enjoy the work that, after all, she had striven for so hard and for so many years. Occasionally, her mind would stray to the Slade and remember how they had tried to convince her to try anything other than portraiture, how they had warned her that so few portrait artists succeeded. *Well*, she thought, *how wrong they were, I am succeeding!*

Her first exhibition was held almost twelve months after her arrival in America. New York Gallery had approached her and suggested a two week stint. To provide variety, and to give herself a break, she had been out and about in the City painting well known landmarks, but always incorporating a figure whether it was someone lying in a gutter in Harlem or a mime artist in Central Park.

The thought of an exhibition in New York was still a nerve wracking experience. Baynton helped her transport all the work, some of which had not been seen. Once again, he was impressed by her dedication and attention to detail and he felt inordinately proud of her achievements.

The exhibition, written up by Suzanne and respected art critics from other publications as well, was an unqualified success. A number of commissions were, of course, reserved. The rest, the 'Scenes in the City' which was the title that the second part of the exhibition went under, were sold almost as soon as people walked past them. Here was their city, sometimes as they would rather not see it and sometimes as they proudly did.

One remarkable picture of the interior of the Statue of Liberty, showing the light from the outside gleaming through, was sold to an unknown purchaser. It later transpired that it had been bought by a woman as a Christmas present for her husband, the Mayor of New York. Fiona could hardly believe her luck.

'It's not luck Fee honey,' Baynton had assured her, 'it's talent.'

Mary and James looked forward to the letters from America. Fiona seemed to be brimming with happiness. She had been gone for almost a year now and her latest letter announced that she and Baynton would be over for three weeks during the summer, hopefully timed to coincide with the school holidays so that they would see something of the children. Could they stay at the farm? Fiona asked in her letter, as they wanted to be en famille.

'You see,' James said, hugging his wife, 'that old cliché of not losing a daughter but gaining a son is right. Won't it be great to have them here?'

Mary nodded. She had missed Fiona more than she imagined possible. It would be wonderful to see her again, and quite soon now.

The stay at the farm was everything they had all hoped for. Baynton threw himself into helping James, and Fiona enjoyed riding with Mary and Alison and sometimes Lynn who wasn't quite such a keen rider.

Sebastian confirmed that he was going to be vet and spent a lot of time inspecting the sheep, telling his father if he found one that was lame or that didn't seem happy. James, fortunately, took the little boy seriously and indeed, a lame sheep is not a happy sheep, so he would take his son with him to clean up the feet and use antibiotic powder to help sort out whatever problem had arisen.

Fiona sketched constantly; it was impossible for her not to. She did a more up-to-date portrait of the children but this time with Mary and James standing behind them. At the end of the three weeks, she gave it to the family as a 'thank you for having us' present with which they were over the moon.

'When I'm a famous actress,' Lynn said, 'will you do a portrait of me, by myself?'

'I most certainly will,' Fiona replied, 'but you might want to commission someone else.'

'No,' the little girl said solemnly, 'you're the best.'

Fiona smiled happily. What a joy it was to belong to this very special family.

During the time they were in England, and after talking it through with Fiona, Baynton decided to sell his house in Church Square.

'We shall never stay there now Fee. You'll always want to be with Mary and James.'

Fiona agreed, so they put it on the market and had offers during the last week they were in England. Baynton left the matter in the hands of a local solicitor suggesting that, as several people wanted it, it should perhaps go into a sealed bid. Just after they arrived back in the States they learned that the house and its contents had sold for considerably more than Baynton had paid for it several years earlier.

Chapter 27

Fiona was surprised to find an enormous amount of mail waiting for her on their return home. There were invitations to lecture art students on the art of portrait painting, invitations to talk to women's clubs on 'Being a Woman Artist in the New Century' and numerous requests to accept commissions, some from people as far away as California.

'It seems,' said Baynton, 'that my English rose is about to launch herself across America.'

It was a combination of the exhibition which had been such a success and Suzanne's column after the exhibition. She had headed it 'A Second Interview with McInnes – the Young Artist with a Big Future'. The article had been syndicated across the States and, combined with the art critics' reviews of the exhibition, had sparked off some serious interest in her work.

America was in the throes of election fever. Fiona had never known anything like it. She found the whole process extremely complex, with all the primaries and the enormous battle for each of the states. Despite herself, she began to find it interesting and Baynton, who was helping and advising the Democratic candidate, was delighted to explain the whys and wherefores and intrigues of the whole campaign.

For Fiona, the most exciting part was the strong possibility of a female President, the first in the history of the United States. Just for the fun of it, she did some fairly simple portraits of the main contenders, not meaning in any way to use them but just because by doing them she found she could read something of the candidate that she couldn't necessarily see from a photograph.

'It's quite uncanny how she interprets photographs,' Suzanne said to Baynton on one of her visits. She and William were over for dinner and they'd been allowed into the studio whilst Fiona finished off the starter in the kitchen.

William had quite fallen under Fiona's spell.

'It's her accent Duchess,' he said to his wife. 'I just love to hear her talk that way and she can draw!'

'Well honey, she is an artist,' drawled Suzanne with just the faintest hint of sarcasm.

'Dinner!' Fiona called as she came out of the kitchen. Baynton rushed to help her with the tray. Their eyes met and held, both knowing what the other was thinking - I love having them here, but I want to hold you in my arms. They smiled at each other, not unnoticed by Suzanne and William.

'Oh you two lovebirds make me sick,' Suzanne said laughing. 'I can't think why you don't get married.'

There was a slightly awkward pause then Baynton said lightly, 'When Fee will have me, we'll get married.' He gave her a warm smile and a wink. Fiona smiled happily at him and started serving. The subject was not mentioned again.

The election was over. There was a woman in the White House. The country was in a state of euphoria; great hopes were placed on this new President. There were expectations that a woman would sort out so many of the problems that had existed during past presidencies – womanising, scandals and even fraud. The hopes of thousands of Americans were held in this woman's hands.

Mary, James and the family came to New York for the promised visit. Fiona and Baynton had taken time off to go to Disneyworld and the Epcot Centre with the family. Alison, Fiona noticed, had grown into quite a serious young woman now, determined to do well in her 'A' levels and equally determined to become a doctor.

Sebastian couldn't understand why Fiona and Baynton didn't have any animals. It just didn't seem like a home he confided sadly to Mary. Lynn's only comment was that she was glad they didn't have any messy babies. With one accord, they all said, 'Oh Lynn!' and there was a lot of laughter. Baynton, though, looked a bit pensive.

'He would like a family,' she confided later that evening to James.

'Mary my love, stop being a mother hen. When they decide they want a family – if they want a family – I'm sure that's exactly what they'll do.'

The apartment felt terribly empty after they had all gone and Fiona paced restlessly, unsettled and missing them all. It was Baynton who suggested she should get away for a spell.

'Why not go and visit Amanda? You haven't seen her for over two years have you?'

'Oh Baynton, what a wonderful idea, but do you mind? Can you manage?'

'I can manage but I'll miss you horribly sweet Fee, but I also know you quite well and you need a change of scene. All that work on the President's picture, then the family here to stay. I'm not wrong am I?' he finished, folding her in his arms.

'No Baynton darling, you're absolutely spot on, though how you knew something I didn't even know myself I'll never understand!'

Fiona telephoned Amanda straight away. The children were at nursery school and Amanda's voice sounded quite odd to Fiona.

'Are you sure it's alright for me to come?' she queried.

'Most definitely Fee, please, please come. I've so much to tell you.'

172

It was strange to be in Paris again. It always brought back memories of her first visit, the weekend just before her fourteenth birthday. Before catching the train to Reims, she decided to revisit some favourite places. She took the metro to Montmatre, leaving her luggage at the Gare du Nord, and soon found herself climbing up the steep streets leading to the Sacré Cœur.

Once again she was immediately soothed by the beauty, the calmness and the serenity of the church. For a few moments she sat quietly letting her mind drift over the years. For the first time she was able to dwell on her childhood, the parts that she had deliberately buried in the recesses of her mind. She saw the young Fiona lying innocently in her bed and then shivered as her body relived the rape. It was strange really, sitting there in such peaceful surroundings, to remember so vividly the violence of that moment. Although she had told Baynton, she had tried to tell him dispassionately, tried to remove her emotions. Now, perhaps because of Baynton she rationalised, she could face up to her past and look it squarely in the eye. She smiled to herself as her mind used mixed metaphors with abandon.

Baynton's love, physical love, had shown her a passionate side of her nature that she hadn't known existed. She revelled in his touch; she desired him to make love to her with all the emotions and energy of a healthy, living, breathing being and their lovemaking had at last released her from the bondage of the past. With a sigh that seemed to come from someone else, but which released all the squalor and misery that had been held in a secret place, she stood up and walked with an air of confidence and composure that had become Fiona since Baynton's love for her.

Opening her purse she carefully put twenty francs in the candle box, took a candle and lit it 'for you Dada' her mind said, and then a second candle 'for you Claire and Stewie'. She hesitated and then took a third candle; her mother had loved her once, she was sure. Now it was easy – one for Mary, James and the children. Thank you, her heart sang, thank you for everything. Finally, and handling it with a smile of happiness, 'for you darling, darling Baynton, the love of my life.'

It was strange walking back down the steps. The world seemed exactly the same only she was changed, ready for anything that life could throw at her.

She arrived back at the artists' square. It had been raining slightly when she had passed through on her way to the Sacré Cœur and the artists, she had noted, had tucked themselves under the canopies over the little restaurants dotted around the square. Now, with a pale sun shining, they were out again, perched on their stools, working in a desultory manner either on a current picture with no client in view or with a client in front of them and attacking the paper with an energy and passion they reserved for a prospective sale.

Fiona meandered around the square, pausing briefly here and there to watch a fellow artist at work and admire the speed with which they transposed a likeness from the expectant face in front of them to the paper. They varied in style and quality and finally she paused to watch the last artist in the square. She watched his strong and sure strokes as he worked with speed and accuracy, hardly seeming to gaze at the young boy whose face he was producing on the paper in front of him.

It was done. He scrawled his signature at the bottom right hand corner and as he did so, he heard Fiona gasp. He looked up, a slight frown on his brow.

'Mamselle?'

'I'm sorry,' Fiona replied, automatically in French, 'but some years ago you did a portrait of me. I recognised your signature.'

As she was speaking, he had shown the youth the picture, placed a sheet of silicone paper over it and deftly rolled it, slipping on an elastic band as he handed it over and accepted payment and thanks. Now he turned and looked at Fiona.

'I'm sorry Mamselle, I see so many I'm afraid I don't remember.'

'Why should you,' she said lightly, 'but it was you who inspired me to become an artist.'

He stood up and stretched, suddenly more interested.

'What sort of artist Mamselle…?'

'McInnes, Fiona McInnes.' Fiona answered his unspoken question. 'I'm a portraitist.'

'Mamselle McInnes, let me introduce myself. Paul Gavroche.'

He held out his hand and they gravely shook hands and laughed as any tension disappeared.

'Coffee I think,' he said.

'But I don't want to interrupt your work.'

'It's not every day that I'm an inspiration Mademoiselle Fiona McInnes. I want to hear all about you!'

The coffee came, was drunk and more ordered. Fiona told him about the Slade and how she was now in America. Their conversation was relaxed, two professionals discussing the merits of their work.

'But,' he said finally, 'to be a street artist, that is a challenge, for in a few moments one must see character, mood and soul and get it down fast, or they will walk away.'

'Yes,' said Fiona thoughtfully, 'I can imagine it must be challenging at times.'

'At times!' Paul Gavroche almost exploded. 'I'm sure you, Mamselle, used to your cosy expensive studio, could not do what I do.'

'Is that a challenge?' she replied with an impish grin.

For a moment, he looked taken aback.

'I suppose it is,' he said slowly, looking at her in a provoking way.

Wordlessly, she stood up.

'May I use your pastels? You will be my subject won't you?'

'How can I not?' He grinned comfortably, convinced that this probably pampered creature would not be able to work under pressure.

'You understand Mamselle Fiona, you have not one minute more than five.'

'Right,' she said, picking up his folding stool and box of pastels. 'Lead me to your chosen spot.'

'Always the same. We have an arrangement between ourselves, you understand.'

'Of course.' She nodded briefly, already mentally beginning to put his face on paper.

Paul Gavroche opened the sitting stool he was carrying. He hoped for her sake that she would not make too much of a mess of things. It took practice to be able to get down on paper in five minutes the 'real' person. He smiled inwardly, already planning how he would let her down gently, not be patronising or superior, as if he would.

'How would you like me Mamselle?' he said, sitting easily on the stool. Pastel in hand, paper on easel, Fiona glanced up.

'A little to the right I think please,' she said.

He moved his head.

'Like this?'

'Excellent,' she smiled at him. 'Are you ready to time me?'

'There is no need,' he replied. 'I judge the time after all these years.'

She was already at work. A quick glance every now and again, her pastel flew over the paper. She changed colour once, then again.

'It's done,' she announced.

'Ah Mamselle Fiona, you are joking. That is quick even for me.'

'See for yourself,' she replied quietly.

Unbeknown to Fiona, as she'd been drawing several of Paul's friends had come to stand behind her to watch this 'unknown' who was challenging him. As Paul stood up, they burst into spontaneous applause.

'Bravo Mamselle!' several voices chorused.

Paul moved the few steps from the sitting stool to where Fiona stood smiling a little shyly, but obviously, he judged, quite pleased with herself. He didn't know quite what to expect. The time had been so short. He looked, and for a moment was taken aback.

'Mademoiselle Fiona McInnes,' he said formally, giving a slight bow, 'please sign your work for one day you will be famous the world over and I shall be a happy and rich man for I will have a McInnes!'

Fiona laughed happily, picked up a charcoal and scrawled McInnes as she always did in the bottom right hand corner.

'And the year Mamselle.'

She obligingly added the year then solemnly took a piece of greased paper, laid it on top and was about to roll it up and put a band on it when he grabbed her arm.

'Ah no, no Mamselle. This one must not be rolled,' and with deference he laid it between two sheets of card that he had in his artist's bag.

It was good. Fiona knew it was good, but she also knew that she had had quite an advantage. She had been talking to him for half an hour, had noticed the exact blue of his eyes, the way his hair sat round his ears and the light lines from his nose to his mouth, and the way his mouth turned up at the corners. She tried to explain, but he would have none of it.

'You took the challenge and you more than met it,' he said, 'it was well won.'

Fiona looked at her watch.

'I must be going. I have a train to catch to Reims.'

Paul Gavroche was horrified. Here he had just met this wonderful English artist and she was to rush away and he would never see her again. With all of his Gallic charm at his fingertips he took hold of her hand and gently brushed his lips against it.

'Ah Mamselle, if you must go you must, but it is so sad, so very sad. I would love you to see my studio where I do my real work, and then tonight, as every night, you could eat at Madame Despardieux with me and my fellow artists. You would see for yourself what is the real life of the artists of Paris, but Mamselle...' he let her hand go forlornly, 'if you must go, you must go.'

Fiona hesitated. She could telephone Amanda and say she would arrive the next day but she would have to collect her case. She had no toothbrush or nightclothes. As if reading her mind, Paul broke her train of thought.

'You can stay with my sister. She lives in the same house, in an apartment. I have only a room. She will lend you whatever you need. I know my sister.' He grinned. 'She will do anything for her big brother!'

'I must make a telephone call.'

'Bien entendu – this way.'

Fiona was lost. This was an experience she couldn't pass up – an evening with the artists of Paris.

Amanda sounded disappointed that her arrival would be delayed, but Fiona promised that she would definitely be in Reims by lunch time the following day.

'But what are you doing in Paris tonight Fee?' Amanda had asked.

'An artists' convention,' Fiona had replied which, as she justified her remark to herself afterwards, was, in a way, what it was.

Paul Gavroche's sister seemed totally unsurprised when her

brother turned up with a young English woman in tow. Paul insisted on showing her Fiona's portrait of him and she had exclaimed with delight and immediately offered Fiona a bed for the night. She was shown a small neat room with a polished wooden floor, a narrow bed covered with a white counterpane, a cane chair, a chest with a mirror on the top and pretty curtains moving in the light breeze coming through the open window. Fiona was enchanted. It was so Paris! The window overlooked a narrow winding street and if she leaned out far enough she would, she felt sure, be able to touch the houses on the other side.

Françoise showed her the bathroom next door and put out a soft, snowy white towel for her to use.

'You are very kind Madame,' she began.

'Françoise, please call me Françoise.'

Fiona smiled.

'Please call me Fiona,' she replied.

'Come on, come on!' a call came from the landing.

'My brother is impatient. He wishes to show you his studio.'

'I'm looking forward to seeing it,' Fiona said, drying her hands and hanging the towel on the rail Françoise had indicated.

The two women joined a, by now, impatient Paul who was muttering under his breath about the length of time it took to show someone where they would sleep. But it was good natured and soon he was leading the way up two more flights of stairs to his attic studio.

It had to be the untidiest room that Fiona had ever seen in her life. Every inch of the walls, every corner of the room, were covered in pictures, and more pictures were propped up against the walls.

An easel stood near the only window but it was turned so that Fiona couldn't see what was on the canvas.

'This is my home,' Paul announced gravely.

179

'You live here too?' Fiona tried hard to keep the astonishment out of her voice.

'But of course.'

'But where do you sleep?'

As a reply, Paul waved vaguely to the far corner of the room and Fiona perceived the shape of a bed, most of which was covered by yet more pictures.

'I do not sleep a great deal,' he continued.

'That I can believe.' Fiona spoke, trying very hard to keep the laughter from her voice. He looked at her sharply.

'You do not like my studio Mamselle Fiona?'

'Paul, please call me Fiona and yes, I love your studio.' She walked to the window. 'The rooftops of Paris,' she breathed. 'It's perfect Paul.'

As she turned to face him she saw the painting on his big canvas.

'Why, it's beautiful,' she said, looking at the full sized painting of a nude figure, sprawled generously out on a velvet robe.

'It's good, huh.' It was not so much a question as a statement.

It was, thought Fiona, almost Rubenesque. The fleshy form was almost palpable, the colours warm and rich, the almost titian hair of the model adding an element of boldness to the already bold painting.

'What do you think?' Paul was beginning to feel nervous. He wanted this English girl to like his work.

'I think it's remarkable,' Fiona said thoughtfully, wondering where a picture like this would ever sell. The right person would want it, but to many people it would be a painting perhaps portraying a period long gone. It was, thought Fiona, although brilliantly executed, old fashioned.

'Show me what else you have,' she said, knowing only too well from personal experience that an artist generally likes to show their work.

The next two hours passed quickly as Paul leapt about like a man possessed, showing her this picture and that. The range of subjects was dramatic, from scenes in an abattoir to the food markets of Paris to sketches of animals in the Paris zoo, many of whose expressions made Fiona want to weep. She knew what she wanted to say to him but she was not sure she could say it in a positive way. She was so much younger, so much less experienced, yet she felt older and wiser.

All she had learned from her tutors at the Slade came flooding back. Paul had never been to college; he had learned on the streets. His skills were natural, even raw at times and yet he needed to discipline himself. Could she, dare she, help him to help himself?

He made a space on the bed and they sat down talking more quietly now. His excitement was spent. He needed to know what she thought, so she told him.

He listened attentively, occasionally shaking his head or raising his hands in protest, but he knew she was right. He must concentrate on what he did best. The portraits in the square were his bread and butter. Some – as the one he had done of her years before – were very good, but a lot were not. No, she was right; it was the animals. Somehow, he had always known that he felt the pain that animals suffered, or he saw the perkiness of the pet poodles and the owners as they wandered around Paris. His portrait, his big portrait, the one on the easel, was, he told Fiona, 'a fake'.

'It was le style Rubens – pas moi.'

'That doesn't stop it being good,' Fiona said. 'You have so much talent but you should concentrate on what you *feel*; at least that's what I believe, what works for me,' she finished quietly.

'Enough Mamselle Fiona, enough! The night is young, we must eat and be merry with my friends and one day, when you are known the world over, we shall say, my friends and I, that one night we ate dinner in Paris with the famous woman artist, McInnes!'

'You don't mind,' she began hesitatingly, 'what I said?'

'Sweet Fiona, you only said what I have known in my heart for a very long time......I will race you to the pavement!' He flung open the door and started for the stairs.

With a final look at the chaos that was his, she closed the door behind her and joined him at the top of the stairs. Of course, Paul won but, as she told him panting as she fell out of the bottom door onto the pavement, he knew the stairs well, so he was a cheat and a fraud.

Still laughing and with his arms artlessly wrapped around her shoulders, they set off for Madame Despardieux. It was, Fiona told Baynton some weeks later, one the most fun evenings of her life and she only wished that he had been there to share it. Baynton thought otherwise, but kept his counsel. He wasn't sure that the evening she described was quite his scene, but the fact she had wanted him there and missed him pleased him inordinately.

Madame Despardieux was a plump, cheerful French woman who, though born and bred in Paris as she told Fiona, looked as though she had just arrived from the countryside. She had apple pink cheeks, no doubt due to her bending over a hot stove, and white hair pulled back in a bun with wisps constantly escaping, much to her annoyance. But it was her laughter that was the most riveting. Her whole frame seemed to shake and her laugh seemed to bubble up and take over. When she laughed, so did everyone else. It was, thought Fiona, the most infectious sound she had ever heard, like great waterfalls tumbling over rocks. Fiona tried to imprint on her memory every line on the face, the way her big hands with their raised veins would carry dishes so hot that no-one else could touch them. Her big blue and white checked apron matched the tablecloths and the café blinds that hung on brass rails fixed halfway down each window. Candles burned in old wine bottles on the tables and although there were electric lights, they were so dim you had the feeling you were only eating by candlelight.

It was the food that kept the artists using the restaurant as their own. There was no choice.

'You eat it or you starve,' Madame said uncompromisingly.

Eat it they did. For a remarkable few francs, they had potage à l'oignon, cassoulet de lapin and a selection of cheeses – French of course. They drank the house wine and Fiona soon lost count of how many glasses followed by innumerable cups of coffee. Paper napkins were used to draw on and Fiona, digging a pencil out of her handbag, did a few lines which would help her later. For some reason she hadn't got the very small sketch book she normally carried with her because she thought she'd be in Reims before she needed it - a fatal mistake she never made again. Several paper napkins later she really wished she had the wretched pad, but carefully folded the napkins and put them between the pages of her diary.

The company that evening was a merry one. Paul's friends seemed to speak all at once, and although Fiona's French was very good and they were talking 'art' for the most part, once or twice she found herself totally lost as the noise rose to a crescendo and there were several conversations going on at the same time. Finally, when she had yawned for the sixth or seventh time, Paul took pity on her.

'You want to go to bed Fiona?' he asked.

There was a burst of laughter and Fiona felt herself blush. She needn't have worried.

'I have the key from my sister. I'll take you home now,' he said gallantly. It was sufficient an explanation and Fiona looked at him gratefully.

She shook hands with each and every one of his friends, then with Madame Despardieux and her quiet little husband who was stacking plates in the sink.

'I do not believe in a dishwasher,' Madame Despardieux said, her booming waterfall of a laugh filling the restaurant. 'I have him.' She said it warmly and Fiona noticed the look that passed between the disparate pair. He wasn't the poor hen-pecked husband he first appeared but a man happy and basking in his wife's abundant love.

It took ten minutes to get to the apartment. Under the light of one of the street lights, Fiona glanced at her watch. It was three in the morning. No wonder she was tired, her body clock all topsy-turvy. In America, she thought as she lay in the narrow bed, it must be about... it was her last waking thought.

Chapter 28

She woke up at eight o'clock feeling as if she'd had a complete night's sleep, not just a few hours. A knock at the door made her sit up. It was Françoise with a breakfast tray.

'Oh, you shouldn't,' began Fiona eyeing the cafetière of coffee and the hot croissant hungrily. *How can I be hungry*, she thought, *after all that food?*

Françoise handed her the tray and was about to go.

'Please stay Françoise. Won't you have a cup of coffee too?'

Françoise hesitated for a moment. She'd had her breakfast already but it wasn't often she had a chance at a second cup.

'Just a moment,' she said, disappearing from the room, only to reappear a moment later with a cup for herself.

'Thank you so much for the nightgown,' Fiona said in between mouthfuls of the most delicious croissant she thought she had ever tasted. She licked her fingers, determined not to miss a crumb. Françoise smiled, enjoying the company of this nice English woman. She glanced idly at Fiona's hands, looking for a wedding ring. Fiona followed the glance and read the thought.

'No, I'm not married,' she said, finishing the last blissful mouthful of croissant, 'but I live with the most wonderful man and perhaps one day I'll marry him.'

What am I saying? she thought. *It must be Paris – all that wine and food – I'm unbalanced.* But deep inside, somewhere, there was a thought that gave her a comfortable, warm and safe feeling.

She settled back into the seat. The train slipped quietly through the French countryside. It wasn't going to be a very long journey. She closed her eyes, tiredness catching up with her at last. It had been kind of Paul to see her off. She would probably never see him again, but he had given her an evening in Paris that was memorable. She realised she had been privileged to be among the artists like that and to meet Françoise who, she made a mental note, she needed to write to to thank her for her hospitality. Ah! And Monsieur and Madame Despardieux! What a wonderful couple, what food! That cassoulet! How could she think about food again after her lovely breakfast?

'Reims, ici Reims.'

She jerked awake. There already? She felt she had only just climbed into the train.

She lifted her case down from the rack and stepped down onto the platform. Amanda had said would meet every train from nine onwards. Fiona hoped it hadn't meant too many journeys. She glanced at her watch. Eleven thirty.

'Fiona, Fee, Fee!'

The girls clung to each other.

'It's been too long Amanda.'

'Yes Fee, it has.'

Amanda looked very pale and she seemed to have lost a lot of weight. The lovely, slightly curvy figure had gone, and a new, rather angular Amanda was in her place.

'You're all bones,' Fiona said lightly. 'You are OK aren't you?'

'Of course I am.'

Amanda turned her head suddenly, but not before Fiona seen the sparkle of tears in her eyes.

Amanda had parked her Fiat quite close by and Fiona's case had wheels so, with very little difficulty, the girls were soon in the car and driving to the arrondissement where Amanda, Bernard and the children had their home.

'Why did you stay over in Paris? What was the convention?' Amanda wanted to know.

Fiona told her the whole story, including the fact that Paul Gavroche had been the artist who had done her portrait when the girls had spent the weekend with Amanda's parent in Paris.

'What an amazing coincidence,' Amanda said, 'M and D will be fascinated.'

'How are they?' Fiona wanted to know.

The conversation flowed as easily as ever between them. Fiona could sense a tension though. She watched Amanda's hands on the wheel. Her fingers kept alternately opening and then gripping the wheel as if she was having difficulty controlling her emotions. Fiona felt worried but knew Amanda would tell her when she was ready. She remembered from their schooldays that trying to get anything out of Amanda unless she wanted to was useless.

Amanda kept up a sort of automatic conversation – the children at school, the garden – but no mention of Bernard.

'How's Bernard? Working as hard as ever?' enquired Fiona gently.

'Bernard is Bernard,' was the somewhat cryptic reply.

The charming house was as welcoming as ever. Amanda had such perfect taste and her choice of colours and fabrics made each room warm and friendly. The small walled garden, from where only a light buzz of Reims' traffic could be heard was, Fiona thought, a perfect oasis in the midst of a busy city. Her mind turned for a moment to the apartment in New York. She adored it and had never felt the need for a garden but now, sitting under the old cherry trees, it made her realise how much she missed being able to walk out of doors and into a garden at will. The sound of water made her glance around. There, tucked behind a shrub, a lion's face spouted water into the tub below.

'Amanda, you've made it so pretty. You've transformed the garden since I was last here.'

Amanda's face lit up.

'I'm glad you like it. It's my solace really, the garden,' she added.

'Do you need solace then?'

Amanda nodded and once again, Fiona saw the glint of tears.

'Are you going to tell me what's wrong?' she asked gently.

There was a silence. Fiona waited patiently. She knew Amanda needed to talk but she had to talk when she was ready. After what seemed an age, but was in reality only a moment or two, Amanda turned back to look at her dearest friend and it came bubbling out.

Bernard, it seemed unsurprisingly, was the cause of her distress. Every summer since the children had arrived, Amanda had gone to Scotland to stay with her parents for two weeks. Bernard, who only had four weeks holiday a year, encouraged her to go on her own, saying that of his four weeks he wanted to spend two weeks skiing en famille, and the other two weeks at his parents' home. They lived by the sea near Nauzan where he and Amanda had first met and where his parents now looked forward to a regular summer visit from their son and his family. Fiona listened patiently, waiting to see where Amanda was leading. Last summer, when Amanda had returned from Scotland and had been looking forward to her time with Bernard and the children at Nauzan, she'd been disappointed when he'd told her that she and the children must go on ahead, at least for the first week, as he was so busy, and that he'd join them for the second week. Although she had been a little upset, she knew how much the children had been looking forward to their time by the sea with grandmère and grandpère, so she'd set off by train on her own with the children feeling very sad to be apart from him for yet another week particularly as, on the two nights she'd been back in Reims, she'd been in bed asleep by the time he'd arrived home.

'In hindsight,' she said, 'I should've realised something wasn't right.'

Fiona squeezed her friend's hand but said nothing, giving Amanda time to control the tears that were now flowing down her cheeks.

The in-laws, it seemed, were most sympathetic, and when her mother-in-law had suggested that Amanda leave the children with them in Nauzan and take the train back to Reims and have a romantic evening or two with Bernard before returning together for the last week of the holiday, Amanda thought this a wonderful idea. She decided to totally surprise Bernard by arriving back at home and organising a candlelit dinner for two. On the way home, she had called in at the market and bought fruit, vegetables and some fish, planning to prepare one of his favourite meals.

To her surprise, she saw that his car was parked on the road and had a slight sense of disappointment that she wouldn't be able to surprise him with a dinner à deux. However, that slight disappointment was matched by delight at the prospect of seeing him and being able to spend some much needed time alone with no fear of interruption by the children. She let herself in, and instead of calling his name as she might usually have done, and still wanting to surprise him wherever he was, she went from room to room downstairs. When he was not to be found, she realised he was probably in his study which adjoined their bedroom, so she went upstairs only to find the room empty. About to go downstairs into the garden, she heard voices in the bedroom and it was at that moment, she told Fiona, and only at that moment, that things became crystal clear. Unhesitatingly, she pushed open the bedroom door and, to her horror, saw Bernard in bed with a very pretty girl who she recognised as his secretary.

By this time, Amanda could hardly speak for the choking sobs which shook her entire frame. Fiona put her arms around her friend, feeling a sense of anger and frustration, anger against Bernard and frustration because she felt so helpless. She let Amanda cry and eventually the tears and sobs ceased.

'That's the first time I've cried Fee, I couldn't before.'

'Crying is good,' Fiona said comfortingly, quoting from she knew not what but convinced it must be true. 'What now?' she asked.

'I don't know Fee, I just don't know. Bernard says it's all over – the affair that is – but can I believe him? I've been so happy being his wife and a mother. Now I feel that if I stay with him I'll never trust him again. And anyway,' she added, 'I'm not prepared to go on being just 'the little wife.'

'Where is he now?'

'Working,' Amanda replied wearily. 'He comes home early, helps with the children, acts the model husband, but …' she added, her voice fierce, 'I won't sleep in that bed ever again, so I sleep with Hélène and he sleeps there alone. What sort of marriage is that?' she finished dramatically.

Fiona was thoughtful for a few moments.

'Have you thought about working Amanda? If you had a job it'd give you independence and freedom and it might be good for Bernard to realise that your life doesn't revolve around him.'

'I've thought about it of course, but what can I do? I haven't done anything for years, nothing since my degree.'

'Precisely.' Fiona spoke in as positive a voice as she could. 'You've got a really good science degree. You could get a research job with a pharmaceutical company. I'm sure there must be an Institute of Research attached to the university. It's up to you to go out and find something.'

'But the children…' began Amanda.

'Your femme de ménage can work longer hours, you told me so. She can take and fetch them from the nursery can't she?'

Amanda nodded. 'You're right,' she said soberly, 'Bernard and me – I don't know what will happen. I'm still so angry and confused and hurt,' she added sadly. 'If I get a job perhaps he'll look at me in a different light. It's worth a try anyway.' Her laugh was rather bitter Fiona felt, but at least there was a more positive note to her voice.

The next few weeks rather dragged for Fiona. If it hadn't been for her sketch pad, quickly unpacked, she felt she'd have gone mad with frustration. The atmosphere between Amanda and Bernard was as cold as ice although, to his credit, Bernard did try to make amends, but the more he did in the way of flowers for Amanda, gifts for the children and plans for a ski trip to America for them all, the more Amanda remained aloof and apparently unmoved.

Be careful, Fiona felt like saying, you'll drive him away. But she said nothing, feeling that the two of them had to sort it out on their own.

As good as her word, Amanda had spoken to Madame Cachet, her femme de ménage, who was delighted at the prospect of extra hours with the children she so patently adored. Fiona found them adorable too, and at night as she read them a bedtime story, their hair still damp from their bath and smelling the sweet smell that small children seem to have, she found herself thinking that to have children of one's own must be a wonder – but one, she added hastily to herself, I can well do without.

Amanda sent off her CV to the university and to two pharmaceutical companies that she had found had a base in the environs of Reims. She was not overly confident but had put in her accompanying letter that she was not looking for a position that was well paid as she knew she lacked experience but that she felt she had a lot to offer and it would be at least worth their while taking the trouble to interview her.

To her and Fiona's surprise, she received two positive and one negative response. One of the pharmaceutical companies wrote that they didn't need any extra personnel currently as they had just been bought out by an American company. However, they would keep her name on file and contact her in a few months. The university said they might be able to find her a technical research position in one of their laboratories, and the other pharmaceutical company said they hadn't anything at present but suggested that she meet with their Director of Medical Research.

'All in all,' Amanda said happily, 'far more than I'd hoped for.'

Fiona was of course sworn to secrecy. Bernard had always liked the fact that his wife didn't go out to work. He always spoke out strongly about 'these career women who leave their children.' It was an area that Fiona felt so differently about that she hadn't even liked to discuss it with Bernard and anyway, Amanda had obviously been so happy with the status quo that it had been unimportant. Amanda, looking jaunty in her very chic navy skirt and jacket with a colourful scarf around her neck, set off for her first appointment. This was the university one which was followed the next day by the interview with the Medical Director. She arrived home from the second interview simply bubbling but determined not to say anything in front of Bernard who had just arrived home. It was after the children were in bed that she came to Fiona's bedroom and the two of them sprawled on the bed, Amanda talking and Fiona listening intently.

It seemed as if both interviews had gone really well. Amanda had received a telephone call two hours after her university appointment offering her a lowly paid but full-time technical research post. The second interview – the one she was now bringing Fiona up-to-date with – had been even more exciting as far as Amanda was concerned. The Medical Director told her at the end of the interview that he was not only impressed with her credentials, but also her personality and positive attitude. He offered her a training post with the company as a marketing assistant 'With,' Amanda said happily, 'quite a respectable salary. Can you believe it Fee, I've got a job!'

'Have you accepted it then? Did you say yes straightaway?'

'No,' said Amanda solemnly, 'I kept him waiting – for about ten seconds.'

For some reason this seemed terribly funny. Perhaps it was a release of tensions, but the girls were rolling about on the bed laughing when the door opened, taking them both by surprise.

'Can anyone join in?' Bernard asked looking hopeful.

It was, thought Fiona, as if an icy blast had entered the room. Amanda's face froze, every bit of life seeming to drain out of it. She spoke coldly.

'You wouldn't want to join in, even if you were invited.'

He took the hint.

'Je regrette,' he said, closing the door quietly.

'Why did he have to spoil things?' Amanda spoke like a petulant child.

'You'll have to let him know.'

'I know, I know – but not tonight. I just want to enjoy it.'

But the atmosphere had changed. They both knew it, and after a little more desultory conversation, they said goodnight and Fiona was left with her thoughts.

More and more she thought about Baynton. She missed him so. Surely now, once Amanda had told Bernard about the job, she could leave her friend. She had wanted to get away from New York but now all she wanted was to be back there. She closed her eyes and imagined herself in his arms, their four-poster bed their oasis of peace and heavenly lovemaking. She almost got up and packed there and then, but she knew she must give Amanda just a few more days.

There was quite a row. Bernard demanded that she didn't take up the job offer. Amanda told him he had no right to demand anything. He told her she was an uncaring mother. She replied he was the most uncaring person in the world taking a mistress in their own bed.

Fiona tried hard not to listen but it was difficult. The children were fortunately asleep when the row happened. Finally there was silence. Fiona stole downstairs, longing for some fresh air. She crept into the garden, unsure where the protagonists were. Dusk had fallen; the muted sound of traffic was a strangely soothing background. Then, to her surprise, mixed with slight embarrassment and delight, she came across her friend and Bernard making love on the small lawn.

Thankfully, they neither heard nor saw her, and she crept back indoors, helping herself to some apple juice on the way back upstairs, and packed her suitcase. She could go home now.

Chapter 29

For some perverse reason Fiona, having lifted the telephone to tell Baynton she was on her way, decided not to. She would surprise him! Perhaps, she acknowledged unwillingly to herself, she was testing him. As quickly as she thought he might behave like Bernard, she banished the thought – but it lingered like an unwelcome guest in a dark corner of her mind.

The journey seemed to drag. She let her mind dwell for a few moments on Amanda and Bernard. They had slept on the rug in the dining room, Amanda had confided. She had vowed she would never sleep in 'that' bed again and it was going, pronto, and a new bed would be delivered by the time Bernard came home from the office. She was due to start work the following week. Bernard was now not only resigned to the fact but had told her he was actually rather proud of her.

'Men,' Amanda had said somewhat caustically, 'like children really, want their own way in everything.' But she seemed happier again. Her eyes had their sparkle back and even the children sensed their parents' happiness and were more joyful and noisy than ever. It was good, thought Fiona, to be on the way back home to the peace of the apartment, her studio and darling, darling Baynton.

New York was as full of life as always, such a different vibrancy to anywhere else in the world. The yellow cab had a particularly cheerful driver who was full of gossip about the new President. He hadn't wanted a woman President 'But she seems OK,' he said. Fiona had smiled somewhat abstractedly, her thoughts wrapped up in Baynton.

The door commissioner seemed pleased to see her back.

'Say there, good evening Miss McInnes. Mr Rivers will be glad to see you back, he's surely missing you.'

'I'm glad,' said Fiona, 'please don't tell him I'm here. I want to surprise him.'

'Sure Miss,' the commissioner replied, touching the side of his nose with this finger and giving her a conspiratorial wink as he did so.

Up in the familiar lift; key in the familiar door. Fiona walked in, breathing deeply as if she could breathe in Baynton. Finally she pushed open the studio door. There, on the easel right in the middle of the room, was a large notice that read 'Welcome home darling Fiona, Baynton.' For a moment she was puzzled. Then she noticed the date at the top – the date she had left. The welcome had been waiting for her ever since.

Still smiling, she ran a bath and opening one of the closets she took out a favourite dress, one that Baynton liked especially too. She lay back wallowing in the foamy suds, humming a tune, happy to be home. There was a sound, a door opening, then, standing in the doorway, Baynton.

They didn't speak, each just looking. Baynton silently took off his clothes and climbed into the big bathtub, their soapy bodies sliding against each other.

'I've missed you so much,' Fiona began.

'Shush darling, I know.'

Wordlessly, Baynton stood up and reached for a towel and as she stepped out of the bath towards him, he wrapped the bath sheet around them both. The feel of him against her was too much for either of them. Dropping the bath sheet, they almost ran to the bed and made passionate love to each other, until they were sated.

Later, both in their robes, they fed each other strawberries and ice cream, neither wanting to do any shopping for 'real' food.

'Are you hungry darling?' Baynton was concerned.

'Only for you.' Fiona laughed, feeling happier than ever. *How*, she wondered, *can I keep loving him any more?*

Life settled back into its regular pattern. Suzanne and William dropped by quite frequently for a drink, a meal or to drag them off to see the latest film or Broadway show.

'If it wasn't for us,' Suzanne said, 'I don't think you two would do anything other than settle down every evening like a middle aged couple.'

'I am middle aged,' Baynton grinned wryly, but he knew she was right. Fiona and he wanted nothing more at the end of a busy day for both of them – he in court, she in the studio – than to stay in and just be together. The evenings when they were 'allowed' this pleasure were the best. The two of them would sit in Baynton's study, he avidly reading and Fiona writing to Mary, James and the family or to Amanda. The latest news from her friend had been particularly happy and she read it aloud to Baynton.

Dearest Fee, how can I ever thank you (it began). *You were such a support during my cri de cœur . I think I would have gone completely to pieces if you hadn't arrived when you did. Anyway, the past is the past and the future is really beginning to look good. For a start, Bernard has a new secretary, very pleasant (and rather plain I'm glad to say!) Secondly, the new bed arrived and it was good to be back together in our own room. We seem to be closer than we have been since the children arrived on the scene. It's funny really. I hadn't noticed what a rut we had got into.*

I'm loving my job. I thought Pierre Lemarche a bit fierce. After two weeks working in the laboratory I'd hardly seen him, and when I did I got a brief 'Bonjour' and that was it. But yesterday he sent for me. He told me he had

had very good reports and now he wanted to broaden my experience. I'm to go out with different sales people. They call at doctors and chemists by prior appointment only. He wants me to see what it's like on the ground. Anyway, he was quite charming and made me feel very good about myself. He repeated what he'd said at the interview – that if I enjoyed the experience he'd arrange for me to spend some time with the marketing director. Where, I wonder, is all this leading? The children don't even seem to miss me! Madame Cachet is so good with them. I drop them at nursery on the way to work. (I love saying that!) I feel like a real person again, not just maman or wife.

It's also interesting how much more Bernard and I have to talk about now and he seems really interested. Long may it last…

Anyway, dearest Fee, I'm feeling incredibly happy. Thanks so much for all your support. I would've totally collapsed without you.

Love to Baynton.

As ever

Amanda.

'She does sound good. You should be pleased with yourself.'

'Oh Baynton darling, she just needed a shoulder – any shoulder probably – and I just happened to be around.'

'Well, I think you did well Fee. I'd never have imagined Amanda working and she's obviously enjoying it.'

He went back to his book and Fiona picked up a pen and began to write back.

Fiona was pleased with the way the brief sketches she'd done on the paper napkins in the restaurant of Monsieur and Madame Despardieux had provided what she needed for a whole series of pictures based on her stay in Paris which were now taking shape.

The best, she felt, was of Madame Despardieux herself, the ruddy cheeks, the beaming smile and the big, blue-veined and capable hands folded over her blue check apron. Baynton was very taken with it.

'It should be the centre piece of a new show,' he said. 'You've enough surely for another exhibition?'

'I suppose so,' Fiona said thoughtfully.

The portrait of Paul Gavroche was good. She wished he could see it. She had done several of Monsieur Despardieux as well, in which she had managed to capture the hard working, happy nature of the slight figure. Other pictures included the Sacré Cœur or rather, the steps leading up to it with the Sacré Cœur looking slightly ethereal, bathed in misty clouds.

Suzanne came to view.

'Wow darling, who's that gorgeous creature?' She was, of course, looking at Paul.

Fiona told her about the amazing coincidence of meeting the artist who had drawn her portrait when she was only fourteen. Suzanne demanded to see it, so Fiona had to explain that it was with Mary and James in England.

'What a story.'

Fiona could sense Suzanne had an idea forming in her mind.

'Leave it to me darling. Read my next week's column!'

Fiona was aghast.

'Heaven's Suzanne, what terrible thing are you planning? I don't want you to write anything!'

'Trust me!' Suzanne's laugh trilled merrily. 'Just wait and see.'

Whatever Fiona had expected, she had not expected this. She looked in surprise at the picture of herself at the head of Suzanne's column. Unbeknown to her, Suzanne had flown to England and collected the picture for her from Mary and James. As she stated in her article, she had borrowed it. Then she went on to explain the extraordinary coincidence of the struggling artist meeting up with his former subject, years after the portrait he had painted of her in the square in Montmatre, and that he had been the inspiration behind the rapidly rising portrait painter, Fiona

McInnes. She wrote of how they had spent time in Paris together recently (the implication of 'together' infuriated Fiona) and that his portrait done by her would be shown at the new exhibition venue to be announced.

Fiona put the paper down rather crossly. Baynton had already left for court. She really felt Suzanne had taken too much on herself. She was, she felt, being shanghaied into something she hadn't actually even thought through.

Before she could telephone Suzanne to vent her spleen, or at least grumble at the slant of the article, the telephone rang.

'Fiona McInnes,' she answered automatically, her mind still on thoughts of Suzanne.

'Ah, Miss McInnes,' a man's voice said. 'I read with interest the article on your forthcoming exhibition. I rather wondered if, as stated, the venue had not yet been arranged whether you might be interested in my gallery?'

He named the gallery and Fiona gave an involuntary gasp. It was one of the best galleries in New York.

'Miss McInnes, are you still there?' The voice, Fiona noted, sounded a trifle impatient. He probably expected a better reaction than a gasp.

'I'm sorry, Mr...?'

'Jonathon Preece.'

'Mr Preece, I really haven't put a great deal of thought into this.'

She heard a faint sigh at the end of the phone.

'Really Miss McInnes, I think you would be wise to. It's obvious that you have some interesting work to show. I've seen several examples of your work by the way. Why don't we meet and we can discuss it further?'

Not giving Fiona a chance to butt in he said, 'Tomorrow, lunch at the Park Plaza, twelve thirty. Alright?' Fiona murmured assent.

'Good,' he said, and hung up.

Hardly had she recovered from his call when another very similar call came from another gallery and then a third. She made appointments to see them all, feeling she had nothing to lose, but still feeling quite baffled by the interest Suzanne's article had engendered.

Suzanne and William dropped round after dinner. Baynton had heard the whole saga by now and read the article.

'You have to hand it to the Duchess,' he said, 'sneaking off to England without a word!'

He obviously thought the whole thing a terrific coup for Suzanne and a marvellous opportunity for Fiona. It was the first time they were on different wavelengths and Fiona felt annoyed with Suzanne again. It was all her fault.

But you couldn't be cross with Suzanne for long. She breezed in, William as ever following on adoring every moment of his irrepressible and charming wife.

'Isn't it wonderful Fiona,' she began, 'I had all these telephone calls from galleries asking for your number including…' she paused, making sure all eyes were on her, '… Jonathon Preece. THE Jonathon Preece! You do realise Fiona this is a real coup?'

'I just wish…' Fiona began but it was useless.

'A drink Baynton, I need a drink. All this excitement, all this adrenalin, has made me thirsty. Now, what are you going to do?' She paused for breath. 'Fiona, you are going to use Jonathon's gallery aren't you?'

She looked at Fiona, perhaps aware for the first time that the girl was unusually quiet.

'I don't know what I'm going to do yet Suzanne, but whatever I do, it's my business.'

'But darling, I want to do a follow-up article.'

'Perhaps Fiona doesn't want you to,' Baynton said, finally realising that his darling Fiona was being run over by Suzanne's

201

enthusiasm.

'Of course Fiona wants…' began Suzanne.

'Actually,' Fiona said, 'actually, Fiona doesn't want anything other than to be left alone. I want to make my own decisions thank you, not be bullied by someone who doesn't know one end of a paintbrush from another.'

'Wow,' said William, somewhat unhelpfully.

Suzanne drew herself up and swallowed her martini in one gulp. 'I think it's time we left,' she said, her voice rather distant and cool.

'I'm sorry,' began Fiona, now feeling guilty. After all, she had got three galleries chasing her, thanks to Suzanne. Suzanne held her hand up as if to silence Fiona and swept past Baynton, hardly even brushing his cheek, instead of her usual, effusive kiss. Fiona was ignored.

'William,' she said, 'come.'

William shrugged his shoulders, somewhat uncomfortably, and kissed Fiona lightly on the cheek.

'Don't worry,' he whispered, 'it will all be forgotten by the morning.'

After they had left, Fiona and Baynton looked at each other. For a moment Fiona was concerned; after all, Suzanne was his dearest friend. She need not have worried. Seeing her expression, Baynton burst out laughing.

'Come here little Fee, what a storm in a tea cup!'

He put his arms around her and swung her up, depositing them both in one of the large sofas.

'You're not angry?'

'What's to be angry about my love? Now, tell me all about these galleries that have been ringing you all day.'

Chapter 30

Jonathon Preece was a real character.

'He wore a velvet jacket to lunch,' Fiona confided to Baynton. 'I swear he was wearing eye make-up too!'

'But what did he say Fee?'

Baynton tried not to laugh. Fiona's slightly shocked description made her suddenly seem so young.

'He wants ten percent of all sales, but I told him I had other people to meet before I could make a decision. But Baynton, he took me – after lunch of course, which was delicious – to look at the gallery. I'd been before with you of course, but this time I was looking at it from a different perspective. Oh Baynton darling, to exhibit there, what a privilege!'

'I'm so proud of you Fee.' Baynton gazed at her. 'Why don't you marry me?'

'Oh Baynton darling, you know I can't, please don't ask me to.'

A slight shadow crossed his face but he smiled at her.

'Joking honey, honestly. You don't want an oldie like me.'

Fiona picked up a cushion and flung it along the sofa, hitting him square in the face.

'So,' he said fiercely, 'you want a fight.'

'No Baynton, no, mercy sir, I beg you!'

'No mercy,' he grinned, and grabbing hold of her he flung her over his shoulder and walked swiftly to the bedroom. She was still flailing about when he lay her on the bed and proceeded to start kissing her.

The next few weeks went by at a gallop. She met with the other gallery owners, had several more delicious lunches and finally decided that Jonathon Preece's gallery was the right one for her. The date for the exhibition was eleven months away, giving her time to finish off her current painting of Amanda set in her garden in Reims and do several smaller pictures that she had in mind. She also had to make arrangements for framing and the weeks ran into months.

Baynton was in California defending a young man accused of date rape. He promised he would fly back for the private viewing before the grand opening. Mary and James arrived from England with all their news of Rye, the children and the local gossip.

Fiona was like a cat on hot bricks. She had written to Paul Gavroche, care of his sister Françoise. She hadn't heard anything, but anyway, she rationalised, he wouldn't be able to afford to come all this way. Still, it would have been nice.

Her mind jumped from one thing to another. The last picture was at the framers; would the framer have it there by tomorrow as promised? The fridge was empty; what could they eat tonight? Suzanne called to say William wouldn't be at the private view; he was caught up at the hospital and was devastated.

Mary took one look at Fiona when she arrived. The girl was a bundle of nerves. She had never seen her like this before. She and James proceeded to calm things down.

'What if Baynton doesn't get here?' Fiona wailed.

'He will,' Mary and James chorused comfortingly.

James was sent out in Fiona's car to do some serious supermarket shopping. Mary put the kettle on to make a cup of tea, her panacea for most things. Soon order reigned. Fiona lay in the bath suddenly more relaxed. Mary knocked and came in with a cup of tea and a biscuit.

'There now, that's better, more like the Fee I know and love,' she laughed.

'Mary, whatever would I have done without you both. With Baynton away this past month and with so much to do, I've just wallowed.'

'I think you've done very well and Baynton should arrive any time now shouldn't he?'

'No,' Fiona said, shaking her head. 'He telephoned just before I got into the bath. He can't get away now, but says he'll come straight to the private view from the plane tomorrow.'

'Well, that's alright then,' Mary said. 'I'll make a start on dinner.'

'I'm not hungry...' Fiona started to say, then caught Mary's expression. 'It's like being sixteen again,' she grinned, 'having you in charge I mean!'

To her surprise, Fiona slept well. She woke feeling refreshed and calm then, at the realisation that this was the day of the private view, her stomach churned and her heart began to beat rather rapidly. Mary walked in with a cup of tea.

'I knew you'd be awake darling.' She bent down and kissed Fiona on the forehead. 'Breakfast in half an hour.'

'It's lovely to be spoilt like this.' Fiona sat up and hugged Mary. 'I can't tell you how happy it makes me having you and James here. I'm sure I would have gone to pieces with worry if you hadn't arrived when you did.'

Mary blew her a kiss as she left the room and made her way to the kitchen. James has already made a cafetière of coffee for them both and the delicious aroma filled the air.

'The croissants are in the oven darling,' James said, looking up from reading the latest article Suzanne had written. The subject matter was political satire, but at the end of the article, in a separate block, she reminded readers about the forthcoming exhibition at the Jonathon Preece Gallery of that rising British artist, Fiona

McInnes.

'You know,' said James thoughtfully, 'I think Fee is very fortunate to have someone like Suzanne batting for her.' He grinned. 'Even though she's a bit unorthodox at times.' He was remembering their surprise when she arrived unannounced on their doorstep and proceeded to charm them into loaning the French artist's portrait of Fiona when she was fourteen.

This prompted Mary to say 'Have you seen Paul Gavroche's picture of Fiona?"

'Um,' said James musingly, 'in Baynton's study. I have a feeling we won't be getting it back.'

'I'd come to that conclusion too. Pity really, it's so much like she was when she first came to live with us.'

'Hi you two.' Fiona came in gathering her robe round her waist with its tie belt. 'I'm starving!'

They all burst out laughing.

'Nothing changes after all,' said James, winking broadly at his wife.

The day passed in a flash. The framer telephoned to say he had delivered the last painting to the gallery. Fiona received a mysterious telephone call from Suzanne saying 'Prepare yourself for a big surprise sweetie,' but wouldn't say anymore.

'That woman,' said Fiona to Mary and James over lunch, 'I love her but she drives me mad. Ever the journalist, but she's a good friend too I suppose,' she added, a trifle lamely.

'Why don't you have a rest after lunch?' Mary suggested.

'I couldn't possibly! I want to go for a good long walk. Will either of you come with me?'

'I'm going to have a rest,' Mary said, 'even if you don't want one.'

'I'll come with you Fee. Central Park?'

Fiona nodded, glad that she was to have some company. She felt the afternoon would surely drag by otherwise.

It was a lovely sunny afternoon, and Fiona and James strolled through Central Park, watching as they did the mime artists, jugglers, runners, children playing and others like themselves, just enjoying the walk. James was fascinated.

'All this space in the middle of New York with so much going on. Do you still jog?' he continued.

'Only when Baynton's here. It's not always a good idea to be alone. From time to time there are attacks on joggers, particularly women.'

'Yes, I've heard,' James said, 'I'm glad you don't run alone.'

It was evening. Fiona was alone in her bedroom. She had changed her mind several times about what to wear and had finally decided on cream wool palazzo pants with gold strap sandals and a cream top with a delicate gold linked belt, with the gold necklace and matching bracelet Baynton had given her on her last birthday. She brushed out her fair shoulder length hair and slid a hair band on, then took that off and put in a gold slide. She took that out and brushed her hair again, shook her head and let her hair fall naturally, framing her face. Mary knocked and came in.

'Darling, you look lovely, so slim and elegant.'

Fiona turned to her gratefully.

'Are you sure?'

But she knew in fact that she looked good. Baynton always preferred her in clothes like these and he preferred her hair swinging loose rather than tied back which is how she wore it when she was in the studio. She would grab an elastic band and pull her hair into a ponytail to get it out of the way.

The three of them left together in Fiona's car. Once again, she was particularly glad that they were with her. Without Baynton's support at this point she would have felt very lonely.

They were the first there apart from, of course, Jonathon and his staff. Jonathon was looking splendid in a midnight blue velvet jacket and pink velvet bow tie. Fiona introduced him to Mary and James.

'My parents,' she said simply.

Jonathon was fussing around impatiently, ordering his two assistants to get the caterers organised 'NOW'. Fiona took a glass of champagne but declined canapés. She was feeling almost sick with fright. She had a sudden vision of her first private view in the Reave Gallery, among all Mary and James' friends. This time was totally different. Critics could be so cruel.

She wondered around by herself, trying to look at the painting through eyes other than her own. The picture of Paul Gavroche was good she decided, and so was the main one of Madame Despardieux. She steadily gained confidence as she looked and looked again. There was Amanda, looking pale and thinner than she should in her Reims garden. Looking at it, she could almost hear the faint sound of the traffic.

A commotion at the door made her turn. It was, of course, none other than Suzanne making an entrance.

'No,' she was saying, 'he does not have an invitation, he's my guest and a guest of Miss McInnes.'

Jonathon's assistant was being officious.

'I'm afraid…' she began.

'It's alright Marion, he's my guest.'

Delightedly, she exclaimed, 'Paul, how on earth did you get here?'

He looked puzzled. She spoke in French and repeated the question.

'Ah, dear Mademoiselle Fiona, your good friend...' He indicated Suzanne. 'She sent me the air ticket. I had to come of course.'

He took her hand and let his lips briefly touch it. It was at that moment that Baynton arrived. For a split second he looked a little surprised to see a man kissing Fiona's hand with obvious warmth, then when Paul straightened up and Baynton saw who it was, he grinned.

'Why, that's great, you must be Paul. Fiona was so hoping you'd come.'

'And you must be Fiona's lover.' This time he spoke in broken English and they all laughed.

Fiona moved nearer to Baynton and hugged him, whispering in his ear as she did so 'Now I can enjoy myself. Thank goodness you're here.'

'As if I would miss this,' Baynton said, returning her hug.

The rooms were soon crowded, with people milling around and drinking champagne, eating canapés and looking at the paintings. Already, several had red stickers on them. It gave Fiona quite a wrench when she saw that some of her favourites had already sold.

'They're my children you see,' she confided to Mary, 'and I don't want to lose them.' She could see that Mary didn't understand, how could she? Mary understood so much but to regard paintings as family was beyond her comprehension.

At the end of two hours, the last person left the gallery. Jonathon was well pleased.

'One of the best private views,' he said rubbing his hands together.

Fiona actually had rather begun to like Jonathon, but at that moment she didn't, for she recognised that his glee was because he was counting his money, and she found that offensive.

Later, when she said this at dinner, everyone smiled benignly. The artist being temperamental their smiles seemed to say, but Baynton squeezed her hand tightly and looked into her eyes, sending her the message 'I understand – you can't expect the others to …'

Mary, James, Suzanne and William who, although he hadn't managed to get to the viewing, was able to join them for dinner, plus Paul Gavroche who was staying with Suzanne and William for three days, were sat around the table with Fiona and Baynton. Fiona was the only one who spoke fluent French and she tried to include Paul in the conversation, but she could sense that he didn't really feel at ease and it made her feel bad. He had given her such a good time in Paris. In order to make herself feel better, she asked him to spend the next day with her and she would show him the sights of New York. She told the others what she had suggested and she could sense Mary and James stiffening and see Suzanne's raised eyebrows, but she really felt she owed Paul a decent day after all his kindness to her.

Chapter 31

It was James who went out to buy the morning papers. He bought every one he could find, then they combed through them. Baynton had already left for an early flight back to California, but had promised to buy the papers at Kennedy and read what the critics had to say during his flight. It was James who found the first one.

'Look at this headline in the art section,' he said. 'British artist captivates everyone.'

The critic went on to describe the realism of her work, the way the characters of her subjects shone through the oil.

'This is a great artist in her embryonic period,' he continued, rather grandly. 'McInnes is a name to buy and hold onto. To buy a McInnes now could be a very wise investment for the future.'

The critics, bar one, were fulsome in their praise. The one that Fiona took notice of, of course, was the rather negative 'I find it surprising that Jonathon Preece allowed his gallery to be used for a fairly average exhibition of work by a British artist when we have so many talented young American artists who he will not give the time of day.'

'It's an interesting point,' Fiona said thoughtfully, 'is it really fairly average?'

'What nonsense.' James spoke firmly. 'He's probably anti-British.'

'I can't expect everyone to like my work though.'

The high of the previous evening was gone. She felt hollow

inside. The thought of spending an entire day with Paul loomed ahead. She fervently wished she hadn't made the arrangement.

The bell rang. It was Paul. Fiona hastily kissed Mary and James and said she would be back by early evening. She couldn't fail to notice their expressions. They were disappointed. It was, after all, their last day in New York. She resolved that she would give them a very special evening.

The day with Paul was pleasant. She took him on a tour of New York, much like the one that Baynton had given her on her first visit. However, the atmosphere between them changed quite suddenly when, on top of the Empire State Building, Paul tried to kiss her. She was so off guard that he actually managed to plant a kiss on her mouth before she drew back, totally shocked.

'Why Fiona? Why stop? I love you. You do not belong here in this cold, grey city. You belong in Paris with me, with my friends. Come back to Paris Fiona, now, today!'

Fiona drew a deep breath. At the back of her mind she had known, but had not wanted to acknowledge, that this was why Mary and James had been cool to Paul and why they had been less than keen for her to spend the day with him. They had sensed something that she had not even acknowledged to herself. She liked him, of course she did. The thought of living in Paris among the artists had an appeal, she couldn't deny it. But her life was here, with Baynton. New York was her home. She had grown fond of Paul during their brief time in Paris, but more than that, nothing.

Now she had the difficult task of letting him down gently.

'Cher Paul,' she began, holding his hand and leading him over to a quiet spot, 'you're a dear friend, a fellow artist.' She held up her hand as he tried to say something. 'Please, don't say anymore.'

They talked for half an hour, standing there hundreds of feet above New York. Finally, he accepted what she was saying.

'Will you promise me Fiona that if, one day, you feel differently

arms.

They sat over breakfast for a long while. He had been able to come home much earlier than expected as the case he'd been defending had been thrown out of court. It had been a set-up. The girl concerned was an ex-girlfriend, determined to exact revenge for being dumped.

'A waste of a lot of time and effort,' Baynton said, 'but darling, the good thing is that I've space in my diary. Why don't we have a holiday?'

'Oh, that would be wonderful, just to be away, the two of us.'

They talked more, trying to make a decision.

Baynton was the one to come up with the idea of riding in Montana.

'I have friends with a ranch there,' he said. 'They have a few log cabins that they let. They also have a pool,' he added, knowing Fiona's love of swimming. 'We could ride all day and swim every evening.'

'It sounds perfect. Can we go in a few days though? I simply have to finish a painting.'

'Is it the one on the easel?' Fiona nodded, looking at him anxiously. 'Do you mind?'

'Why should I?' he asked, leaning across and kissing her full on the mouth.

They stood up as one.

'Come and have another look now,' she said, and laughed. 'Actually, I haven't seen it myself in the light of day.' Hand in hand, they walked to the studio.

'You know Fee, I probably shouldn't say this, but I think it's the best picture you've ever painted.'

'I wondered if you actually liked it,' Fiona said, squeezing his hand.

'How could I not? The only trouble is I'm not sure I'll ever want to go to sleep again in case you're watching me.' But he smiled; how could he help but be pleased? The picture showed him sprawled on their bed, eyes closed, hair tousled, expression peaceful, with the suggestion of a smile on his lips.

'I look as if I've fallen asleep after making love,' he teased.

Fiona blushed. 'Actually, that is how you look.'

'Satisfied definitely, that's what the expression says to me. You're a clever old soul aren't you?'

Baynton put his arms around her.

'Do you think you could cover me up a little more though?'

'An artist has to be true to herself,' Fiona answered solemnly, but with a grin denying her mock serious tone. 'Anyway, the critical bit is covered!'

'Only just my love. Any less and it would be censored.'

'It's only for us actually darling. I painted it as a welcome home present for you and also to keep me company when you're away.'

Chapter 32

The next few days were hectic. Fiona spent every moment on the portrait. Baynton made seemingly endless telephone calls, first to Colin and Judy in Montana, then to various airline companies. Car hire was arranged. They more or less finished together. The painting was left on the easel to dry. Looking at it, Fiona knew it was good, but what was even more important was that now, if Baynton was away, she would not have to conjure him up in her mind. She could lie in bed and look at the picture. Baynton was thrilled with it. It seemed so alive, even though he was apparently asleep. He was strangely touched by it too, for in a wonderful way it seemed to him that only someone who loved him deeply could have somehow let his inner soul show on his face.

'You haven't signed it.'

She picked up her paintbrush and wrote F. M. McInnes.

'I've packed,' he said, 'for both of us.'

'Baynton, you can't possibly have packed for me!'

'Trust me darling.'

She hesitated, but only for a moment.

'Well,' she said, 'I'll trust you, but woe betide you if you've forgotten anything I need.'

They were to leave in a couple of hours.

'That's good,' Fiona said, 'I must go and sort out one of my drawers in the studio. I've been putting it off for ages.' She disappeared into the studio. 'Call me when it's time to go!'

Baynton nodded, deciding to do the same thing in his study.

Fiona opened a drawer that she hadn't looked in since arriving in New York. It contained mostly photographs and negatives of pictures she had painted at various stages of their development, or of paintings she had sold which she kept for her own records. She had been meaning for some while to put them into chronological order. At the moment, they were in a rather chaotic state. One by one, she took out the packs of photos, glancing through, and where they weren't dated, putting the date on the corner. After about half an hour, when she was not displeased with the progress she was making, she opened up another pack and out fell the pictures she had taken of the portrait of Amanda with her first baby. The look on Amanda's face hit her somewhere in the solar plexus. That look was one that would feature on most mothers' faces as they gazed at their first born. It was a look of deep and unselfish joy, a look of the purest love there could be.

Even though she, Fiona, had painted the picture, seeing it again years later gave her a feeling of deep emptiness. She sank on the floor still holding the photograph. She realised that more than anything in the world she wanted a baby, Baynton's child. She could hardly believe her own emotions, could hardly even trust herself to think what she was thinking. What would Baynton think? Because she had said she never wanted to marry him, they'd never discussed children. He knew all about her childhood and how awful it had been, how it had coloured her thinking. Now, she would have to tell him how she had suddenly, at the sight of a photograph, changed her mind completely. She wanted to marry him. She wanted a child, his child. Somehow, she pulled herself together when he called. She had a hasty wash and put on a fresh sweater and trousers and joined him by the front door.

'You look gorgeous darling. Are you ready for our great escape?'

'Ready,' she replied lightly, thrusting her most recent thoughts down deep inside her, waiting for the moment, the right moment, to tell all to the man she loved.

The journey had gone smoothly. The hire car was ready for them when they arrived and before long they were driving through the beautiful autumnal countryside of Montana.

'It's stunning,' said Fiona, overwhelmed by the beauty. 'It is a wonderful country. I suppose I'll have to ride with a western saddle though?'

'I wouldn't worry,' Baynton laughed. 'It's a darn sight easier than riding eastern! Whenever I go to England, I have to adjust. It's as bad as having to drive on the left in England. What an odd nation you are!'

There followed a good natured argument which lasted until they turned in the gate to Northridge. Colin and Judy came out to meet them. Judy, with her flaming hair and freckled face, hugged Baynton warmly then turned to greet Fiona.

'Well, you must be the girl we've heard so much about from Baynton and read about in the papers too. Welcome to Northridge.'

Colin, who was a bear of a man, hugged Baynton then turned his attention to Fiona.

'Why, you're sure a little beauty!' And he hugged her, as he had Baynton. He smelt, thought Fiona, of hay and horses and both his and Judy's welcome was so warm and friendly that Fiona felt instantly at home with them.

'I'll show you the cabin,' Colin said.

'Then come and join us for dinner in an hour,' Judy added, 'give you time to freshen up, right?'

'Right,' they both chorused.

Colin led the way across the yard and up a slope that was studded with trees and there, with its breathtaking views, was the log cabin that would be their home for the next ten days.

219

'We thought you'd like this cabin best,' Colin said as he threw open the door. 'The other one doesn't have such a pretty view.'

Fiona was amazed. From the outside it really looked like a simple cabin with a covered porch on which two rocking chairs were strategically placed overlooking the view. But inside, they saw a large room with a big fireplace piled with logs, two comfy looking sofas covered in bright rugs and even a stereo system and television.

The bedroom too was a pleasant surprise, leading directly off the main room. It was a much smaller room, almost filled with a king sized bed. Along one wall there was a cupboard and hanging space and leading from the back of the room, the final surprise: an outdoor spa.

'Water's hot if you want a spa to freshen up,' Colin said. 'See you in an hour,' and he was gone.

Fiona was thrilled.

'Oh Baynton, why didn't you say it was so glorious?' Fiona had discovered the tiny kitchen and bathroom. 'It's wonderful. Shall we spa?'

Of course they did and were half an hour late for supper in consequence, as one thing led to another. Full of apologies, they arrived for dinner. Judy and Colin were totally unfazed.

'You're here for a holiday. What's half an hour?'

Fiona was grateful for Judy's understanding. She so badly had not wanted to start off on the wrong foot with these old friends of Baynton's.

The dinner was wonderful; their own beef with sweet potatoes and cabbage, followed by cheesecake and coffee. It was whilst they were eating Judy's delicious cheesecake that Baynton choked. He put it down to too much talking, but his throat was obviously uncomfortable and Fiona noticed that he kept sipping water. However, the incident was soon forgotten in all the catch up chat.

Fiona learned that Judy and Colin's two daughters were away at university and that they both wanted to work in the tourist industry.

'Pity really,' Colin mused. 'I had hoped one day they'd take over from me.' He shrugged. 'They have to do what they choose I guess.'

'It's a hard life out here in the winter,' Judy contributed. 'I think they just felt they wanted a more urban life - not that I'd change it for anything,' she added fiercely, 'I love the ranch.'

Before long, Fiona and Baynton, plus a storm lantern provided by Colin, made their way back to the cabin. Fiona went into the tiny bathroom to shower and clean her teeth. Automatically, she felt in her sponge bag for her birth-control pills. They weren't there. Baynton had forgotten to take them out of the bathroom cabinet. She smiled to herself. How she could tease him, and how it might have mattered, how it might have ruined the holiday.

'Baynton,' she began cheerily, going back into the bedroom.

'Oh Baynton darling, what is it?'

Baynton was sitting on the side of the bed sipping a glass of water. He looked up and smiled.

'Nothing my love,' he said easily, 'my throat's a bit dry after that choking, that's all, honestly!'

He was so positive that Fiona felt immediately reassured.

'Now, what were you going to say Fee?'

Fiona started to laugh.

'Actually, I was going to pretend to be very cross with you,' she began.

Baynton looked puzzled. She sat down beside him on the bed and told him about the photograph she had taken of her painting of Amanda with Henri. Baynton sat, looking at her, wondering what she was leading up to. When finally she told him, he could hardly believe his ears.

'Are you sure darling, really sure?'

'I'm sure,' she replied, 'and Baynton, will you marry me?'

There was a pause.

'Why were you going to be cross with me?'

'Because,' said Fiona, starting to laugh helplessly, 'you said you'd packed everything I needed but darling, you forgot my birth control tablets, and,' she added, almost convulsed with laughter, watching his expression and trying to speak indignantly, 'you haven't even said if you'll marry me yet.'

Baynton reached over and put his arms around her.

'Yes, I'll marry you, you great big bully, if – and only if – you'll forgive me about the pills. Actually, of course, it was deliberate.'

She pulled away from him, for a second almost believing him. Then, seeing his look, she reached round and grabbed one of the pillows and started hitting him with it.

'Mercy, mercy!' he pleaded, as they both fell backwards on the bed. Suddenly, they were serious, looking intently into each other's eyes.

'A baby and marriage, I can hardly believe it,' Baynton almost whispered.

'Let's make a baby now and get married tomorrow please,' Fiona whispered back.

In fact, they couldn't get married the next day, but drove into town and made an appointment for two days later.

'Gosh, it's easier than in the UK,' Fiona said, agreeably surprised.

Baynton insisted on taking her to the jewellers and bought her a big, square sapphire surrounded by diamonds. The ring was too large, but the jeweller promised it would be ready on the day of the wedding. They chose matching wedding bands and arranged to have them inscribed with the date and place. Then they drove back to Northridge to break the news to Colin and Judy and invite them to be their witnesses. After all that, there was still time for a short ride, enabling Fiona to get adjusted to the western saddle which, to her surprise, she found extremely comfortable.

'Told you so,' said a complacent Baynton.

Chapter 33

Two days later they were married. Fortunately Baynton had packed one decent dress for her and she wore that with its matching shoes.

'I must have known,' Baynton said, 'I only put it in at the last moment. I really thought you wouldn't forgive me if I only put in jeans and trousers, but I didn't think you'd actually wear them!'

'You're brilliant darling, I'm sure I wouldn't have put it in for a riding holiday. If it had been me packing I'm afraid it would probably have been a trouser suit today, and this is so much nicer!'

Colin insisted on taking a few photographs and Baynton insisted they have lunch in town at the most upmarket restaurant he could find.

'So now,' said Judy happily, 'you're on your honeymoon.'

'So we are,' Fiona responded, slight surprise in her voice, 'and I couldn't think of anywhere I'd rather be than in Northridge.'

Colin and Judy smiled at them, happy that their dear friend Baynton had finally found himself such a lovely bride.

That evening, Fiona wrote to Mary and James. She had thought of sending them a fax, but decided instead to write a much fuller letter. She hoped they would understand how it had all come about and that they wouldn't be hurt that she hadn't come back home to be married, like the almost daughter she was to them.

Baynton wrote to them too, which Fiona thought was particularly nice. She would have been surprised at the contents of his letter though.

Dear Mary and James, I know that Fiona is writing to you about our marriage. I hope you will be as happy for us as we are ourselves and that our sudden, and perhaps surprising action will meet with your approval.

As you may remember, I sold the house on the square some time ago and I feel I would like Fiona to have a place of her own, a bolthole, security, what you will, and I was wondering whether you would consider selling Round Window Cottage to me (for Fiona) when your current tenant leaves. I would, of course, pay the full market price. It would be a wedding present to Fiona and would mean she would always have a place of her own.

With love to you both.

Ever,

Baynton

Their reply was waiting for him when he and Fiona returned to New York. Mary had written:

Very dear Baynton, what a lovely surprise! Your letters arrived on the same day. Fiona's happiness was on every line. We couldn't be more delighted.

On the subject of the cottage, our tenant is due to leave next month. As you know, we only do six month lets and he has now found a house just outside Rye, so James has asked me to say we would be delighted to sell the cottage to you. We could never bear the thought of parting with it, but for you and Fiona to have it is keeping it in the family.

James is having it valued this week and we will let you know the valuation figure. It does, of course, need the odd thing doing to it – all old houses do! Anyway, we shan't breathe a word to Fiona. What a lovely wedding present!

All our love

Mary

The holiday had been a wonderful break. The riding had been both relaxing and, at times, exhilarating. Colin rode with them quite often, showing them trails they would never have ventured onto on their own. Judy didn't ride these days. She had had a riding accident a few years earlier when the horse she was riding had bolted, spooked by a snake. Judy had been knocked off her horse by the branch of a tree and had fallen awkwardly, breaking her leg badly and hurting her back. She wasn't afraid she'd assured them, but it made her feel vulnerable and she now only hacked around the ranch and didn't do any trail riding.

Once or twice during the happy ten days, Baynton had choked again, but put it down to a sore throat. He made so light of it that Fiona had stopped worrying, or at least she pretended to herself and Baynton that she had.

Mary's letters awaiting their return home were full of delight at their marriage.

'Why has Mary written to you separately?' Fiona wanted to know.

'Because I wrote to them silly,' Baynton replied.

She had wanted to read the letter, but Baynton managed to distract her for sufficient time for him to dispose of it. His secret wedding present was safe.

Fiona missed her period. She was convinced she was pregnant, but she hardly dare believe they had managed it straightaway. She also noticed that she didn't enjoy her morning coffee any more, but tried to conceal it from Baynton who, unusually, seemed a little withdrawn.

It was when they were out to dinner with Suzanne and William that the next choking attack occurred. This was by far the worst and although Baynton made light of it, Fiona sensed he was worried. She knew he was. When he went to the men's room, she turned anxiously to William.

'Something's the matter William, I'm sure. What should I do? He says it's nothing. He won't go to the doctor.'

'It's probably nothing Fee,' William said easily. 'If you like, I'll have a word with him. Not tonight,' he said, seeing her eyes light up. 'Leave it to me will you? I'll speak with him in the next day or two. Trust me.' He lowered his voice as he said the last two words and she realised Baynton was nearly at the table.

The rest of the evening passed in the usual happy way. Suzanne and Baynton bantered as they were wont do to. William teased Fiona about their escape to Montana to get married.

'Couldn't face all your friends in New York eh?' he said.

'I shall put you in my column,' Suzanne informed them.

'Oh no,' they chorused, 'anything but that!'

Suzanne pretended to be miffed. It was the usual happy foursome, an evening Suzanne and William always remembered.

William had persuaded Baynton to see a colleague of his and although Baynton made light of the coming appointment, Fiona sensed his worry. On the day of the appointment, she wanted to go with him, but he was adamant.

'Finish the picture Fee,' he said, 'I shall be much happier if I know you're painting away!'

Reluctantly, she agreed, but found herself wandering around the apartment unable to pick up a paintbrush. On sudden impulse, she telephoned Mary and James. She couldn't bring herself to voice her fears, just said she felt like a chat. After the phone call, a worried Mary looked at James.

'James, it's midnight. Fiona knew that yet she still phoned. Something's wrong. I know it is. There was something in her voice.'

'Come back to bed my love. Whatever it is, she telephoned us and if there's anything wrong, she'll tell us in her own good time.'

Mary lay awake for a long while, longing to fly to New York and comfort Fee. She knew, some mother's instinct told her – adopted mother anyway she rationalised – that something was very wrong.

Baynton was quite a long time at the hospital. William's oncology colleague insisted on all sorts of tests and finally, he sat Baynton down in his office, looking serious.

'Tell me the worst.' Baynton's tone was light, though he had the most horrible feeling in the pit of his stomach. He knew in his heart of hearts that he had cancer. Bill Green confirmed his fears but then went on to explain that radiotherapy and chemotherapy would help enormously and there was no reason that with a good balance, they could 'kick the wretched thing.'

'No operation!' said Baynton, relieved. He had imagined a voice box being inserted or something even worse. Bill Green looked relieved too. It was so much easier to talk to someone both positive and who was trying to get to grips and understand the whole procedure.

They spent an hour together whilst Bill explained in greater detail what would be happening over the next few weeks. Just as he was leaving the office, Baynton was struck by an awful thought.

'Bill – Fiona, my wife (how he liked saying that) and I are hoping to have a baby. Does this make any difference?' As he asked the question, he already knew the answer, but he waited to hear what Bill would say. His fears were confirmed.

'Not during treatment Baynton, I'm sorry.'

It was almost the worst blow of all. He climbed into his car and stared bleakly ahead. He should never have married Fee, he knew he was too old for her and now this. She so badly wanted a child, as indeed did he. He drove slowly out into the sunshine, away from the sanctuary of the underground car park. For the first time ever, he dreaded going home.

Fiona heard the lift and was at the front door before he could even get his key out. One look at his face, even though he was desperately trying to conceal his feeling, told her that her worst fears had been realised.

'Oh darling, tell me everything,' she said.

They walked hand in hand to the study and sat on the soft leather sofa, hardly a space between them.

'Tell me,' she said quietly, 'everything.'

Baynton lifted her hand to his lips and kissed it.

'How I love you dearest Fee,' he began. Word for word, he told her what Bill had told him. He explained about the treatment and that Bill was optimistic about a cure. He saw Fiona's face light up.

'But darling,' she began. He didn't want to get her hopes up too high. He still had to tell her about the baby business. He started again and as he spoke, she started to smile. Baynton was startled, then he saw the happiness in her eyes and the truth dawned on him.

'Yes darling, I'm sure we started a baby in Montana!'

'Oh Fee, how clever you are!'

'How clever we are you mean. I haven't seen a doctor or done a test, but I know Baynton, I just know.'

He frowned. 'Why didn't you say anything?'

'I wanted to be sure, but I am darling – I know I am!'

Later that evening, she used the pregnancy kit she'd bought earlier. It confirmed what she already knew and as they sat quietly having dinner together, they talked of the future, their future and their child. Baynton felt confident that he would get through all the treatment alright, and with Fiona and their child by his side, he had so much to fight for, more than ever before, more than any court case he had ever fought. This was a case he was going to win.

Chapter 34

The treatment started three days later. Fiona drove Baynton to the hospital every morning. Every day he felt worse and worse. He started being sick regularly and tried to laugh about it, saying it was supposed to be morning sickness for the mother-to-be, not the father-to-be.

Fiona loved him for his bravery and after four weeks the radiotherapy ceased. He had lost some weight and his face looked a trifle gaunt, but his spirits were high on the last day of the treatment. He had explained to Fiona how he was dealing with the whole thing like a court battle and felt he had certainly got the prosecution very edgy.

The chemotherapy started a month later, a balance of drugs pumped in through a vein in his hand. To his mortification, his hair had fallen out in clumps, and catching sight of the picture of himself that now hung in their bedroom, laying asleep with his full head of hair, gave him on odd jolt.

Fiona had virtually no morning sickness and was ever more aware of the little baby growing inside her. Baynton came with her for her first scan and they both felt moved to tears at seeing their little child so safe and protected in his mother's womb. The second scan showed that it was boy and Fiona immediately called him LB.

'Why LB?' Baynton wanted to know.

'Why, Little Baynton of course, silly!'

'Of course,' he said, and from that moment LB was not just a baby, but a little person with a name.

It was Fiona who noticed the lump on the side of Baynton's neck. He was lolling about in the bath feeling much happier than of late, for he felt so much better. They were both looking forward to LB's arrival in about six weeks. Where had the months gone? He had won the battle, walked away from the court with the prosecution's face a picture of disappointment. In Baynton's mind, the prosecution had developed unforeseen characteristics. He had grown horns; indeed, he had become Lucifer.

Baynton laughed aloud at the silly games one's mind plays to deal with problems. Good guy versus bad guy. Good guy wins! It was at this point that Fiona came in looking heavily pregnant, wearing her painting shirt that she was no longer able to fasten down the front.

'I heard you laughing darling. Share the joke.'

Baynton told her how he had viewed the prosecution in his court case. Fiona knew all about his method of dealing with his treatment. Now, as he described the prosecutor as Lucifer, challenged and defeated, she smiled and sat down on the corner of the bath.

'Sit up darling, I'll wash your back.'

She soaped his back generously and ran her hands over his smooth flesh and feeling a longing for him to make love to her when he had finished his bath, despite her pregnancy. She ran her fingers up and down his spine, teasingly, knowing he loved her to do that.

'Hey woman, cease these attentions!'

He caught hold of her hand, twisting round to do so and it was at that moment she saw the small lump between his ear and the back of his neck. She felt the blood drain from her face. A secondary. William had told her about the danger of secondaries.

'What's the matter Fee? Are you alright?' Baynton had seen the change in her skin tone. He stood up and reached for the bath sheet, full of concern. Was the baby coming early? Fiona pulled herself together. Not now, not yet. She couldn't say anything, not tonight, one more night please God, one more night when he thinks he's safe.

She managed to reassure him.

'I felt a bit faint darling, that's all – probably too hot in here for me in my state.'

She was so convincing that his fears were allayed.

'Let's go to bed early,' he suggested. 'You need a rest and I need to feel you and LB in my arms.'

They lay curled up together, her head resting on his chest. Every now and again, LB would give them a good thump.

'He's had long enough in there by the feel of it,' Baynton said, smiling in the darkness. Suddenly, he felt a wetness on his chest.

'Fee darling, whatever is it? Are you crying?'

'I just love you so much,' she replied through her tears, 'I love you Baynton, every part of me.'

He tightened his arms around her and kissed her gently and with a sigh, drifted off to sleep. Fiona lay, not moving for fear of disturbing him. Then, when she could tell by his deep and even breathing that he was asleep, she eased out of his arms and sat up, leaning on one elbow.

The moonlight shone through the open window. They never bothered to close the curtains as no-one could overlook them. Now, she was glad that with the moonlight bathing his face she could look at him unobserved.

For some reason, his hair hadn't grown back – not all that uncommon the doctors said. Now, looking at him with his gleaming head, his face thinner than it used to be, she was reminded, most horribly, of looking at her father all those years before. Choking back a sob, she got out of bed and fled to the studio. Once there, she threw herself on her big comfy chair, pulled the rug that she kept folded on the back of it over herself and, burying her face in her arms, cried silent tears.

It was several hours later that she climbed back into bed beside the still sleeping Baynton. She kissed him lightly on the mouth and he reached for her from deep in his sleep. Thankfully, she settled in his arms and, worn from all the tears, drifted into an uneasy sleep.

Their son was born four weeks later, two weeks premature. Despite his prematurity he was a lusty, healthy baby weighing in at seven and a half pounds. The delivery had been quick and easy and Fiona was delighted to find that she had even got away without having stitches. LB looked what he was, a little version of Baynton. He had Baynton's eyes and mouth but Fiona's fair hair. He was, fortunately, a happy and contented baby, only crying when hungry or uncomfortable. Baynton couldn't believe him; the tiny perfect fingers and toes, the soft down of his hair, the noise he made when he wanted his mother's breast.

'Lucky fellow,' Baynton said fondly as Fiona unbuttoned her blouse and released a nipple for her hungry son to suckle.

Mary and James had flown over to help Fiona when she returned home with the three day old baby. Fiona had followed up her mysterious phone call with a letter, updating them on Baynton's health problems, but they were nonetheless shocked at the change in him. His skin had taken on a jaundiced appearance, his neck was now heavily swollen on one side and he was back on chemotherapy. His appetite was almost non-existent and had it not been for the demands of LB, Fiona felt she would have gone to pieces. As it was, when Mary and James arrived she at last felt she had someone with whom she could share her sorrows as well as her joys, for she knew that Baynton was dying.

James spent a lot of time with Baynton who liked being in his study during the day. They had some serious conversations about the future.

'Please encourage Fiona to go back to England when I'm dead,' Baynton said one day.

James looked down at the floor uncomfortably. He found the talk of the future when Baynton would be dead very difficult.

'I mean it James,' Baynton continued, 'she has the cottage.'

He leaned back on the sofa, his mind drifting back to the day the deeds for Round Window Cottage had arrived from England. He had written a notice and put it on an easel in the studio. Follow the sign to find your wedding present with an arrow pointing to one of the drawers. He had heard her squeal from the study and continued to sit at his desk, a grin on his face. He heard the flying footsteps as she ran from the studio towards the study.

'Baynton, darling, darling Baynton, what a wonderful, wonderful wedding present! I'm stuck for words to say thank you!'

'It doesn't sound as if you're stuck for words.' Baynton had swivelled his desk chair round to face her.

'Happy?' he enquired.

'Happy?' she replied, 'I should just think I am,' and she had wanted to know how it had all come about.

Now, thinking back to those happier, healthier days, Baynton felt a deep sense of relief that Fiona and their son would be living close to Mary and James. She would be near family, which is what she would need.

At night, now, they lay in bed just holding hands, his poor emaciated body so uncomfortable that Fiona got up several times a night to help him turn, or to put a pillow in the middle of his back to support him. She wept, but never in front of him. For him, she wanted to be happy. He knew about the tears; he always knew when she had been crying. He loved her for her gallantry, her determination that right up to the end she would be the loving, warm, giving Fee that she had always been.

He could hardly hold their son now; he was fearful of dropping him. But Fiona sat close to him and, together, they marvelled at his development. Every day a new expression seemed to cross the baby's face, his hands ever more active, seeking to reach out and find out about the world about him.

The end came quite suddenly. William wanted to move him to the hospice, but though frail, Baynton's determination didn't waver. He wanted to die in his home, with his wife and baby son.

He died on the day that LB was three months old.

James had been back to England to check on the farm but Mary stayed in New York. She telephoned James when Baynton seemed to be deteriorating and he had flown back, arriving twenty four hours before Baynton died. Fiona didn't know how she would have coped without them.

The funeral was very well attended: all Baynton's fellow lawyers, his many friends, Suzanne, for once quiet and shocked, William providing a supportive arm for his wife as she mourned her dearest friend. But for Fiona there might as well have been no-one there but herself. LB had been left in the care of a kindly neighbour. Now she stood, watching as the coffin was slowly lowered into the grave. There were no swirling mists, but she felt the loneliness she had felt that time before, when Dada's coffin was lowered into the grave. Then she had known her childhood was over. She had Claire and Stewart to look after. Now she knew her life was over, but she had LB. For a moment she almost hated him; she wanted to be in the grave with Baynton. She felt a touch and glanced around.

'Come on darling.' It was Mary.

Automatically she let herself be led to the waiting car. She stopped and turned to look at the grave, the flowers, the people, then, responding to the pull of an arm around her shoulders, she walked slowly forward and climbed into the car.

Chapter 35

The next few months passed in a blur for Fiona. She tended to LB, comforted by his smiles, so sweet they tore her heart – they were so like Baynton's. Mary stayed on. She didn't feel she had any choice. She missed James terribly and they spoke to each other several times a week. Fiona spent most of her time in Baynton's study, as if, by being there, she would be nearer to him.

Mary knew Fiona needed time, but she was becoming concerned that Fiona seemed such a lost soul. The studio door was firmly closed, and on the rare occasion Mary had suggested that Fiona might start painting again, Fiona had simply said, 'I can't.'

The sound of a crying baby woke Mary one morning. She looked at her bedside clock: seven thirty. Usually, LB would be in Fiona's bed at this time, having his first feed of the day. Fiona still breastfed him morning and evening, and he had a bottle and baby rice or pureed vegetables at lunch time.

The small dressing room off the main bedroom had been converted into a nursery and Mary, on finding Fiona's room empty, headed for that. The nursery blinds were still closed and LB was crying hungrily, but of Fiona, there was no sign. Picking up LB, Mary carried the baby back into the main room. It was then she was aware that the studio door was slightly ajar. *She's painting again* Mary thought thankfully, *but what to do with a hungry baby?* It was only a momentary hesitation. LB was hungry. There was a bottle and baby milk in the kitchen.

'Alright poppet,' she cooed, 'soon have something in that empty tummy.'

Holding the baby firmly with one arm, she filled the kettle and plugged it in, measured out the powder into the bottle and topped it up with boiled water. Taking some ice cubes from the ice maker and putting them in a small bowl, she plunged the bottle in to get cool. Fortunately, LB was sufficiently interested in all the preparation that he stopped crying and soon he was sucking away at the bottle in a contented fashion. Mary looked down at him fondly, her first 'almost' grandchild. It was a good feeling. She'd almost forgotten how good it was to look after babies.

By the time Fiona emerged from the studio in the late afternoon, LB was playing contentedly in his playpen whilst Mary sat with her feet up on the sofa, writing to Alison. She wrote to all three children weekly, and these days, there always seemed so much to say.

Fiona yawned as she walked into the room.

'Gosh, what time is it?' she said, seeing little Baynton and Mary dressed.

'Three o'clock.' Mary looked at her watch as she spoke. Fiona sat down suddenly. Mary noticed the shirt. It was the old one of Baynton's that Fiona always painted in. She also had the usual smudge of paint on her face.

'You were very busy darling in the studio, so LB and I looked after each other.'

'My God, I forgot all about him!'

Fiona looked horror struck. She bent down over the playpen and picked up her cooing son.

'It's a good job we've got someone responsible around here,' she said, kissing her beaming son as she pulled him close. 'Would you like to see what I've been painting?'

Mary rose with alacrity.

'Of course,' she said. This was good news. If Fiona was painting again, she could start talking about the future, for up till now all Fiona had been doing was to dwell on the past.

Fiona pushed open the door of the studio. Mary walked in, longing to see Fiona's latest painting, but for once she was taken completely aback. It was a dark picture, full of foreboding. There was, it seemed, a courtroom; a figure, slightly shadowy, stood in the witness box. It was Baynton, wan and pale. The judge sat with a kindly smile, but it was the man in red and black with the menacing eyes, as hard as coals, a sardonic grin on his narrow lips, that arrested Mary's attention.

'What a dreadful painting.' Mary almost bit her tongue, wishing she hadn't spoken so impulsively.

'It's life,' Fiona answered tonelessly, 'or rather, death. Poor Baynton, he didn't stand a chance against him.' She indicated the figure in black with the red bow tie and waistcoat. 'I always thought Mr Lennard was the devil and look, there he is.' She pointed dramatically. 'Dada, now Baynton. The people I loved the most. How can they say good triumphs?' Fiona started to weep.

'Well, at least you've started painting again.' Mary felt her response was totally inadequate, but she felt out of her depth.

The telephone rang. She thrust LB into Fiona's arms and left the studio somewhat thankfully. For the first time in her life she didn't like one of Fiona's paintings.

It was William. He telephoned regularly and up to now, Mary had respected Fiona's wishes not to see anyone, but enough was enough.

'William,' she said thankfully, 'will you come round?'

Something in her voice alerted him.

'Something wrong?'

'Everything. I think she needs help.'

238

'Give me an hour,' said William quietly.

Fiona took LB off with her. She was going to bath and change. LB could lie on the rug and keep her company. She seemed more cheerful, but Mary couldn't throw off the awful feeling of doom she had felt when she had first seen the painting. Fiona must have been up all night to complete it; such a strange, dark picture.

William arrived just as Fiona emerged from the bedroom. She had washed her hair and put on some twill trousers and a cream shirt. Mary had not seen her look so bright since Baynton's death. When the bell rang, it was Fiona who was at the door first.

'William, how lovely!' she greeted.

'Hi Fee,' he returned, hugging her and raising a quizzical eyebrow at Mary over her shoulder. Mary shrugged. She couldn't account for the sudden change in attitude.

'I'll put the kettle on, or would you prefer a drink?'

'I'd like a cup of tea followed by a drink!' said William, knowing how much Mary liked her 'cuppa'.

'Why don't you show William your painting darling,' Mary called from the kitchen.

'Good, you've started painting again Fee.'

Fiona nodded. 'I couldn't before.' She spoke slowly. 'It was as if I was in a steel box. I hate what I've painted,' she continued vehemently, 'but I had to!'

'Show me,' William said standing up.

Fiona put LB in his playpen. He rolled about reaching for a favourite toy. William followed Fiona. He stopped in front of the painting.

'It's very powerful Fee, but Baynton didn't ever give in.'

'No,' said Fiona sadly, 'he didn't have a chance. He lost the case. He really thought he could win it.'

William looked puzzled.

'What case?'

'The final one, the life or death case.'

William began to understand. He looked more closely.

'And that,' he said, 'is death – the Prosecutor?'

Fiona nodded.

'And the Judge?'

'I suppose that's God,' she said slowly. She smiled suddenly. 'You know William, this painting just 'happened'. I was laying on the bed looking at the painting I did of Baynton when he was asleep, so relaxed, so happy, and suddenly, I knew I had to do the final painting, but I've only just realised that the Judge…' She paused, then started again very slowly, 'The Judge, I've given him my father's face. Isn't that strange? And see, he's looking at Baynton with compassion, even though the prosecution won.'

'And the Prosecutor? Is he a figment of your imagination?'

'No, he isn't. But don't ask William, please.'

'You know Fee, I think this is a good painting you've done. It's done. It's over. From now,' he continued,' you can start putting your life and LB's back together. There's a whole world waiting for you out there Fiona McInnes Rivers or whatever you call yourself these days. Get out there, paint the world! That's what Baynton would have wanted above all.'

Fiona bit her lip.

'I know William. I'm going home, back to England, to the cottage he bought me as a wedding present. You will come and see me won't you, you and Suzanne?'

'I've always wanted an excuse to visit the UK. You just try and stop me, and Suzanne feels the same.' He kissed her on the cheek.

Chapter 36

Mary flew back to England a few days later. Fiona was full of energy and was organising the move and sale of the apartment. Mary knew it was time to leave and, as she told Fiona, it would give her a chance to take a few pieces of furniture out of the cottage so that Fiona would have space for a few of the things she wanted to bring from the apartment: the bed, Baynton's desk and chair, the nursery furniture that she and Baynton had chosen together with such care and, of course, the contents of the studio. Once again, she was moving her studio across the Atlantic, but this time in the opposite direction.

Suzanne, who, true to her word, had not written a column about her for ages, did a piece on the young widow moving back to her homeland. A loss for New York, she wrote. She reminded them of the exhibition at the Preece Gallery and continued that Fiona McInnes, after a period of not painting after her husband's death, was now painting again. Let us hope, she continued, that England will appreciate her as much as we shall miss her.

Fiona pulled a face when she read the column. Suzanne really did go over the top at times, but she knew she would miss her friend.

Fiona settled into the cottage with ease. The shabby familiarity of the place made her feel instantly comfortable. Mary had borrowed a cot for LB's use until their goods arrived from the States. People dropped by with flowers or an occasional bottle of wine to welcome her back. All Mary's and James' friends knew about Baynton's death and remembered how much they had enjoyed Fiona's very first exhibition at the Reave Gallery and her subsequent successes.

Now she was a famous artist and there were all sorts of plans afoot to get her involved in various local activities, including the annual professional artists' exhibition. They were even wondering if she might be prepared to give some lectures to the amateur Art Club. Fiona thanked them all warmly, but said she needed time and space. Apart from one or two waspish comments along the lines of 'who does she think she is', people were, on the whole, sensitive to her needs.

The occasional postcard arrived from Paul Gavroche. *I've joined the circus* he wrote on one. He always wrote in French and never gave her an address. Very occasionally, Fiona wrote to Françoise, but ever the bad correspondent, Françoise wrote back even less occasionally. The circus rather puzzled Fiona. Whatever was he doing in a circus?

Six months later, she had another postcard. I started as crew he wrote now I'm artist in charge! He had done a tiny sketch of a tiger in one corner of the card, and although it was diminutive, it was perfect in every detail. So, he had listened to what she had said. He was doing what he did best, drawing and painting animals.

LB started at the local school. Where had the last five years gone? She was now Fiona McInnes Rivers RA. Of all things, the painting she could hardly bear to look at, 'The Trial', had been accepted by the National Gallery. It was on permanent loan; she couldn't contemplate having it in the cottage. Several portraits were currently featuring at the National Portrait Gallery in an exhibition entitled 'Female Artists of this Century'. She had been amazed and flattered to be asked to submit works, despite Mary and James telling her that they were not at all surprised.

242

It was a lovely walk home from the school. LB's first term was nearly over. He had settled in happily and seemed to be making friends easily. He had Baynton's easy charm and a secure and happy home life. Briefly, Fiona's mind darted back to her early school days and the loneliness she had felt at times. By the time she arrived home, she knew that Janet would be cleaning away and she would, after the almost mandatory cup of coffee with her cleaning lady, be able to work undisturbed on her current commission – the local Mayor in all his regalia: red fur-trimmed robe, chain of office and cocked hat; all rather medieval but, thought Fiona, so appropriate for this medieval little town with so much of its thinking still somewhere in the past.

Her mind was full of her painting. She let herself in through the door of Round Window Cottage. Janet came out of the kitchen.

'Mrs Rivers, there's a man. He says he's your stepfather. I showed him into the sitting room. I hope that's alright?' She looked a bit flustered, but nothing to the feelings that were threatening to overwhelm Fiona. How dare he? It had to be Mr Lennard. How had he found her? Why had he come? A myriad of questions raced through her mind and at the same time, like a drowning man, flashbacks of her childhood came unbidden and unwanted: the awfulness of the rape, the emptiness of life without Dada and the increasing rejection she had suffered from her mother.

Making a valiant effort to pull herself together, and taking a deep breath, she moved like an automaton towards the sitting room door.

'Coffee Mrs Rivers?' Fiona shook her head, unable to speak for all the emotions that were threatening to overwhelm her again.

Another breath, a hand on the door and she was inside the room. He stood with his back to her, looking at a small water colour she had done of LB in his school uniform. He turned at the sound of the door opening.

Her first reaction was astonishment; he seemed smaller, less powerful. Then she saw his eyes, hard and cold as ever, and an involuntary shiver shook her body.

'Why are you here?' she asked, her voice cold and somehow calm, despite the almost painful thump of her heart beating in her chest.

'Still the same Fiona, welcoming as ever.' His tone was sardonic as his eyes raked her up and down in the familiar way he had of making her feel vulnerable and used.

'I asked why you're here. You're not welcome, will never be welcome. Please leave my home.'

'Fiona, my dear Fiona, strong willed as ever, despite your fame. Yes,' he answered in response to her raised eyebrows, 'I tracked you down quite easily and now I need your help.'

Fiona's laugh was dry and bitter. 'You don't really think I'd ever do anything to help you do you, after all you did to me and how you treated us? I'll never forgive you and I'll never help you.'

'Surely you'd help your sister?'

'Claire? What's the matter? Where is she? What have you done to her?'

'My dear Fiona…'

'I'm not your dear! Just tell me what it is about Claire.'

'Ah, I have your interest now.' He sat down and undid his jacket, revealing a slightly grubby shirt with a fraying collar.

'Claire, you know,' he began, 'was not as averse to me as you were. She went off me for a bit after your Paris thing, but after you left the little bitch quite threw herself at me.'

Fiona couldn't hold in a gasp of sheer horror. What had she done, leaving Claire in the clutches of this dreadful man?

He smiled a slow, cruel smile.

'She wanted it! She would put on a bra just after she started

244

wearing one and wander around the kitchen asking me if it looked good.'

Fiona bit her lip. She could all too vividly imagine the scene.

'Anyway, one evening when your mother was asleep – she slept a lot towards the end. She was so different from the early days when she enjoyed lots of sex.'

Fiona noted sex, not lovemaking.

'Anyway,' he continued, his voice almost purring at the memory of the virginal Claire, 'I came out of the bathroom and there she was, standing in front of her long mirror, admiring herself in the glass. Not a stitch on! What would a man, any man, be expected to do? She knew I'd be passing her bedroom.'

Fiona exploded. 'How old was she?'

'Fourteen, nearly fifteen.' His tone was casual. It had obviously been of no concern to him.

'She pretended she didn't want me, but she did really. She fought a bit. Not like you though, you wildcat!"

'Get out, get out of here!' Fiona could contain herself no longer.

He made no attempt to move.

'I thought you wanted to help your sister?'

Fiona sank into a chair, burying her face in her hands, defeated again by this man.'

'Tell me,' she said, her voice subdued.

'We became lovers. I think your mother may have known, but she wouldn't have minded. She wanted me to be happy. Then, as you know, your mother died and Claire wanted to get married and have a baby. Why not? I thought. The mother and the daughter. We got married and she had a baby. You know that of course, she showed me your letter.'

Fiona nodded.

'Then she started playing me up. She was out all the time,

buying clothes, seeing other men.'

'You weren't man enough for my little sister then?'

He glared. 'I'm all man and happy to prove it little Fiona.'

She pulled herself together, determined to climb back out of the abyss. Thoughts of Baynton filled her mind, gave her strength; she felt powerful, a woman, not a child.

He saw the change, the stiffening of the shoulders, the calm expression and the coldness emanating from her that was almost tangible. He became conciliatory.

'Let bygones be bygones Fiona, please.'

He had never said please in his life; he must be desperate. It strengthened her resolve. She stood up.

'Get out,' she said, 'now.'

Her tone was final. He stood up and looked her squarely in the eyes.

'She's left me,' he said, and for the first time ever, she heard emotion in his voice.

'Good, I'm glad. I hope she has the sense never to come back to you.'

She walked resolutely to the door and opened it.

'Goodbye,' she said pointedly.

'I did love your mother you know.'

'You're pathetic,' was her response, amazed at the calmness she felt. He was just a slightly shabby, greying man who had no power to frighten her or hurt her. She was protected from him, Baynton had seen to that, surrounding her as he had with such loving care, tenderness and kindness that it had finally wiped out the last vestige of fear.

Janet came into the hall just after Mr Lennard had left. Mrs Rivers, she noted, looked rather flushed.

'Would you like some coffee now?'

'What a good idea Janet. Do you mind if we don't have it

246

together this morning? Could you bring mine up to the studio? I've wasted enough time.'

She climbed the stairs to the studio and looked at the painting The Mayor looked defiantly back at her. Proud as the proverbial peacock, she thought, smiling as she picked up her palette and started mixing her ermine red.

Her time was very committed now. She had a number of commissions constantly in the pipeline. The Army seemed to have taken her on and a number of regiments had commissioned her to paint portraits of retiring Generals or Brigadiers. She had also been commissioned to paint the Prime Minister and his attractive wife and, as she walked up the staircase inside Number 10, deliberately letting her hand run up the smooth banisters, she wondered at all the people who had climbed these stairs before her. She looked at one portrait after another as she climbed up the imposing staircase. Many of the previous Prime Ministers were there, but this was the first Prime Minister who had asked that his wife be included. Fiona enjoyed their company and in all, went there on twelve separate occasions, managing to do much of the work in her cottage studio. They became friends and chatted easily, envying her slightly, they said, for her freedom of movement. It was the only thing they regretted about their position.

Chapter 37

The telephone call from Claire came a week after Mr Lennard's visit. She sounded very weepy. She was in London with her son; she had no money, and could Fiona help. Fiona put the telephone down and immediately picked it up again and telephoned Mary.

'I have to go to London. I should be back by this evening but could you collect LB and keep him overnight if I don't get back?' Mary was intrigued. 'I'll explain when I get back,' was all Fiona would say.

Claire was waiting for her as arranged, in the Charing Cross Hotel. She sat with a tray of coffee in front of her. A slight, dark haired boy, bearing an uncomfortable resemblance to his father, sat in an adjacent chair reading a comic.

Fiona stood for a moment, unobserved by the pair. Claire had dyed her hair deep auburn, she wore quite heavy makeup and, despite herself, Fiona found herself thinking Claire looked rather tarty. Her clothes and accessories didn't help: a short – very short – black leather skirt, a tight fitting red jacket, lipstick the same red and big dangly earrings.

Claire looked up.

'Fiona.'

The sisters clung to each other for a moment. The boy watched his mother embracing this stranger. His eyes were dark and his lips, unlike those of most ten to eleven years olds, were thin and rather mean looking. Fiona looked at him; her nephew. Despite feeling a

248

slight revulsion that she was extremely ashamed of, she bend forward to kiss him.

'I'm your Aunt Fiona,' she said lightly.

He drew away from her, holding the comic in front of him like a barrier.

'I don't have an Aunt Fiona, Daddy said so,' and he returned to his comic.

Claire murmured an apology of sorts, but Fiona was not much concerned. It was Claire she had come to see, Claire she wanted to help. She waited, deciding not to tell of Mr Lennard's visit. What good would that do – and she had tried, reasonably successfully, to banish him from her mind.

It all came bubbling out. Claire's version differed slightly, but she conceded that she had been rather smitten with Len for a long time.

'His real name was Julian,' she confided, 'can you imagine! Anyway, Len suited him better. Then one day he told me that Mummy and he hadn't had sex for years and I decided I'd make it up to him. At first it was fun, but after Mummy died he got nasty at times.'

'He hit you?'

'Not too much. Sometimes he said it was for my own good. After we were married he tried to keep me in. I thought I might like a job, but I wanted a baby too. So we had him.' She nodded coolly in the direction of her son who was seemingly engrossed in another comic.

'After that he got so possessive, I suppose a bit like he got with Mummy. You know how they met?' she suddenly broke off.

'No, tell me.' Fiona had always wondered how he had first come into their lives.

'Well,' said Claire, 'do you remember she used to go to bridge evenings? I didn't understand when she said she going to bridge. I always wondered which bridge! Anyway, she met Len there and they became lovers. Daddy was having chemo then, though I don't remember that at all. Len said Mummy complained she didn't have a sex life anymore and according to Len, she was a very sexy lady, despite being in a wheelchair. In fact,' she concluded, 'I think that added a certain frisson for him.'

How disgusting and how typical thought Fiona, feeling almost physically sick listening to this sordid tale. *All this going on whilst Dada was ill, in pain and dying.*

'Then, when Daddy died he moved in,' Claire continued the saga, apparently unmoved by the awfulness of it. 'I remember that a bit. Do you?'

'I remember,' Fiona said soberly, remembering the slow, insidious way he had wormed his way into their lives, changing them forever.

'Anyway, I can't stand him any longer. He said he'll track me down wherever I go and he will too. So, I want to go to Canada, Vancouver. Well, Vancouver Island actually.'

'Why Canada and why so specific?' She didn't like to suggest that taking a boy away from his father might be unfair or even wrong. Perhaps her nephew would benefit from being as far away as possible from the man. Fiona repeated the question. 'Why Canada?'

'Do you remember Philly Green? She was in my class. Anyway, she emigrated with her parents and has married a wealthy man, a dentist who has a big house and a yacht. They live on Vancouver Island. It looks beautiful. She's sent me lots of photos and is always asking me to visit.'

'It's one thing to visit but how long will you survive once you've left there?'

'I intend to find a rich husband too.'

'But you're already married…'

'So what! Canada's a long way from the UK, no-one will know.'

Fiona's eyes swivelled towards her nephew.

'He'll do as he's told,' said Claire, matter-of-factly, in response to the unanswered question.

How did I ever have a sister like this? Fiona couldn't help thinking.

'How can I help?' she asked.

'Money, it's as simple as that. I only have a few pounds. I need money for tickets and some money to tide me over until I find a rich husband, or at worst, have to get a job for a few months.'

Fiona was silent for a few moments. It was not that she didn't trust Claire, but she thought it would be best if she got the tickets and then gave Claire some travellers cheques just before she flew. Claire watched her sister's face anxiously. Would Fiona help her? She always had when they were children.

'Right,' Fiona said positively, 'I'll book us in here overnight then we'll go to the travel agents and organise tickets.'

An immense look of relief crossed Claire's face. She had not misjudged her sister – she always came through in the end.

Later that evening, in her own room, Fiona telephoned Mary and briefly filled her in.

'I want to see them off tomorrow then I'll come straight home. Is that alright Mary?'

'Darling, of course it is. LB's told us all about his day at school and is sitting at the kitchen table drawing. He's inherited some of your talent Fee.'

Fiona smiled. She could picture her little boy solemnly drawing away and 'being good', just as his Mummy would want him to be.

The sisters hugged briefly as they said goodbye the next morning. Claire was dry eyed, just relieved that she had managed to swing things her way. Fiona had just thrust a book of travellers cheques into her hand, and glancing quickly, she realised it was around two thousand pounds, more than she had anticipated. Fiona also gave her a hundred Canadian dollars for taxis and other immediate necessities when she arrived. For Len, she had bought a book on Canada that contained many beautiful pictures that she hoped might excite him, and a few comics which she felt would probably interest him more. He took the book and comics and gave her a reluctant, brief smile, almost, she thought, as if he was receiving what was his due.

The plane taxied down the runway and up into the sky like a great bird. Fiona walked slowly out of Heathrow, thinking about her father. *I've tried Dada, I've tried to look after the bairns.* Then she remembered what Claire had said earlier, one of her kindlier remarks.

'You know Fiona,' she had said, 'I resented you leaving us. I thought it was so unfair that you could go away just like that, but one day I realised that you really did look after Stew and me for about nine years. That was pretty amazing. I took advantage of you, I know that, but perhaps it's not too late to say thank you.'

It was that statement of Claire's that now entered her mind. She was free. Dada had asked her to look after the bairns. She had given her best for as long as she could. Quite suddenly, the last fettle in the chain snapped. They had been snapping for years, Mary and James, and then Baynton, had seen to that. But now, quite suddenly, she knew Dada's wish had been fulfilled. She knew from Stewie's occasional postcards that he was alright. She was free, totally free at last.

Back in the centre of London, she went into Dillons and chose a book for herself and two for LB, and espied a lovely Country Kitchen cookbook that she knew Mary would adore. Mary read cookery books like novels.

Walking into the station she was delighted to find a train due to depart in the next few minutes. She settled herself into a window seat and started reading 'Captain Corelli's Mandolin'. Every now and again, thoughts of being home with her son again made her smile.

The next morning at breakfast, LB announced that he wanted to be called Baynton. It was school of course, and Fiona was not altogether surprised.

'Do you mind darling,' she said, 'if Mummy calls you LB?'

The little boy was thoughtful for a few moments, then he smiled in that charming way of his, the smile so like his father's.

'You can call me LB Mummy, but when my friends come over, can you call me Baynton please?'

It was hard at first. In fact, for several weeks Fiona managed to avoid calling him anything when his friends were round to play, but one day she found herself calling him in from the garden.

'LB,' she called, then remembered. 'Baynton, Baynton.'

He came running, a happy grin on his face.

'You called me Baynton,' he said. He looked so happy about it that she resolved to try and call him Baynton as much as she could. Having said it out loud twice, she had broken some sort of silent pact with herself, but surprisingly, she felt happier for it.

Chapter 38

Lynn's course at drama school had, at first, seemed to be going very well. She seemed to have dozens of friends and brought a number of them home for weekend breaks. Their noisy roistering would drive James to his study and Mary to shrug her shoulders in despair.

'I love Lynn dearly,' she confided to Fiona one day, 'but she does worry me, us, both. There's something different about her these days and I don't seem to be able to get close to her any more.'

'I'm sure there's no need to be worried,' Fiona said, trying to sound comforting, although she too thought Lynn was getting wilder by the minute. Even her soft, brown and naturally wavy hair which used to fall over her shoulders – providing a delightful frame for her extremely pretty face, or done in French plaits when she was riding or trying to look more sophisticated – was now short and spiky and a very strange mixture of colours.

'She needs to try out her wings,' Fiona added, wondering if it would do any good to talk to Lynn herself.

A golden opportunity occurred a few days later when Lynn turned up on the doorstep, for once not surrounded by a crowd of friends.

'I've just had a major row at home,' was the greeting as Fiona opened the door.

'Come in Lynn, tell me all.'

It was obvious the girl had been crying. Her eyes were still full of tears and the pupils surprisingly dilated. They went through into the kitchen. Fiona glanced out of the window. LB and his friends were playing with Tweeny, the kitten. She had just taken out lemonade and biscuits, so she knew she and Lynn would be able to talk uninterrupted.

'It's this,' said Lynn, dramatically pulling off her black tee shirt. Fiona managed not to gasp out loud, but she had to put a hand over her mouth to prevent it. There, round Lynn's neck like a necklace, was the tattoo of a snake, its heading pointing downwards and its tongue darting out of its mouth, as if anticipating a bit of the luscious young breast below.

'It's … amazing,' Fiona said.

'You don't like it?' demanded Lynn in a tone full of resentment.

'I think it's been beautifully executed, but a tattoo Lynn? Will you always want that there?'

In response, Lynn turned round.

'You might as well see the rest.'

There, with its tail curled round the first snake was a second snake, this time following the line of her spine, disappearing into her jeans.

'It goes to my bum,' she announced triumphantly.

For once, Fiona was stuck for words. Poor Mary and James; this would be difficult for them.

'Coffee I think,' she said, trying to busy herself while she marshalled her thoughts.

Lynn sat, her defiance ebbing away.

'I've done it this time, haven't I?'

'Poor Lynn, did you get carried away?'

'It was a dare. I was the only one of the girls who went ahead with it.' She started to cry. 'I've never seen mum and dad like that before.'

'It must have been a shock darling. They'll get used to it.'

'They haven't much option.' Lynn's laugh was bitter. 'I'm stuck with it now.'

They talked together for quite a long time and when she had gone, Fiona was left with an uncomfortable feeling that Lynn had wanted to tell her something else. There was something she couldn't quite put her finger on, something about Lynn that gave her a sense of unease.

Later that day, Fiona telephoned Mary.

'Lynn is so upset with herself for upsetting you.'

'I know,' said Mary sadly, 'but why Fee, why? What did she have to prove?'

She sounded so upset and worried that Fiona hadn't the heart to voice other fears that were worrying her.

On a grey summer's day some weeks later, Alison turned up at Round Window Cottage. LB was playing at a friend's house so, once again, Fiona led the way to the kitchen to make some fresh coffee.

'I need to talk Fee,' Alison began. She sat at the kitchen table twisting and twisting the gold bracelet that had been Fiona's last birthday present to her, around and around.

'It's Lynn,' she blurted out as Fiona put the mug of coffee in front of her.

'Not more tattoos!'

'No, far worse. Drugs, I'm sure she's using drugs. I don't know what to do about it. Should I tell mum and dad? What do you think Fee?'

Fiona's heart sank. It was, she realised, not a total surprise to her, though she had been trying not to acknowledge her fears, even to herself. With an awful sense of foreboding, she sensed that Alison was right.

'You have no choice Ali, you must tell Mary and James. Even if you're wrong, they should at least be aware that it could be a possibility. They've been so worried about her lately.'

At three the following morning, Fiona's telephone rang. Sleepily, she answered. It was Alison.

'Fee, Lynn's in hospital. They think she's taken ecstasy or something similar. Mum and dad are at the hospital but they wanted me to telephone you.'

Fiona was immediately alert. 'I'll be there as soon as LB's at school Ali. Try not to worry, she's young and strong and she's a fighter.'

'I know, but I'm frightened for her.'

'Of course darling. Is Seb with you?'

'No, don't you remember? He's in France for a week's exchange.'

'Well, why don't you come here, spend the rest of the night with me and we can go up to the hospital together.'

'Oh Fee, can I? Thank you!'

LB was delighted to see Alison the next morning.

'I don't think you were here when I went to bed, were you?'

Alison shook her head.

'Did you come in the middle of the night? Was it scary?'

The little boy's questions kept them somewhere near normal, but once he was at school and they were alone, the shutters were down and they both wept with fear as they drove into Hastings.

Lynn was in the Intensive Care Unit. Mary and James sat, ashen faced, on one side of the bed. All around, machines bleeped and Lynn seemed to have tubes and wires both going in and out of her body. Her face was as white as the pillows she lay on. Her poor spiked hair looked more freaky than ever in the orderly and pristine atmosphere of the hospital. Staff bustled in and out, never leaving her without a member of staff present or in the immediate vicinity.

To Alison's dismay, they wouldn't let her in. She and Fiona had to be content with looking at her through the viewing window.

'Oh Fee! What if she dies? I should have spotted it before, I'm a medical student.'

'Wiser heads than yours have missed the signs before,' Fiona answered, feeling as much to blame as anyone. Why hadn't she noticed the perhaps more obvious warning signs?

James came out, looking very grim.

'It's touch and go. She's in a coma. We don't know, we just don't know. I shouldn't have been angry over the tattoos.' He shook his head despairingly. Fiona and Alison moved closer and he put an arm around each of them.

'Thank you for being here,' was all he could say, before he returned to the bedside of his wayward daughter.

For Mary and James, the next few weeks were a living hell. The hospital insisted they went home to rest once the first few days were over. Lynn showed no sign of consciousness. They played her favourite music on tapes by her bed, they talked to her, they stroked her hands and face. All Mary's motherly instincts to hug her daughter were not possible. At night she lay, dry eyed and awake in James' arms, feeling that she was in some awful black limbo and that life could never ever be the same again.

James too lay still, trying not to disturb his wife who, he thought, might be sleeping. They were talked out now. All they could do was cling to each other and pray for a miracle. The local paper and even some of the nationals covered the story – 'Brilliant drama student in a coma', 'Ecstasy strikes again!', 'Will they ever learn?'.

Leah Bett's father whose own daughter had so tragically died several years before, wrote to them, but they neither opened letters or newspapers, unable to cope with anything additional in their lives. They showered and dressed, their total direction just to get Lynn through another day.

Fiona fed the animals and prepared meals, most of which were barely touched. She and LB had moved into the farm to be on hand as needed. For once, her studio didn't beckon, all thoughts focused on Lynn. The doctors were grave, their gravitas not helping, yet smiles would have been worse, but there was worse to come.

Mary was sitting quietly by Lynn's bed one afternoon. James had gone for a walk around the grounds, to clear his head he said. A woman, much of Mary's age, came in. For a moment Mary was puzzled – yet another consultant? There was something vaguely familiar about the face. Mary glanced away, not really interested. Her whole attention was focused on Lynn. She heard a chair being drawn up by her side and her hand was taken hold of.

'Do you remember me? We were at school together I think; you were in the year above me. Sue McLaren.'

Mary's attention was caught. She turned. No wonder the face was familiar.

'Why are you here?' she asked, not really interested in the answer, but politeness as ever prevailed, even under these circumstances.

'Mary, I'm a consultant in charge of infections.' Mary started to speak. 'Let me finish Mary, please. This isn't easy.'

Mary studied Lynn's sleeping face. She looked so peaceful. Her hand went out and stroked her daughter's cheek.

'Mary, there's no easy way. Because of certain indications, an ulcer on her leg and signs of needle use, we've done some additional tests.'

Mary gasped in horror, blackness threatening to overwhelm her. She tried to stand, but her legs failed her. Sue looked at her, every instinct wanting to leave unsaid the words she had to say.

'Mary, I'm afraid Lynn is HIV positive.'

Mary stood up. 'No,' she almost shouted,' don't tell lies Sue McLaren.'

It was at this moment that James returned. He moved quickly to Mary and put his arms around her protectively as he turned angrily to face this new white coated doctor.

'Go away,' he said, controlling his voice as best as he could, 'can't you see you've upset her?'

'Of course I'll go, but we need to talk. Please ask Sister to direct you to my office before you leave tonight.'

Perhaps it was Mary's raised voice, perhaps it was just the right moment, but Lynn groaned. A member of staff came in response to James' urgent call. The staff didn't stay with Lynn all the time now, but were always within earshot. Lynn's eyelids fluttered. She couldn't speak for the tube that had been down her throat until the tracheotomy had made it sore. Mary squeezed her hand and kissed her. Lynn's eyes opened and Mary looked into her daughter's eyes for the first time in three weeks. James moved his wife gently aside and kissed Lynn as well.

'Come on kitten.' He hadn't called her that for years and Lynn gave a tiny smile. 'We've been waiting for you, keep awake for us now.'

Doctors and nurses came and went. Lynn opened and closed her eyes in response to questions. They all recognised, with immense relief, an intelligent response.

Lynn was making good progress. There was some liver damage, but fortunately not as serious as they had first thought. The HIV was still a well kept secret with only Mary, James and their children, including Fiona, knowing. It had been hard for James to come to terms with and even harder for Mary. The thought of Lynn using needles made her shudder with horror, and the alternative scenario of it being sexually transmitted was, for James, equally hard to bear. The thought of someone out there spreading HIV made him for the first time in his life acknowledge a violent side to his nature. He felt, for a time at least, that he could commit murder, either to the drug dealer or the HIV carrier.

Sue McLaren proved to be a calm tower of strength, explaining that HIV might never develop into full blown AIDS, because of the cocktail of drugs they were using now. At the time, Mary found difficulty in taking in all that Sue told them, but when the time came when Lynn was deemed strong enough to be told, it was what Mary repeated and repeated, like a mantra, until it became totally believable.

Lynn's homecoming was a quiet affair. She was still subdued, unsure of herself in every way. She was bored and restless, yet she didn't have enough strength to do anything other than lay about listlessly. It was Fiona who found a solution. She arrived at the farm one day armed with two large pads of lined paper and some well sharpened pencils.

'Write Lynn,' she said, 'write it all down.'

'I can't,' said Lynn, pushing the pads away. 'I've never been any good at that kind of thing.'

'You've never nearly died before,' was Fiona's quiet response as she left the room.

She would have been surprised and gratified had she been a fly on the wall. Lynn picked up a pad, chose a pencil and, hesitatingly, started to write, slowly at first, but gradually her hand started to move quickly over the paper. Mary came in, saw Lynn absorbed for the first time and ran to hug a delighted Fiona. Together they danced noiselessly around, hugging each other and crying. James heard the news later and took what he felt was his first proper breath for weeks. They weren't out of the woods yet, but at last his little kitten and her snake-surrounded neck were on the mend.

Chapter 39

It was nine thirty. Fiona put down the newspaper with a sigh; time for a bath and bed. She didn't like the evenings. Baynton was already in bed and asleep. She couldn't paint, the light was wrong. She liked the daylight and had had an extra skylight put in the attic room that was now her studio. Every night she went to bed with a flask of coffee and a book. She often read until three in the morning. It wasn't the coffee that kept her awake; she often didn't even touch the flask, but she had to read until her eyelids drooped and the book fell from her grasp. If she lay down before that moment, she would just toss and turn for hours.

She stood up and stretched and as she headed towards the kitchen, the door bell rang. She glanced at her watch again; nine thirty five, how odd. She opened the door and looked out, then up and down the street. No-one appeared to be there. It was then she noticed the flowers on the doorstep. Picking them up, she went back indoors and closed the door. Red roses. The last person to give her red roses had been Baynton. Who on earth was leaving red roses on the doorstep? She saw a note tucked among the flowers. She opened it slowly, hardly wanting to know who delivered flowers in such a mysterious way.

Remember me? she read. It was signed Paul. *Paul? Who was Paul?* It didn't for one moment occur to her that it might be Paul Gavroche, for he always wrote and spoke in French. She racked her brain, running through the various people she had met over the years by that name.

'How odd,' she said out loud.

The doorbell rang again. Now what, she thought. She opened the door, wondering what, or who, she would find this time.

'Hello Fiona.'

'Paul!' Fiona said in astonishment, and then, 'what a surprise!'

'Are you going to invite me in?'

She stepped aside, still a trifle bemused. He was speaking English, heavily, rather attractively accented, but English. That was what had thrown her about the note. Had it been in French, she would have instantly known it was him.

'You look good,' he said.

'So do you.' She still felt strange. *What was he doing here? In England? In Rye? And at this time of night?*

Seeming to read her thoughts, he said, 'Look, I'm sorry, arriving like this, unannounced, but I have wanted to see you for so long. My plane from Africa...'

'Africa?' Fiona repeated in a surprised tone.

'It's a long story chérie.'

'You speak English now Paul!'

'You noticed.' He laughed. 'I learn it for you Fiona, it is one of my surprises for you.'

'Come into the kitchen. Are you hungry?' He nodded. She took a bottle of red wine from the rack.

'Here,' she said, 'you open that. I'll make an omelette.'

They sat companionably at the kitchen table, drinking wine whilst he ate the omelette, then they went on sitting and talking. Or rather, Paul talked. He wanted to tell her of his good fortune.

'All because of you Fiona.' He seemed more confident, more assured Fiona thought, happy to see her old friend again after all these years.

'The last thing I heard from you, you were an artist in a circus!'

Paul laughed. 'Ah, the circus, that was a life, that was an experience. What an experience, but I learned, I learned so much. I saw the animals closely. The tigers, their wonderful muscles; the lions, the monkeys.' For a moment, he was lost in thought.

'Then what?' Fiona prompted.

'Then I met a man who bought my entire collection of paintings. For the first time in my life, I was rich!'

Fiona nodded encouragingly. 'Then?'

'Then I decided I must see these magnificent animals in their natural habitat. So I went to Africa.'

'Africa,' Fiona repeated, 'then what?'

'Well, I learnt English because I met a young English vet who was spending a year in Africa. I moved in with him. I watched him operate on a zebra. I saw him give medicine to baby elephants. I saw the animals in the bush. You've no idea how big a bull elephant can be Fiona, bigger than your kitchen!' They both laughed.

'And now?' Fiona asked.

'Now Fiona, I have money in the bank, now I have a future and I wanted to share my story, my story of success with you. For without you, I would still be sitting in that square in Montmatre doing portraits of boring tourists.'

'Boring, that's how they are? Come with me Paul.' She led him by the hand into the dining room and pointed to the wall over the fireplace. 'So, I was a boring tourist was I?'

He looked at the picture he had done of her when she was fourteen.

'There is an exception to every rule Fiona,' he said gravely. The atmosphere between them was suddenly tense. Fiona stepped backwards and looked at her watch; it was two thirty in the morning.

'Where are you staying tonight Paul?'

He looked at her blankly. 'I hadn't thought,' he began

264

'It's alright, you can stay here.' Then she added hastily, 'I have a guest room,' determined not to give him the wrong idea.

He had left a small case in the hall which he collected and together they went up the narrow stairs and she opened the guest room door. It was the room that Alison and Lynn had shared years before and the wallpaper with the design of rosebuds, faded now almost to pink, was still on the walls.

'Thank you,' began Paul, stepping nearer to her.

'The bathroom is here, a fresh towel…' She walked to the airing cupboard and lifted out a big fluffy bath towel. 'Here,' she said, handing it to him. He stood there, by the bathroom door, holding the towel in his arms.

'Goodnight,' Fiona said purposefully.

'Fiona…' He dropped the towel and stepped towards her. His arms came round her and hugged her to him. Her face was buried in his chest, the faint smell of Dior aftershave assailed her nostrils. She recognised it as one that William always wore. She pulled away.

'No, Paul, please!'

'Of course.' His arms dropped by his sides, they both bent to pick up the towel, bumped heads, stood up and smiled slightly awkwardly at each other.

'Goodnight,' Fiona said finally and walked back down the landing into her own bedroom and closed the door firmly behind her.

She lent back against the door, her heart thumping as she acknowledged to herself that the feel of his arms around her had been good, too good. James often hugged her. William too, when he and Suzanne visited, and other local friends too. But tonight, this hug had set her pulse racing. She hated herself. How could she? She felt as if she had been unfaithful to Baynton. Tears filled her eyes as she let herself think about him.

Every night, as always before getting into bed, she stood and looked at the picture of him sleeping. A sob tore at her; she still missed him so. For once she didn't read. She turned off the light and lay down, sure she would toss and turn for hours. Once she thought she heard a sound on the landing. No, not Paul, he mustn't come to her room. But the sound was the closing of his bedroom door and her reaction was a mixture of relief and, to her dismay, disappointment.

She was walking in the meadow, the meadow where Baynton had first kissed her. There was Baynton. She tried to reach him but every step she took nearer he seemed further away. She held out her arms trying to reach him.

'It's good,' he said, 'it's good.'

'What's good Baynton? What's good?' As she spoke, he faded and she was alone in the meadow.

When she woke up she lay still for a while. She had had a dream. If she lay very still, she knew she would remember it. She closed her eyes tightly. The meadow, there was a meadow. Gradually, her mind conjured up the dream. She opened her eyes. He hadn't told her what was good. With a sigh, she got out of bed and walked into the bathroom. She stood under the shower, letting the water fall over her hair and face until her face ran with rivulets of water mingled with tears.

LB broke the spell. He burst into the room.

'Mummy, mummy, there's a strange man in the bathroom. He speaks in such a funny way. Who is he? He told me he's a friend.'

Fiona wrapped a towel round herself and walked into the bedroom. LB looked so sweet, his hair all tousled, a worried expression on his little face. Fiona swung him up and deposited them both on the bed.

'He is a friend darling. He comes from France. That's why he speaks English like that. His name is Paul Gavroche.'

266

LB repeated the name.

'You'd better go and wash darling and get dressed or you'll be late for school.'

He kissed her on the mouth as he always did.

'I love you mummy!'

'I love you too darling,' she replied, squeezing him gently before pushing him away.

'Go on, hurry now. I must get dressed too.'

'Alright mummy,' and he was gone.

Paul walked with the two of them to the school. Fiona passed a number of people she knew, all of whom looked curiously at her companion.

'The gossips will have a marvellous time,' she told Paul.

He grinned. 'Let them gossip,' he said, then, as an afterthought, he added seriously, 'If this is an embarrassment for you Fiona, for you and Baynton…'

It gave Fiona a bit of a jolt hearing Paul refer to LB as Baynton. It shouldn't have done, for most people, including herself, called him Baynton these days. She only called him LB when they were having a morning or evening cuddle. He still allowed it.

They had decided over breakfast that Paul would stay for a day or two, but now he was worried about her position. He wouldn't have been that thoughtful once she mused, remembering how he had tried to persuade her to leave New York with him, all those years before.

With LB at school, they wandered around Rye together. It was good seeing the place through a stranger's eyes; things that one took for granted at times took on a new dimension. It was one of those lovely clear spring mornings; the sky was blue and the air had a freshness to it. They climbed the steps of St Mary's Tower, squeezing past the big bells which Fiona told him, laughingly, had been stolen by the French at one time.

'I'm surprised we let you have them back!' but his tone was bantering.

The view surprised even him. 'Why, I think I can see France,' he said, 'well, perhaps not, but almost!'

'On a really clear day you can,' said Fiona. 'I think you're right, that is France, not the horizon.'

He marvelled over the beautiful countryside and the variety of tiling on the roof tops.

'What's that?' he asked, pointing to a square piece of lawn.

'Oh, that's the garden of Lamb House.'

'Lamb House?' he queried.

'A famous American writer, Henry James, lived there, and Benson and Rumer Godden.'

Paul looked somewhat bemused. 'It looks beautiful anyway,' he said.

It was Market Day, so they walked through the tightly packed stalls, listening to the music from the record stall, or the fruit and vegetable vendors calling out their prices, and finally, after wandering round the shops and into the art gallery, they headed back to Round Window Cottage for a much needed cup of coffee.

Cups of coffee in hand, they climbed the two flights of stairs to the studio.

'This is great,' Paul said, waving his hand to the extra window, 'plenty of light. Now, show me.'

They spent the next few hours going through Fiona's canvasses, many of which she did for her own amusement, and a number that she was collecting for her next exhibition. He wanted to see her photographs. She had told him years before that she always kept a photographic record of her work at various stages of completion. Paul thumbed through her neatly catalogued photos, stopping briefly here and there with a comment. But he gave a low moan when he came across the photograph of 'The Trial'.

'Chérie,' he said, reverting unconsciously to French, 'how sad you were when you painted this, sad - and angry too,' he added with perspicacity. Fiona nodded.

'I hadn't touched a brush for nearly four months. I think my sadness and – you're right – my anger came out in this.'

'I read about this you know,' he said thoughtfully. 'In Africa, I came across an old art magazine that someone had brought out from England. Anyway, your painting was being written up as one of the finest examples of modern oils, with great depth of feeling. I did wonder when you painted it.'

Chapter 40

The few days turned into a few weeks. Almost to Fiona's chagrin, Paul had not touched her again. Her friends now included him in invitations, and even Mary and James were curious about his visit but hesitated to ask how long he was planning to stay. Fiona seemed to be a strange mixture of being contented and edgy.

'It's Paul holding back, that's the problem,' James remarked as he and Mary lay in bed having their usual catch up of the day.

'No,' said Mary, 'perhaps it's the reverse. Perhaps he'd come on too strongly and she doesn't want him to.'

'In which case he'd have been asked to leave,' said James. 'Trust me, I reckon our Fiona is one frustrated female!'

'James, you horror,' Mary thumped him hard.

'What? Are you frustrated too? Come here woman.'

He clicked the bedside light out as they cuddled closer.

At Round Window Cottage they were playing cards with friends who had joined them for an evening of supper and bridge. It was eleven thirty when goodnights were said. Fiona declined the proffered brandy and made excuses about a slight headache as she said goodnight to Paul.

Paul sat in the dining room; one small lamp cast a slight shadow. He was wondering what do to. For the first time in his life he felt unsure what was expected of him. He decided that tonight he would pack. It was time to go back to France, to get on with his work and his life. This had been a nice, very nice, interlude, but

Fiona had made it clear that first evening – as indeed she had made it clear on the top of the Empire State Building – that she was not interested. The fact that he loved her, had loved her for years, was beside the point. She didn't love him and the longer he stayed, the harder it would be to leave.

That's it, he thought, his mind made up at last, *I'll leave in the morning*. He took his brandy glass out to the kitchen and washed it, smiling to himself as he did so. There was a time when he wouldn't have washed a glass until the next time he needed it. How a woman changes a man he mused.

Upstairs, Fiona lay on her bed, still fully dressed. She had looked in on LB who had thrown off all his covers. His hair was damp round his forehead and she ran her fingers through the soft clinging waves. So like Baynton, she thought, with a lump in her throat. She bent down and kissed him. He stirred in his sleep and reached for her hand.

'Night night darling,' she said softly, turning to leave his bedroom.

'Night night mummy,' came the sleepy response.

Now, lying on her bed, she wondered what to do. Paul couldn't go on living here much as she liked and enjoyed his company. He wasn't interested in her any more, that was obvious. He hadn't made a move towards her. Her mind turned back to the first evening. He had put his arms around her on the landing. She blushed slightly, remembering how she had smelled Dior. Part of her had recoiled, but she knew that part of her wanted to stay like that, close to him. Then there was the dream. Baynton had said, 'It's good.' What had the dream meant? Perhaps it meant that it was good to move on, not to dwell in the past? Perhaps the dream meant that she was ready for a new relationship. She got off the bed slowly and walked into the bathroom. Automatically, she showered and pulled on her cotton nightshirt. She caught sight of herself in the mirror. The cotton nightgown was hardly glamorous. She went to the tall chest of drawers and pulled out another flimsy nightgown. She'd never worn it before. It was one of the many presents Baynton had given her. She'd laughed when she'd unwrapped it.

'Oh Baynton darling,' she remembered saying, 'you keep buying me these gorgeous nightgowns and then you never let me wear them!'

He'd grinned and said, 'Well, when I let you wear them, start getting worried honey!' The conversation had ended, as it so often had, with them rolling around naked in bed.

She bit her lip, for a brief moment uncertain. Then, with a sudden resolve, she pulled the cotton nightshirt over her head and the gossamer nightgown on in its place. She walked back to the mirror and looked at herself dispassionately. Her hair was still fair and shining, albeit the odd grey hair was creeping in. Well, I am thirty six, it's allowed, she said to the mirror. She went back to the bathroom and opened the cabinet. Taking a bottle of Calèche, she sprayed herself, her wrists, behind her ears and one general all over. Putting the bottle back in the cabinet, she picked up her hairbrush and brushed her hair thoroughly. Then, without a backward glance, and with her heart thumping like a young girl, she walked slowly along the landing.

Paul's bedroom door was open. He was bending over the suitcase, packing, when he heard a sound. He glanced up and drew a sharp breath. Fiona stood there, looking at him, her nightgown tantalisingly transparent, so as to leave little to the imagination.

'You're leaving.' It was more a statement than a question.

He nodded. 'I thought perhaps it was time.'

'Oh.' Fiona turned away, sheer loneliness and disappointment replacing the feeling of excitement that had sent her heart thumping.

He was round the bed and holding her in a flash.

'Chérie Fiona.' He spoke only French now. 'I love you, I've always loved you since that time, the second time you came to Paris and I'd hoped, chérie, that you would learn to love me a little, perhaps?'

She hadn't allowed herself to think of love, not like that. All she knew that was suddenly, she had wanted Paul. She had wanted him to make love to her. She found herself responding to him in French; it seemed the natural thing to do. He led her into the room and closed the door. He lifted the suitcase off the bed. Looking at her steadily, with love in his eyes, he took off his clothes. She stood motionless, unable to move, waiting for him. She watched his every move, and as he walked towards her, his eyes holding hers, she trembled as she felt his arms engulfing her to him. She lent against his chest, breathing in the smell of the man. He groaned, and with a quick movement swung her up onto the bed.

'It's beautiful ma petite, but can we take it off?' he whispered and wordlessly, she sat up and pulled the nightgown over her head, letting it fall to the floor.

'I have waited so long for this moment,' he said, 'I'd almost given up.'

'Were you leaving?' She felt him nod, as he started to kiss her, gently at first, then with mounting passion. She felt her body respond, the awful emptiness of the past years melting away as he kissed and caressed her. Finally, when they came together, they both felt as if they were coming home.

273

Chapter 41

Fiona and 'that French chap', as some people called him, were really an item these days. Why, he had been there almost two years. At first, Round Window Cottage was cramped. Alison's old bedroom had become Paul's studio but it was too small and the light was not good. So, when the cottage next door came up for sale, they decided to buy it straightaway. Paul insisted that he would buy it and Fiona was glad in an odd sort of way. It made their commitment seem more formalised. The cottage, which was called appropriately The Cottage Next Door, gave them the extra space they needed. They knocked through a door on the ground floor and converted the downstairs into a big family style kitchen, leaving the small kitchen in Round Window Cottage as a laundry room. Upstairs, they knocked the three small bedrooms into one big room and this provided Paul with a decent sized studio which, with windows on three sides, gave him the light he needed.

From time to time they talked of marriage. LB was now eight years old. He loved Paul.

'Really,' Fiona said to Paul one day, 'you're the only father he's ever known.'

Neither of them saw any need to get married, 'unless we have children,' Paul said. Fiona was surprised.

'I didn't know you wanted children.'

'I didn't know myself until recently, then I thought how lovely it would be to have a diminutive version of you!'

It gave Fiona food for thought. Baynton's illness had meant that her pregnancy and LB's birth had been surrounded with sadness, but now, why not? Time was marching on and if she didn't have a child now it would be too late. Without telling Paul she stopped taking the pill, and after several months had gone by with nothing happening, she concluded that either she or Paul were not particularly fertile. She didn't bother to start taking the pill again and put the whole thing out of her mind.

Fiona was sitting at the desk, Baynton's desk, in the studio, going through the mail. The usual circulars were put to one side. There was a letter from Reims. Fiona opened it eagerly, she so enjoyed hearing from her old friend. Reading today's letter, it was hard to remember what a low state Amanda had been in after the Bernard debacle, but now, with her very successful career and Bernard – perhaps because of it – the apparently doting husband, Amanda was as happy as she had ever been. She was now Marketing Director, having shown a real flair on the marketing side, and had built up one of the most successful marketing teams in the pharmaceutical industry. She wrote that she had a business meeting in London and wondered if Fiona could join her for dinner before she flew back to Paris, never wanting to be away from Bernard and the children for long. Fiona looked at her diary. She could squeeze a quick trip to London, though her schedule was quite tight. She telephoned Reims and left a message on Amanda's answer phone.

At supper that evening, Paul told LB that he had a surprise for him in the studio. Fiona knew what it was and was longing to tell the excited little boy, but she treasured the relationship that had grown between her lover and son and knew Paul wanted to show LB himself.

Paul continued to be a very successful artist. Having got Africa out of his system, he now concentrated on domestic animals. He was currently working on a water colour of two Dandie Dinmont terriers whose owners lived in Rye. He had begun his work on domestic pets by drawing Rob, Fiona's black Labrador, and Tweeny, the Siamese cat. This picture had pride of place in the sitting room and was viewed by all Fiona's friends who immediately asked Paul to paint their animals. Word spread and now he seldom had a free spot.

After supper was over, Paul took LB by the hand and led him up to the studio. Fiona followed at a discreet distance. She heard the little boy exclaim excitedly 'Oh Paul, my own easel!' Fiona entered the room in time to see Paul swing LB up into the air and hug him. 'I wish you were my daddy instead of being Paul.'

Paul looked steadily at Fiona, waiting for her to respond to this. It gave her a jolt. LB had always been told about his father. Indeed, he had a small painting of him on his bedroom wall that Fiona had done especially for him. But of course he had never known Baynton. Now, like any other child, he wanted a daddy of his own.

'If Paul would like to be your daddy darling, I think that would be a lovely idea.' She smiled at them both.

'You know Baynton,' (Paul always called him that), 'in France, the children call their daddies papa. Perhaps that might be a good idea. What do you think?'

The little boy beamed and ran to his mother.

'Is that alright mummy?'

'Of course it is darling, I think it's a splendid idea!'

She left the two of them together. LB loved copying what Paul was doing and he was showing signs of some real talent.

The telephone rang as she reached the foot of the stairs.

'Miss McInnes?'

'Speaking,' Fiona said automatically, wondering how she could possibly fit in another commission. Whoever it was, they would have to wait.

'Ah Miss McInnes, I'm glad to have caught you. Let me introduce myself. My name is Richard Lewis. I'm the Personal Private Secretary to His Majesty' Fiona gasped

'You're kidding,' she said, thinking someone was playing tricks with her.

'On the contrary Miss McInnes, I'm very serious. You've been recommended to His Majesty by both the National Portrait Gallery and various regimental officers whose portraits I believe you've painted.'

Was it really the King's Private Secretary? Perhaps it was.

'What can I do for you?' she said, trying to sound more composed than she felt.

'In the first instance, we'd like you to come to Buckingham Palace to meet His Majesty and then we can make whatever arrangements are necessary.'

'I'm rather busy, that's the only problem.'

'I'm sure you'll find a way of delaying any other pieces of work,' Richard Lewis replied smoothly.

Amazingly, the date he suggested was the day before she was due to meet Amanda, so at least that would all tie in quite well. She explained she would be staying at her club and he informed her that a car would pick her up at eleven a.m. on the day in question. That was the end of the conversation. With her heart thumping, she sat down at the foot of the stairs. How extraordinary that she, Fiona McInnes, be asked to paint a portrait of the King! It was a commission beyond her wildest dreams but for now, until she had adjusted to the idea, she would keep it to herself - until the letter of confirmation arrived anyway she concluded, just in case, although she didn't doubt it any longer, but just in case.

It was a time of surprises. Late the following day, the doorbell rang. Fiona put down her brush with a sigh, almost wondering whether to leave it unanswered. A second ring. She would have to go. Paul was out. He'd taken the finished Dandie Dinmonts picture round to show the owners. The completed picture of the little dogs was a delight. One was sitting up, the other lying down. Their big eyes, such a feature of the breed, were full of character and intelligence.

A tall good looking man stood on her doorstep. By his side was an attractive young woman with the blackest hair Fiona had ever seen and eyes a startling shade of green.

'Hi sis, remember me?'

It was Stewart. Fiona could hardly believe it. She would have recognised him even though she hadn't seen him for over ten years. He's grown to look so like their father.

'Stewart,' she exclaimed, 'come in, come in!'

'This is my wife, Maureen.' He put an arm protectively around the lovely girl by his side.

'We met in Ireland when I was posted there,' he said by way of explanation.

'But this is wonderful!' Fiona spoke as she led the way to the sitting room. 'I can hardly believe my eyes.'

She turned to Maureen and moved closer to kiss her sister-in-law.

'It's lovely to meet you Maureen.' She indicated a chair. 'Please, sit down.'

For a moment there was a slightly awkward pause, then all three of them started speaking at once; suddenly there was so much to say, so much catching up to do.

Paul walked into the hubbub of conversation.

'Hello,' he said, his French accent as strong as ever.

Fiona teased him that he put it on because he knew how attractive the sound was to all her women friends, but she loved it too and it certainly wasn't put on, just part of dearest Paul.

Fiona introduced them.

278

'Paul Gavroche,' she said. She normally said 'my partner'.

Paul interrupted. 'We live together,' he explained easily, 'have done for several years now but you'll never believe it Stewart, I first met your sister when she was fourteen when she came to Paris.'

A shadow crossed Stewart's face. 'I remember that.' His tone was bitter. 'I was only a kid but I remember Claire crying and Uncle Len didn't even help her…'

Maureen looked puzzled. 'You didn't tell me about that Stewie.'

Fiona smiled, hearing again the name she herself had always called him.

'This calls for a celebration,' said Paul, 'brother and sister re-united!'

'Another celebration too,' added Stewart, 'we're on our honeymoon!'

There were shrieks of delight from Fiona, and Paul disappeared to the cellar to find a bottle of champagne and some glasses.

'He seems nice Fiona, why don't you get married? I was sorry,' he continued, 'about Baynton. I did send you a card to the States when I found out, but that was probably ages afterwards when I was reading about you in the paper, some award or other.'

Fiona nodded. She hadn't received the card, but that was water under the bridge. At least he had written.

'We went to see some of your paintings yesterday, in London,' Maureen said shyly in her soft Irish lilt. 'You're ever so clever, aren't you?'

'I'm sure you're good at things I can't do,' said Fiona, charmed by her new sister-in-law and delighting in seeing Stewart again after all these years.

'Where are you staying?' she asked suddenly.

'We go back to Ireland tomorrow,' they chorused together.

'And tonight?'

'We'll find somewhere local.'

'Why don't you stay with us?' Paul said, coming back into the room with a tray of glasses and the champagne.

'Please do,' Fiona said quietly. 'It would be lovely to get to know you again Stewart and you too Maureen. And you can meet LB.'

'LB?' Stewart raised his eyebrows as he took a glass from Paul. 'What, or who, is LB?'

'He's your nephew. His real name's Baynton. LB is just a sort of nickname.'

'Hey, I'm an uncle! That's great!'

'You're an uncle already though. Claire has a son.'

'Claire and I have lost touch with each other. She left Uncle Lennard. I had a postcard from Canada to say she was living with a farmer in Vancouver. Then she wrote again to say she'd left him but I haven't heard since. I feel sorry for the kids, but it's her life.'

Fiona was quiet. All this talk of Uncle Lennard and Claire was bringing back memories she would rather forget. She decided not to tell them of Mr Lennard's visit to Rye or of her helping Claire to 'escape' to Canada. She'd heard nothing further from either of them. Perhaps, one day, she might be able to talk to Stewart about them both, but not yet. She got up suddenly.

'I'm going to walk to the school. Anybody like to come with me?'

Paul looked surprised. LB came home on his own these days, but a glance at Fiona's face and he realised something was amiss. She's told him a bit about her childhood, but not as much as she'd told Baynton. He knew she'd been unhappy but now, intuitively, he knew there was more, much more. Perhaps, one day, in her own good time she would tell him.

Maureen said she'd like a walk.

'Is it far?' she said, looking down at her shoes. Fiona smiled understandingly.

'It's alright Maureen, nothing's far in Rye!'

If LB was surprised to see his mother at the school gates, he didn't show it.

'Hi mummy.' Fiona hugged him.

'LB, you've heard of Uncle Stewart, my brother? Well, he's come on a short visit and this is Maureen, his wife.'

She felt so proud of him. He held out his hand and gravely said, 'How do you do?'.

Maureen was enchanted.

'What a lovely boy. I hope I have a son like you one day.'

'I'm not a little boy actually,' LB responded firmly, 'I'm actually ten.'

'Well, you're a fine fellow, that's for sure.' Maureen smiled as she spoke.

'Why do you speak like that, all singy songy sort of?' he wanted to know.

'Well, it's because I'm from Ireland.'

'It's nice isn't it mummy?'

'I think it's very nice darling. Now, let's go home before Paul and Stewart have drunk all the champagne.'

Chapter 42

Next morning they were off. LB had enjoyed meeting his new uncle and aunt and had been reluctant to leave for school.

'We'll come again,' Stewart promised him, and Maureen added, 'You must come and visit us in Ireland, for it's a beautiful place to visit, that's for sure.' She seemed to get more Irish the longer she was with them Fiona thought; she was obviously not trying to control her lovely accent now and the Irishness of it charmed them all.

Stewart gave them the address of the farm. Maureen's father farmed it and now that Stewart's army service was over, Stewart was helping him. They even had a small cottage of their own Maureen told them. Her granddad had lived there when he retired from the farm and one day, her mother and father would move there and then she, Stewart, 'with all our children,' she said, 'we'll go to the farmhouse.'

'It all sounds wonderful,' said Fiona. 'I've never been to Ireland. We'll certainly come and visit you, won't we Paul?'

'Of course. Anything Fiona wants, we do!' Paul said, but he said it so charmingly that they all laughed.

Now she was alone in the studio trying to marshal her thoughts. She almost resented Stewart coming back into her life. It had disturbed her in a way she hadn't wanted to be disturbed. It had brought back all those dark thoughts that she didn't want to remember. She tried to paint but couldn't.

'Paul, I'm going to the farm,' she called. She was gone before he could even make any attempt to join her. He shrugged and returned to his studio. She would, he felt sure, tell him eventually.

Once again, it was Mary who helped her. She didn't cry; after all, there was nothing to cry about, but she did need to talk, to talk to someone who knew the whole story, someone who she didn't have to explain anything to. She felt mean. She knew she was shutting Paul out. She could tell by his expression this morning when she disappeared so rapidly after Steward and Maureen had left. She saw his look, half questioning, half concerned, but she couldn't, didn't, want to talk to him.

Mary knew the minute Fiona walked into the kitchen that something was wrong. Her heart missed a beat.

'LB?'

'He's fine Mary.' Fiona smiled, thinking of her son.

'Coffee?'

Fiona nodded absentmindedly, picking up an apple from the fruit bowl and turning it round and round in her hands.

'Where's James?'

Mary started to tell her, but Fiona wasn't really listening so she didn't continue. Instead, she sat down with two mugs of steaming coffee.

'What is it darling?'

She reached across the table and took the apple from Fiona's fingers and enclosed Fiona's hands in her own. She loved Fiona as much as any of her own children. She knew Fiona was deeply troubled. She waited. Fiona would tell her in due course.

In a way, it was such a relief that Mary almost had to stop herself laughing. She didn't know what she had imagined and she knew that, to Fiona, old ghosts raising their heads were no joke. But it was the past, the long gone past at that. Fiona had so much to be happy about. She had found love again with Paul. Not everyone, Mary thought, is fortunate to find love twice. She had a darling son. She was a well-known and respected artist, and yet she was miserable because the past had caught up with the present.

'It's not that actually,' Fiona said slowly, 'I thought it was. I thought it was because Stewart was there that I was remembering all those awful days in my childhood, but it's worse than that.'

'How could it be worse?' Mary spoke softly, wanting the girl to continue what she had started.

'It's worse because I wish he hadn't come at all.' There, now I've said it out loud, she thought to herself.'

'I can understand that, in a way,' Mary said, not quite sure what Fiona was getting at.

'It's just that my life was well ordered. I knew what I was going to do. Now, suddenly, because of Stewart and meeting Claire in London, and seeing 'him' again, I'm confused and I don't like how I feel. Oh Mary, please help me.' She began to cry.

'There, there Fiona darling, Stewart stirred those old ghosts, that's all. You don't resent Stewart, you resent the memories he brought with him.'

Fiona nodded through her tears.

'But they won't go away, Mary. I feel surrounded. I feel I'm being buried in them!'

Mary bit her lip, trying to find the right words. What did Fiona do when she had a problem?

'Fiona.' She spoke firmly. 'Paint away your ghosts. I don't know how, only you'll know how to do it, but shut yourself in your studio and let it all out.'

Fiona picked up her mug and drank deeply. 'Mary, how is it you're so wise? I knew you'd help me.'

'Isn't that what mothers are for darling?'

Her tone was light, but as ever, she felt so close to Fiona that she did indeed feel like her own flesh and blood.

'Thank you Mary, for so much.'

They smiled at each other and Mary handed her a clean handkerchief. Fiona had always found it amazing that in any crisis, with her or any of the children, Mary always produced a neatly folded handkerchief. She wiped her eyes and blew her nose and pushed the borrowed piece of fabric into her pocket.

James chose that moment to come in and Mary said a quick prayer of thanks that he hadn't come in five minutes earlier.

'I saw your car,' he said. 'Had to come and have a word with my favourite artist. Any chance of a cuppa m'dear?'

Mary got up and poured him some coffee from the jug and the three of them sat companionably round the table for the next hour.

Paul heard the front door; he heard her coming up the stairs to his studio. He went on painting, determined to appear unconcerned.

'Paul, I'm sorry, I can't explain, not yet, but I've got something I've got to do in the studio. I really don't want to be disturbed. Do you mind awfully? Could you see to LB when he comes home?'

Paul didn't understand. He wanted more than anything for her to share her problem, or whatever it was, but he knew she had to deal with it her way.

'Fine,' he said in a non-committal tone, 'don't worry about Baynton chérie.'

She went down the stairs from his studio and up the stairs in the other part of the house to her studio. Once again, she closed the door. She put on the painting smock that Mary and James had given her the Christmas after Baynton died. She had found that she couldn't concentrate when wearing his old shirts; it was just too painful.

Today, automatically, she picked up a new canvas and moved the one she had been working on. Not even aware of the colours she was mixing and without an idea in her head, she started to paint.

She stood back and looked at what she had been painting. It said it all, everything she knew and felt. Time had stood still. She remembered putting on the lights and now she realised darkness had fallen and the street below was silent. For the first time, she felt a prick of conscience. She had thought only of herself and her needs, all thoughts of LB and Paul having gone during the past hours.

Fiona cleaned her brushes and palette and with one last look at the still wet canvas, she left the studio. She hesitated for a moment outside LB's room, then quietly opened the door. The little boy lay as he always did, on his back, his hair tousled and on his face, the look of wonderful innocence that sleeping children always have. She crept out again and went quietly down the stairs, wondering if Paul would be there or in his studio.

The stairs led directly into the sitting room. The room was in darkness save one lamp that cast a pool of light over Paul. He sat, book in hand, Tweeny curled up on his lap and Rob stretched out at his feet. Hearing a sound, he looked up and saw Fiona. He put down the book and stretched his arms. With a protesting mew, Tweeny leapt off his lap. Fiona smiled at the scene: so domestic, so reassuring.

'Better chérie?'

Fiona smiled again, not just at the question, but at the kindness that had left her the space she needed when she needed it.

'All better,' she replied, walking over to give him a hug.

'Hungry?'

'Um, I am rather.'

'Good,' said Paul, 'I waited to eat with you. Come on, you can sit and watch while I make supper.'

He pronounced it 'suppaire' which Fiona found rather endearing. He had, he told her, already made the sauce bolognaise.

'The spaghetti will be just a few minutes.'

He poured her a glass of Valpollicella and pushed her down into a chair.

'Don't interfere, just relax and let me look after you.'

'It's a good job English women don't know how good French men are in the kitchen,' Fiona said happily, 'or they'd all go to France to find…' – she nearly said husbands but managed to say, 'a man.'

Paul had always avoided the subject of marriage and Fiona, who had originally not wanted to marry Baynton, was quite happy with the thought of living together. They were independent spirits who chose to share their lives. Perhaps if there had been a child? But it seemed that it wasn't to be.

Paul turned down the stove.

'Hey, wake up!'

Without knowing it, she must have closed her eyes during her brief reverie.

The spaghetti bolognaise was good. Fiona hadn't realised now hungry she was. She pushed her plate away with a contented sigh.

'Now, chérie, dessert.'

'Not another thing!'

Paul stood up and opened a cupboard.

'How about one of those delicious liqueur chocolates with our coffee?'

'I might possibly be tempted!'

They both laughed happily.

Paul carried the coffee into the sitting room and threw another log on the fire to stop it going out. During the day it was warm enough but in the evenings during the late summer, they enjoyed both the look of the fire and the smell of the burning wood. They drank their coffee in companionable silence, broken finally by

Fiona.

'Paul, do you mind me not talking about..?'

'… whatever was worrying you,' he finished for her.

She nodded.

'Fiona chérie.' He often spoke in French when they were alone, particularly at the end of the day, and always in bed. 'Whatever happened in your life before we met, or rather before we lived together, is your business. I haven't told you about all the women I made love to, have I?'

'True,' she countered, not for the first time wondering how many there had been.

'Well, when and if either of us feels the need or wants to talk about things in a previous life, the life before 'us', then that is when it will happen, not before.'

Fiona nodded.

'Let's go to bed Paul.'

Wordlessly, they stood up and, hand in hand, went up the stairs. Once in their bedroom, Paul started to undress her. He was unhurried and kissed her thoroughly with the removal of each article of clothing.

'I must have a shower,' she said, shivering slightly in her nakedness.

'Me too,' he replied, pulling off his clothes with none of the finesse he had shown in removing hers.

The hot water cascaded over them. She held her head up, feeling the water running over her head and down her cheeks. Paul lathered his hands and gently washed her all over. She did the same for him. They stood close together, letting the water pour over them.

'I'll be in bed first,' he boasted, grabbing a towel and throwing one towards her. She turned off the shower and caught the towel in one deft movement.

'No you won't!' she laughed.

They arrived either side of the bed at the same moment, both still damp. Paul pulled back the duvet and they dived for the mattress. At first they were laughing, but his gentle caresses became fiercer and soon they were both caught up in the passion that engulfed them.

Afterwards, lying contentedly in his arms, she had a sense of peace she had not felt for a very long time. His lovemaking was different from Baynton and she recognised that she had put Baynton on a pedestal. Now the realisation dawned that she was truly in love with Paul, and not, as she had convinced herself before, that she just loved him. It was more than that. She was truly in love for the second time in her life.

Chapter 43

At breakfast the following morning, Fiona told Paul about the telephone call from the Palace.

'I shan't actually believe it until the letter arrives though,' she said.

Paul was impressed. 'I'm not a bit surprised chérie. Who else would the King choose for his first portrait since the Coronation but my clever Fiona, the best portraitist the world has ever known!' he added extravagantly. He pronounced clever 'clevaire' just like he did 'suppaire' – Fiona loved that.

'You could be biased you know!' but she was smiling, happy with his pride in her achievements.

The letter duly arrived.

'This is a letter to keep,' Paul said seriously. 'As a good republican, I nevertheless applaud the good taste of your monarch.'

The arrangements were made and two days before the first sitting, Fiona drove to London with her camera and modest sized sketch book. Unsure what the exact protocol would be, she determined she would treat this commission as any other. But first, of course, she had her date with Amanda.

Fiona arrived at her Club and registered Amanda as her guest. Amanda had an all day meeting and had said she would arrive between five and six p.m. Deciding to have a quick shower, she first ordered some tea and toast and hearing a knock on the door a short while later she grabbed a towelling robe to cover her naked and damp body, assuming it was the waiter with the much needed refreshment. To her delight, it was Amanda, and the friends fell into each others arms both talking at once.

'You're early. I didn't expect you for at least an hour.'

'My meeting finished early. I couldn't wait to see you!'

It was as if they'd been together only a day or two before. It didn't matter how long the gap was between seeing each other, they always picked up where they left off. Baynton always used to tease them saying that if they were half way through a conversation on the telephone, the next time they spoke they'd pick up from where they left off. It was a slight exaggeration, but Fiona had known just what he meant.

The tea and toast arrived with plenty of toast for two and the waiter obligingly brought them another cup and saucer. Then the two of them got down to the serious business of girl talk and general catching up.

It was obvious to Fiona that Amanda's life was happy and successful, the children, so bright and doing so well at school and Bernard, still with the same company but talking of early retirement and looking forward to being a kept man.

For all the laughter, Amanda's work was obviously very important to her.

'I'm terribly impressed,' Fiona said, listening to her friend's chat about flow charts and bottom lines.

'The only bottom lines I know,' Fiona chortled, 'is the one I put under my signature on a canvas.'

This seemed hysterically funny to both of them and they rolled about on their beds.

'I've got to pee!' Amanda got up suddenly from the bed and dashed for the bathroom. 'All this laughing and I don't have the control over my pelvic muscles that I used to!'

'Not enough sex?' Fiona asked innocently.

Amanda came out of the bathroom and pulled a face.

'Funny you should say that,' she said, but she was still laughing and Fiona got the message. All was well with Amanda and Bernard.

It was after dinner and they were once again talking, this time more quietly. Fiona decided to trust Amanda with the big secret about the next day. She swore Amanda on their eternal friendship not to breathe one word of what she was about to hear.

'Should I check the room for bugs?' Amanda enquired tongue-in-cheek.

Fiona frowned for a moment.

'I suppose walls do have ears.'

'Tell me now before I die of suspense. These walls most certainly don't have ears.'

Lowering her voice almost to a whisper, Fiona told her friend about the mysterious phone call that she had momentarily thought was a hoax but that, by the end of the conversation, she had believed.

'Then, when the letter arrived, well...' She opened her handbag and passed the letter over. 'See for yourself.'

'Phew.' Amanda read the letter through twice. 'What an honour. You must be over the moon.'

'I'm actually surprisingly nervous,' Fiona replied. 'I just keep telling myself it's like any other commission, but it isn't really is it?' she finished quietly. 'I've even had to put off one or two other jobs and I've made the lamest of excuses.'

'Well, I think it's terrific! What a pair we are. Two wee girls from Edinburgh have gone a long way in the world.'

At the gate the next morning, Fiona was asked for identification. She handed over the letter and was waved in. The taxi drove her directly into an inner courtyard away from prying eyes and there she was led up a flight of stairs and up numerous corridors. The sumptuousness of the Palace was overwhelming. Every wall had paintings that she longed to stop and look at. Instead, they moved at a steady pace until they arrived at a set of double doors. Her heart was beating faster than usual. *The King*, she was thinking, *me, Fiona McInnes, meeting the King!*

She need not have worried. As the footman opened the door, a man, very clearly not the King, rose from behind a desk and came round to greet her.

'Ah, Miss McInnes. Richard Lewis,' he said, holding out his hand.

He was a man somewhere between fifty and sixty, slim, tall and distinguished looking. He waved her to a seat and offered her coffee. Not really wanting coffee, she felt it would be a little rude to refuse. It was easier to say yes, so she nodded her head and smiled assent.

He was surprised at how young she appeared. Having read up about her he had assumed she would be older, she had painted so much of note. Indeed, he had visited the National Portrait Gallery to see some of her work that was on semi-permanent display there. She was about the same age as His Majesty in fact. He thought that this was possibly a good omen. Fiona was thinking that it was a useful opportunity to ask some questions. Yes, photographs of the location would be fine and yes, His Majesty would be wearing naval uniform and she could photograph it. However, he was not able to confirm whether Fiona could take pictures of the King.

'His Majesty will make those decisions,' he said, adding that the number of sittings would be six.

Fiona was horrified. 'It's not enough,' she protested.

'That's all the schedule allows.'

The information was politely but firmly given.

Finally, it was time to meet him. They went through more double doors and into a large yellow room.

'The Yellow Drawing Room,' Richard Lewis informed her unsurprisingly.

A door opened at the far end of the room. The King walked in with an air of someone who had his mind on something else.

'Miss McInnes, Your Majesty.'

His fair hair flopped over one eye. He pushed it back and held out his hand. His grip was surprisingly firm and his blue eyes met hers steadily.

'How kind of you Miss McInnes. I hope I'll be a good subject matter.'

Still holding his hand, Fiona made a half curtsey. *Why*, she thought, *he's as nervous about this as I am*, and suddenly she felt at ease. She was here in a professional capacity and she knew she would do a good job and it was, she decided, going to be an enjoyable experience.

The first meeting set the scene. They discussed various venues, finally deciding on the Throne Room, with the hanging velvet curtains and just a hint of the Throne framing the background, and decided that he would stand at a very slight angle. Fiona took photographs of the planned location and did some preliminary sketches and, after saying goodbye to His Majesty, returned with Richard Lewis to the study to make appointments for the sittings starting the following week.

'All in all,' Fiona told Paul that evening, 'it was a complete mix of awe-inspiring and the ordinary. He's just a very pleasant man, my age almost exactly.'

It was arranged that she would do one sitting a week for three weeks. The final three would be spread out over the next three months. Fiona found that the background and the uniform photographs were of real help, but it would be the final three sittings when the absolute perfection she wanted for the face and hands would be critical. She had, at least, put into perspective the whole portrait now and was able to treat the commission as she did every other one with her usual attention to detail.

The King himself was a delight to paint. He had a young open face, and although sometimes Fiona detected a sadness in his eyes, his nature was happy and caring and this began to shine through on the canvas.

It was on the third visit that, somewhat hesitatingly, she asked if it might be possible to take a closer look at the art works. She was now familiar with the art on the route she followed and had paused to admire certain paintings. She had also joined one of the guide tours of the Palace, both to see parts of it she'd not previously seen and to listen to the guides descriptions of the magnificent rooms and art work. However, for Fiona, it had been understandably superficial. No guide, however well trained, knew the answers to the many questions she would liked to have asked about some of the rare and precious art.

The King's response was so typical of him.

'How thoughtless of me. Why didn't I think about it? Please Fiona, leave it to me.' He had dropped the Miss McInnes very early on.

A few days later, she received a telephone call from the Keeper of the King's Pictures. It was arranged that she would make a special visit when he would be delighted to show her around and hopefully answer her questions.

It was a day Fiona would always remember, an experience beyond her wildest expectations. There were Titians, Canellettos, Constables and Turners; family portraits by Gainsborough and Reynolds; paintings by Degas and Monet, as well as a complete room of Dutch Masters. She was shown paintings in the private quarters of the family. Still, after one complete day, there was still so much more to see that another day was put in the diary.

Every room had its own special atmosphere. She would always remember the colours; vivid yellows, deep reds, blue rooms, green rooms, each with co-ordinating curtains and wonderful Abusson, Chinese, Indian and more traditional carpets. From an artist's point of view, it was like a never ending plethora of colours, shades and depths that she felt privileged to see, and with which she would enthral audiences for years to come.

As she was driving through the now familiar gates on the last but one visit, she suddenly felt an odd sensation in her stomach. She drove on, parked the car and then placed her hand on it. For a moment she thought she had imagined something. No, there is was again! It felt like the faint wings of a butterfly. She knew that feeling. She rested her hand on her stomach again. Yes, it was unmistakable – the slight but definite movement of a baby. Her baby; a baby for Paul. She was filled with a wonderful sense of wellbeing. She hardly knew how she'd get through the next two hours. All she wanted to do was to turn the car around and drive home to share the news with Paul and tell LB that in a few months' time he would have a brother or sister.

The sitting went well the first time the King asked to see the portrait. Before, when Fiona had deferentially asked him if he would like to see the progress that was being made, he had declined. Today, he stepped down the two steps of the dais and came around the easel. He looked at it silently. For a moment, Fiona was disappointed. It was good, she knew it was. It was exactly as she saw him. He smiled suddenly, that big smile of his.

'It reminds me of my mother.'

Fiona felt the tears pricking her eyes. He was indeed like his mother. His face was stronger, but the resemblance was there.

'I like it Fiona.'

'Thank you Sir, I'm glad. I do have another sitting though, there's still some detail to do.'

He smiled. 'Then I'd better get back to my spot.'

He had been a good subject and she had enjoyed meeting him. She hoped that others would like the portrait as much as he did; critics could be so cruel at times. Strangely enough, Fiona wasn't worried for herself, but felt rather defensive about the young King. She still thought of him as young; he seemed so much younger than her somehow. She wouldn't like people pulling the portrait apart because it was him as he really was.

Chapter 44

Paul couldn't believe his ears.

'Chérie, how clever of you.'

'You too Paul,' she teased.

'How didn't you know?'

'It's crazy really. I've been so busy I sort of lost track of things, and I'd given up all thoughts about a baby. I thought it wasn't going to happen.'

'You're sure?'

I'm always sure she thought to herself, remembering how Baynton had asked the same question.

She took his hand and placed it on her stomach.

'Wait,' she said as he went to draw his hand away. Sure enough, there was a faint move, then another. Paul's face lit up.

'It's a miracle,' he breathed, 'Yes, it's a miracle.'

Their baby daughter, Francesca Mary Gavroche, was born in the same week as the unveiling of the King's portrait. Few people reading the announcement in the birth columns would have realised that the new arrival, the daughter of Fiona and Paul Gavroche, and a sister for Baynton, was one and the same artist Fiona McInnes who was being feted as the new Annigoni. All the quality newspapers had similar headlines: the best portrait of a royal since the one of the late Queen Elizabeth by Annigoni. A Mori poll indicated that the people liked it too. 'It's just like him' was the general feeling on the streets.

In Rye, the celebration was more intimate as Paul and LB fussed over Fiona and the new baby.

Downstairs, Mary and James were in the kitchen. Mary was getting lunch ready whilst James was reading a pile of newspapers he'd bought earlier.

'What a girl she is,' James said, looking at a picture of her in The Times alongside the portrait. 'It's not many that can produce a baby girl and a King in the same week.'

'Ah,' said Mary, turning to him and giving him a hug, 'she's always lived a different kind of life.'

Printed in Great Britain
by Amazon